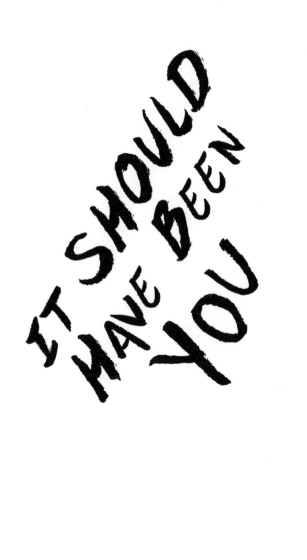

LYNN SLAUGHTER

IT SHOULD HAVE BEEN YOU

PAGE STREET
PUBLISHING CO.

PAGE STREET
PUBLISHING CO.

Dedication

For:

—My husband, Alan;

—My mother, Gertrude Slaughter, who passed on her love of books and reading to me;

—And the teens I've worked with over the years who opened their hearts and shared their stories with me.

This book is for you.

Once I decided to kill her, the rest was surprisingly easy.

I waited in the dark, my back pressed against the cool exterior stones. When she stopped playing, I knew what the silence meant. She was scribbling another note in the margins of her music.

I tapped on her studio window. She started, dropped her pencil, and snapped her head toward the sound. Rising from the piano, she took a few tentative steps, the hike in her shoulders disappearing when she saw it was me. Her hand lifted in greeting and gestured toward the back door off the kitchen.

I stepped inside. She smiled. Only the slight twitch in her left eye let me know she was less than thrilled to see me.

She led me back to the love seat in her studio.

"You scared me," she said. "What's up?"

"Sorry, I didn't mean to. I was on my way home and thought I'd return this to you." I pulled out the biography of Horowitz.

"It's good, isn't it?" She walked over to her bookcase and shelved it with the other biographies of renowned pianists. She had an extensive collection. Alphabetized, of course.

"Extremely well written. So where is everybody?"

"My parents are at rehearsal, and Clara's up in her room listening to that insipid jazz she's so crazy about. She knows not to bug me when I'm practicing."

"I didn't mean to interrupt, either. How's it going?"

She shrugged. "Good. Having a little trouble with the last movement, but ... "

"Mind if I sit and listen for a minute?"

"That'd be great." She jumped up and eagerly moved to the Steinway. I wondered if she was relieved she didn't have to make any more small talk. Who knew where that would lead?

I studied her as she launched into the opening notes of the Barcarolle. She was beautiful. Not as beautiful as her music, but close. Her dark curls cascaded down her long spine. She swayed to the music, lost in its beauty and power.

I congratulated myself on how thoughtful I was, letting her die doing what she truly loved. All those dramatic speeches I'd fantasized giving her weren't going to happen. Surprise was everything. She'd never know what hit her.

Moura played on, oblivious as usual to everything except her music.

Like I said, it was surprisingly easy.

Chapter One

FIVE MONTHS LATER

There are one hundred thirty-two steps from my locker to our high school newspaper office. I know, because I've counted them.

"Hey," I said to Brett, at step 29. We'd gone out a few times last spring. Until he suddenly lost my phone number. Permanently.

His eyes darted around, as though he were searching for cover. "Hi Clara," he mumbled and sped past me.

When I turned the corner at step 57, Emily, Monica, and Amber were huddled together giggling. They became silent and stared at me. Then they turned their backs and started whispering.

Subtle.

I tried not to look like I was hurrying, but I was. Forty-four steps to go.

Oh God. Was that Lester Thompson hurtling toward me?

"Hey," he said, as he fell into step beside me. "You're lookin' fine."

"Gee, thanks. Is that a new tattoo on your neck?"

He pulled a toothpick out of his mouth. "Satan's spawn. What do you think?"

"It's certainly big."

"Yeah, I got a great deal on it. So, like, I was thinking, you want to go out Friday night?"

I pulled up to an abrupt stop at step 117. "Lester, why would you possibly want to go out with me? I'm not exactly your type." I pointed at my pale blue hoodie and jeans. "See? No black."

He crinkled his forehead. "Yeah, but babe, you're so pretty, and like … a dangerous chick."

Great. Now I was Leonard High's new pinup girl for danger—Date her if you dare. "Thanks, but I'm not your babe. And I'm about as dangerous as your grandmother."

"Not what I've heard." He ran his tongue along his lower lip.

Eww. "Don't tell me you believe everything you hear."

"Oh, come on." He grabbed my arm and stroked it. "A tattoo of Satan would look great right here."

"Leave me alone." I wrenched my arm free and pushed past him.

"Bitch," he yelled after me.

I shivered and kept walking. Almost there.

Three. Two. One. I thrust the door open and spun inside, relieved to be back in this broom closet of an office with its ancient radiator.

As I booted up my computer, Lester's voice calling me a bitch echoed in my brain. Funny. I used to think I was pretty nice. But it was getting harder and harder to be Ms. Warm-and-Friendly when half the student body treated me like a leper who'd escaped from the colony.

I reached for my backpack, pulled out my compact mirror, and stared glumly at myself. I didn't get it. How did one lone zit on a heart-shaped face scream "dangerous"? I scrunched up my face and tried to look badass.

CJ poked her head in the door. "What the hell are you doing?" she boomed out. Her vocal volume seemed designed to make up for being vertically challenged. She claimed to be five feet, but that was a definite stretch.

"Practicing looking tough. You know, changing my image. Getting that 'Mess with me, and I'll kick your butt' look." I gave her my best hairy eyeball.

She giggled. "Trust me. This is not a good look for you. You don't look scary—just deranged."

"Not what I was going for." I tossed my mirror on the desk. "So what's up with you?"

"Covering the Spanish Club meeting. They have the best food. Want to come?"

"Bring me something? I want to work on my column."

She must have heard the slight tremor in my voice. "You okay?"

I swiveled my chair around. "Not really. Lester Thompson just asked me out—said he wanted to date a dangerous chick."

CJ gave me a hug. Then she snorted, and her shoulders shook.

"Are you laughing?" I pulled back to look at her.

"I can't help it! He worships Satan, for God's sake. The thought of the two of you together … well, it's hilarious."

"Maybe for you. How would you like to be known as a 'dangerous chick'?"

"And this matters because … why? The guy's a douche. And he's like one of the biggest dealers around."

"You're kidding."

"You really don't know? You've led a sheltered life."

I raised my eyebrows. "Now *you're* kidding."

She bit her lip and blushed. "Sorry."

"The last few nights, I've been getting these weird phone calls. When I pick up, there's no one there. You don't think it could be Lester, do you?"

"No idea. But I thought you changed your phone number."

"We changed both—my cell and our landline after … you know …" I squeezed my eyes shut, trying to push away the memories of those threatening calls we'd received in the days after my sister's murder.

"Well, shit," she said.

"Double shit." I eked out a smile. "But don't worry. I'll be fine. You need to go cover that meeting and write such an amazing article that Tony can't help but notice you." Tony Sweigart was our newspaper's swoon-worthy editor in chief. He looked like Chris Hemsworth. I wasn't one of his fans, but he had plenty of them, including CJ. Half the girls in our class had crushes on him.

She shrugged. "Like that's going to happen."

"Hey, don't sell yourself … short."

"Ha, ha."

"Okay, okay—Go! You're gonna be late."

After CJ took off, I turned back to my computer and imagined sending Lester's ask-out to my mental trash bin labeled "Awkward." Just as I was typing in the password to access my column, Wolfman dropped by to pull up some stats on the basketball team, but he didn't stay long. Neither did CJ when she returned with a heaping plate of enchiladas for me. I was the only one who preferred working in the office rather than hanging at Starbucks. Or going home.

By the time five o'clock rolled around, my eyes were starting to glaze over. I pulled out my thermos and poured myself a cup of hot chocolate laced with hazelnut coffee, enough of a pick-me-up to tackle the email that had just come in:

Dear Since You Asked,

My boyfriend and I have been together for the past nine months. He's everything I ever dreamed about—romantic, thoughtful, and a great kisser!

Lately, though, he's been acting kind of distant and spending a lot of time talking with "Kimberly," a girl from his neighborhood he's known forever. Then on Sunday night, my BFF's sister told me he was at the movies with Kimberly, and they were all over each other.

When I confronted him, he insisted his mother "made him" take her out, because she's a family friend going through a hard time. He says he still loves me and wants to be with me, but Kimberly's his friend, and he also needs to spend time with her right now.

What should I do? This just doesn't feel right.

—Confused

I twirled my pencil, liking the feel of its ridges against my fingertips. After a few minutes, I typed:

Dear Confused,

You think it doesn't feel right? You know it doesn't feel right because it's not. Your skunk of a boyfriend may be a great kisser, but it's only his aftershave that's covering up the smell of what he's shoveling.

Kimberly may be having a tough time, but does your A-1 kisser really expect you to believe that his mother ordered him to cheat on you to "comfort" Kimberly?

It's up to you, but if it were me, I'd be running, not walking, away from this relationship. For one thing, it's getting mighty crowded, what with Kimberly and your boyfriend's mother horning in on the action. Why not unconfuse yourself by finding a nice guy who wants to be your friend first and foremost?

—Since You Asked

I read my response several times, changing a word here and there. I couldn't help giving myself a thumbs-up after I pressed "Save." Yup, I was definitely getting my mojo back. Time to send a silent prayer of thanks to the Writing Gods who were clearly hanging in with me.

Maybe I couldn't solve my own problems, but it sure felt good to lose myself, even for a few hours, in someone else's. When I was writing, it was like I could push all my anger, guilt, and grief over Moura's death into a tiny room, turn off the lights, and close the door.

Moura and I hadn't had much in common—well, other than our looks. We weren't identical, but we might as well have been—same dark, curly hair, wide mouths, and violet-blue eyes that people always commented on. Lately, though, I'd been thinking there was something else we'd shared. Writing catapulted me into the zone, and music seemed to take her to another universe, where everything else fell away.

Moura. I could still see her, still hear her, playing her beloved Chopin, the notes pouring out like rain from the heavens. My eyes burned, and I pressed the heel of my hand against my forehead.

My twin would never play the piano again. She'd never go to Juilliard or fall in love and get married.

So why was I still around? Why did I get to write and hang out with my BFF and binge on *Law & Order* reruns and ice cream from the Mellow Moose? It didn't make sense.

I took one of those deep cleansing breaths the therapist had taught me. *Keep going. Focus on now. You can do it.*

Pretty ridiculous, but hey, it was all I had.

Peeking into the adjoining classroom, I spotted Mr. Bradford, our advisor, who almost always stayed late, too. Just knowing he was around made me feel better. With his stooped shoulders and button-down shirts that looked like they'd never seen an iron, Mr. B. looked like a crumpled pretzel with a bad comb-over. But he was one of my heroes. He'd never given up on the newspaper business—which wasn't dead yet, but was definitely on life support—and these past five months, he hadn't given up on me, either.

I emailed my response to Mrs. Rivera, our senior counselor, who checked my columns over, then scrolled through my column inbox to see if anything new had come in. That's when I saw it: "Confidential for *Since You Asked*." Nothing very unusual about the message heading—nearly everyone who writes thinks his or her problem, and especially his or her identity, is highly "confidential."

But this wasn't a typical request for help. For one thing, it was only seven words long.

It Should Have Been You
… But soon

The room swam around me. It was like a hideous rerun of the stuff people had posted on Facebook and Twitter right after Moura died. I'd closed all my accounts and sworn off social media, but the messages were branded into my brain. "The wrong twin died." "How can you live with what you've done?" "Watch your back, you worthless piece of shit."

This wasn't supposed to be happening again. Not now, not when I was finally making it through a whole day without heavy meds.

Meds. I still had a stash at home. The thought of sinking back down into that fuzzy numbness where I felt little, and cared even less, was so tempting.

No. Not going there. Not going to give in, not when I was just starting to get my life back. Whoever had sent this email hadn't only meant to scare me but to sock me hard where it already hurt—where it always hurt. Wasn't this the refrain that played over and over again in my head, the one I was sure my sister's legions of admirers were thinking? *It should have been you, Clara, not her.*

And maybe they were right.

But it wasn't me. I was alive, and Moura was dead. Murdered.

Was I next? Oh God, what should I do? I couldn't lay this on my parents. Mom was a walking zombie, wearing her grief around like a heavy shroud. And between trying to hold Mom together and doing his own grieving, Dad was on overload.

Mr. B. was like a second father to me, but I couldn't tell him about this. If he knew I'd been ID'd as the *Since You Asked* writer by someone out to hurt me, he'd pull me off the column so fast I'd be spinning out the door.

I could call 911. But if I did, the police would hook me

back up with my least favorite excuse for a human being, Detective Luis Martino. In the days after Moura's murder, he'd put me through hours and hours of hell, trying to get *me* to confess. As far as I could tell, he'd gotten exactly nowhere with finding my sister's real killer, and I was still his favorite suspect.

I forwarded the message to my personal email account and texted Jenny, who'd talked me off a ledge, literally, more than once: *Emergency! Can I come over?*

Chapter Two

As I raced toward Jenny's house, I pushed the speedometer on my VW Bug so high my car shook, right along with me. Definitely not a good combination. I was so distracted I nearly sideswiped a delivery truck as it pulled out of the back entrance of Ralph's House of Pancakes. So much for priding myself on my responsible driving.

Jenny was waiting for me in the lobby of her chrome and glass-covered high-rise that was so shiny it made my eyes hurt. But it was one of *the* addresses to have in Springbrook, Ohio. Jenny's parents were hotshot attorneys, who worked such long hours that Jenny referred to seeing them in passing as "newsworthy sightings." Our parents were close to being absentee—hers, physically, and mine ... more emotionally. Sometimes I think that's why we understood each other so well. We knew what it was like to be an afterthought.

Rick, the ancient doorman, swept the door open for me with a flourish. Jenny took one look at my face and pulled me into her enormous arms for a giant bear hug. As she liked to say about herself, "I'll never be a small girl."

She was over six feet tall and outweighed me by a good fifty pounds of solid muscle.

But the biggest thing about Jenny has always been her heart.

"Come on," she said, pulling me toward the elevator. "Stay for dinner? We can order Chinese."

My stomach lurched. "Not sure how much I can eat, but sure…. I'll check with my dad."

Fifteen minutes later, the knot lodged in my gut tightened, as we sat side by side staring bleakly at the damn message on the computer screen. "It could just be another one of those creeps that went after you before," Jenny said, "one of Moura's weird groupies, trying to freak you out. Maybe they're mad that you're still here, and she's not."

"Well, consider me freaked!"

Jenny squeezed my arm. "That's what this jerk is going for, so my advice to my favorite advice expert is to show him you're *not* freaked."

Just then, Rick buzzed. The Golden Pearl deliveryman had arrived with our order. "Clara, this delivery guy is so hot!" Makeup kit in hand, she dashed to the ornate gilded mirror in the foyer, quickly ran a brush through her hair, and put some lip gloss on before descending to the lobby to retrieve our food.

When she got back, she was practically glowing. "He winked at me!"

Usually, this would launch us into a strategy session on how to make a love connection with Mr. Hottie Deliveryman. But not tonight. As Jenny worked her way through two helpings of vegetable lo mein and sesame chicken, I picked at my food and pushed it around my plate. I couldn't stop obsessing about the message. "No one on the staff is supposed to breathe a word that I write the column." God, would I ever be able to trust anyone again? The paper had been the one place I felt safe.

"Uh … you told *me*."

She had me there. I'd promised, along with everyone else on staff, to keep quiet about who wrote *Since You Asked*.

She held up three fingers. "Scout's honor, I haven't said a word. But chances are you're not the only staff member who blabbed to their BFF and swore them to secrecy."

"You're right." I sighed and slumped down. "What should I do? I feel like I want to write back."

"Are you sure that's a good idea?"

"I don't know, but I can't let this creep think he—or she—is getting to me."

We headed back to the computer and I pushed "Reply": *Gee, thanks. Be sure and let me know a date and time so I can pencil you in.*

I hesitated, then pushed "Send." For a moment, I felt better.

But seconds later, a return message popped up: *This account is no longer in service.*

I swore. Jenny, who'd been looking over my shoulder, threw a comforting arm around me.

"Clara, you've got to talk to the cops."

Less than an hour later, I was in the police station making a report. It took the callow-faced sergeant less than five minutes to connect the dots and send me up to Detective Martino's office. I'd hoped I could avoid him, but he'd either pulled night duty or was working late.

Amazing how little his office had changed in the last few months. Scribbled notes, piles of folders, and old Styrofoam coffee cups littered his desk. The familiar bars crisscrossed his dirty window. Even if he wanted to look out at the city, I doubted he could see much through all the grime.

"So," he said, staring at the computer screen where he'd pulled up the message, "you don't recognize this address?"

"No. And when I tried to reply, I got a message that the account was no longer in service. Can you figure out who sent it?"

"We can try. But how did this person even know to send it to the column? I thought you told me no one knows who writes the column." His dark, hooded eyes stared at me with their usual mixture of suspicion and semi-contempt.

"I don't have a clue. We're all supposed to be on our honor not to say, but maybe someone on staff talked—or someone guessed."

"All right, I'll have one of our tech guys check it out." He paused and lifted his mangy eyebrows expectantly. "I'll need all the ISPs for your devices."

"What? You think I sent this to myself?"

"Look, all I know is I've got an unsolved murder on my hands. Witnesses say you were yelling at Moura two nights before the murder. Your own family was aware there were tensions. I've got no signs of forced entry, yet she gets bludgeoned to death, and you claim you didn't hear a thing. You see why I'm having a little trouble with this?"

"I've told you over and over again. I was listening to Dixieland jazz riffs on my iPod with my earbuds on. My bedroom's up on the third floor. World War III could have been going on downstairs, and I wouldn't have heard a thing!"

"You don't have to yell, Clara. I heard you … Dixieland jazz, huh? I don't know too many teenagers who go in for that kind of music."

"So now I'm suspicious because I like jazz? This is ridiculous!"

"Just an observation." He paused, and I could almost see the wheels in his miniature brain turning, as he went for his version of a sympathetic smile. I wanted to tell him to stick to his day job and forget acting, but I knew I couldn't stop him from giving Good Cop mode another whirl.

"Clara," he said in a markedly softer tone. "I know it couldn't have been easy being the sister of a superstar."

I cut him off just as he was about to launch into his favorite version of my sister's murder—that starred *me* sneaking up behind Moura while she practiced Rachmaninoff's *Barcarolle* and smashing the back of her head with the bookend bust of Clara Schumann, the famous pianist I'd been named after, no less.

"How many times do I have to tell you? I did not kill my sister! And if you had a shred of evidence, you'd have

17

arrested me a long time ago."

"This investigation is far from closed."

I pushed my seat back and stood up. "I don't know why I bothered reporting this to you guys. I thought your job was to find my sister's killer, not torment me."

Detective Martino pulled himself to his feet, his beefy super-sized frame looming above. "I'm just doing my job, Clara," he said, evenly. "And we'll definitely check this out. Call me immediately if any more threats come in. Understood?"

I nodded and stalked out, unable to resist the urge to slam the door behind me.

Chapter Three

I yanked open the door of my battered Bug. I was losing it, first driving to Jenny's like an IndyCar driver and then not even following that Safety Precaution 101 rule: Lock the damned car.

I banged my fist against the steering wheel. Martino was such a jackass. Why had I thought he'd be any help? Why couldn't he feel any sympathy toward me?

It wasn't just Moura's death I grieved. It was the pitiful relationship we'd had while she was alive. We hadn't even been close. Not really. Nope, no cozy late night sisterly chats for us. Every time I tried to talk to her, I got absolutely nowhere. My mind flashed back to the last time I'd tried, about a week before she died. She'd come into the kitchen to grab a drink after practice. I was munching on some crackers and poring over the handouts Mrs. Olivet had given out that day at the Psychology Club meeting.

"How did your practice go?" I asked.

She shrugged. "There's always more, but the opening is getting a lot better." She pointed to the papers I'd spread out all over the table. "What's all that?"

"Handouts from this workshop Mrs. Olivet gave us on Myers-Briggs. This is so cool!"

"What's Myers-Briggs? Sounds like a mouthwash."

"It's a type of personality assessment that helps people understand themselves and others better."

"How so?"

"Well, for one thing, it measures how extroverted or introverted you are. Extroverts get energy from being around other people. Introverts need alone time to refuel, and they can get super drained if they don't have enough time to themselves."

"Sounds like total crap. You can't put people into boxes like that. I get energy from being with other people at rehearsals, and I also like being left alone, especially when I'm practicing."

"Well, sure," I said, feeling defensive. "We're all a bit of both. It's just that a lot of us really do have a tendency to be one way more than the other. Let's say you're an extrovert and you realize your friend's an introvert, then you might take it a lot less personally when she doesn't want to party with you a lot.... So I was thinking, maybe we should take this quiz to help us understand each other better?"

She downed the rest of her drink and set it in the sink for someone else—*me*—to clean. "Thanks, but no thanks. We don't need some stupid quiz to tell us we're different. Total waste of time."

Yup, that was my dear sister in all her glory—the ultimate Queen of the Putdown when it came to anything I was excited about. She was always telling me I needed to "do something meaningful" with my life. Of course, meaningful to Moura meant dedicating my every waking moment to music, which hadn't been my thing since I'd unceremoniously quit piano lessons at age seven.

From the get go, music captured Moura and swept her away. Suddenly she couldn't care less about playing *Chutes and Ladders* or running under the sprinkler with me in the backyard on hot summer days. She preferred the company of our piano. Within six months, she had so many gold stars in her piano books and was so far ahead of me I knew I'd never catch up.

Truthfully, I didn't want to. Why practice scales when I could be outside climbing trees? Or reading a good book?

I'd long since ceded both music and our parents' attention to Moura. When she'd played, it was breathtaking, and even I, the musical Neanderthal in the family, had gotten chills. And while it sucked to be a blip on the familial radar screen, I could usually quiet the voices inside my head that said I was nothing special compared to Moura. Jenny let me know I wasn't some expendable blob taking up space on the planet, and Mr. B. thought I had a great shot at getting a scholarship to Ohio State, where I could double major in journalism and psychology.

But now it was like there was a tapeworm inside my gut—gnawing at my insides, eating me alive. I willed myself to stop the endless litany running through my brain—*you didn't even like your sister.* But she was the winner, the shining star.

So why is she dead, while I'm alive?

Alive. Well, at least for the moment. I shivered. Sitting

here alone in my car was not the brightest move. Would anyone really try something in the parking lot of the police station? I peered around. Nothing but a handful of parked cars. Still, my skin prickled like someone was watching me. I locked the doors.

An engine started up with a deep growl, and headlights blared at the far end of the row in front of me. Instead of moving toward the exit, a dark van turned in to the row of cars where I was parked.

It got closer and closer. The driver wore a baseball cap with the bill pulled down, hiding his face. My hands shook as I grabbed my backpack and dug down into a mass of paper and books to find my keys.

No go. The van had stopped with the engine running and the lights on just a few cars away from me. I gasped for breath as I reached for the switch on my overhead light and twisted it. Nothing.

In desperation, I overturned my backpack on the passenger seat and pawed through my stuff. Finally, my fingers connected with cool metal. I fumbled with the keys as I tried to fit them into the ignition.

Success on the third try. My Bug roared to life.

When I looked up, the van was gone.

By the time I got home, my breathing was almost back to normal. If some creep was trying to send me into cardiac arrest, he was well on his way. All I wanted to do was slip upstairs and call Jenny for some tea and sympathy—minus the tea. But the minute I walked in the door, my dad's deep music conductor's voice boomed, "Clara, get in here. Now!"

Great. Reluctantly, I walked into the kitchen. Mom sat in her usual spot at the breakfast bar, nursing a vodka and tonic. As far as I could tell, she had substituted vodka for food since Moura's death. She'd lost so much weight that her skin sagged around her bone-thin frame. She glanced up, lifted her hand in greeting, and then quickly lowered her gaze. It seemed pretty obvious that looking at me was painful for her—so basically, she didn't.

Dad's gray-eyed gaze, on the other hand, had no problem latching on to mine. "Detective Martino just called. How is it that I have to find out from the police that my own daughter reported getting a threatening email?" The vein in his neck throbbed, as he slammed his coffee mug down on the counter.

I swallowed hard. "I'm sorry! I didn't want to make things worse."

"Worse would be having something happen to you. How can your mother and I protect you if we don't know what's going on?"

Wow? They wanted to protect me? Apparently, I'd moved higher up their priority list by default. "Dad, it's probably just an empty threat. Some jerk trying to spook me. Moura had a lot of fans, and let's face it, there was a lot of talk, a lot of rumors, that I had something to do with her … her death." Out of the corner of my eye, I saw Mom's hand tremble as she took a big swallow of her drink.

"Rumors" were the understatement of the year. It went

way beyond the threatening calls and all the social media crap. For the first two weeks, I couldn't get out of the house without being bombarded by photographers and reporters shoving microphones in my face and asking me if I'd killed my sister.

Dad took off his glasses and shook his head wearily. "We live in a sick society, Clara. People think and say stupid things. Now tell me exactly what this message said."

My stomach clenched, and I leaned against the counter for support. "It said, 'It should have been you ... But soon.'"

"What? I don't believe this! That's disgusting."

"Yeah. I'm pretty freaked. But maybe that's the point—to get under my skin, engage in a little recreational cyberbullying. Hopefully, nothing more."

"Listen to me. If you get any more messages, or anything else happens, you tell us immediately. Understood?"

"Yes," I said, even as I wondered how keeping anyone safe was possible. Moura had been the star of my parents' universe, and they certainly hadn't been able to keep her safe.

"Check the security alarm and the locks every time you enter the house. Be careful getting in and out of your car. Always lock the doors."

"Dad, I know all that." I tried not to sound impatient, even as a trickle of guilt worked its way down my spine about forgetting to lock my car at the police station.

"Text me every day when you get to school, when

you're leaving, and when you get home, so I know you're okay. Are we clear?"

"Crystal."

The next day after school was more of the same. Apparently, Detective Martino had been busy last night after I'd stomped out of his office. No sooner had I headed to my spot in the newspaper office than Mr. B. summoned me to his adjoining classroom.

"Sit down, Clara."

I sat.

"Detective Martino called me last night and filled me in about this email. Obviously, I'm very concerned about you and your safety. But frankly," he said, lowering his chin and staring at me over his wire-rimmed glasses, "I'm also very disappointed that you didn't report this to me immediately. I thought we had an understanding, that you knew I was in your corner."

"I do know. I'm so sorry! I was scared you'd take me off the column, maybe even the staff. The column is so important to me. It's keeping me sane."

"Sanity is great, but not if it puts you in harm's way."

"But this jerk can come after me whether or not I'm writing the column. And maybe we'll be able to ID the creep from his—or her—messages."

Mr. B. slumped forward, putting his right elbow on the desk and resting his chin on the back of his hand. The bald patches on his head shone beneath the classroom's fluorescent lights. He looked like the middle-aged version of that statue of *The Thinker*.

He didn't say a word, so I plunged ahead. "I promise I'll show you any more messages that come in. And I'm supposed to let Detective Martino and my parents know as well. Dad read me the riot act last night when I got home from the station."

"Well, he should have."

"True."

Mr. B. straightened slightly and jabbed his finger in my direction. "I need to inform the principal about this. For the time being, *Since You Asked* will remain yours. But if you ever pull something like this again and don't let me know what's going on, you're out. Understood?"

"Yes. Thank you, Mr. B." I wanted to hug him, but that kind of stuff embarrassed him—and worried him. Last year, a student on the debate team accused another teacher of sexual harassment because he gave her a hug after she won regionals. Personally, I thought that was taking political correctness a little too far.

He glanced at the huge clock above the doorway to his classroom. "Staff meeting in fifteen minutes."

I headed for the drinking fountain and nearly crashed into CJ, who stood rooted in the middle of the hallway, staring at something at the far end. I turned to look. Sure enough, there was Tony, hand leaning against a locker while he whispered into the ear of a tall blonde.

Whatever Tony was whispering was apparently hilarious, because Blonde Girl tittered away.

"How am I supposed to compete with that?" CJ

muttered.

"Oh, come on. You are fabulous inside and out. It's Tony's loss if he can't see that. Besides, from what I hear, he's a three-time wonder. Ever since Sheri, it's three dates and he moves on to the next girl with legs up to her neck. How shallow can you get?"

CJ stiffened and I mentally kicked myself. I should have known by now that she couldn't stand any criticism of Tony.

"I hate it when you say stuff like that," she said. "He's the farthest thing from shallow. I wish you could have seen him last summer with those kids in Honduras on our mission trip. He made every one of them feel special, important. Those little guys hung all over him. He was like a rock star."

Now *that* is something I could imagine Tony eating up. As far as I could tell, he loved being the center of attention. But no way was I going there with CJ. Besides, what did I know? I was hardly part of Tony's inner circle.

"You're right," I said. "You know him a lot better than I do. But … it's just … Don't you think sometimes he comes across as a tiny bit arrogant?"

"Trust me. It's a cover. Underneath it all, he's really insecure. His dad's a hard-ass. Nothing Tony does is ever good enough."

"That sucks," I said, feeling more sympathetic toward him. "Okay, you've convinced me." I gazed at her with newfound respect. "You should be the one writing *Since You Asked*, not me. You're amazing."

She squeezed my arm. "Not on your life. The column's

perfect for you. To be honest, I wouldn't want the responsibility."

We crammed ourselves around the big work table in the back of Mr. Bradford's classroom. Mr. B. sat at one end, and Tony at the other. I was between Donny Masden, our roving investigative reporter, whose recent piece on widespread cheating had set off a major firestorm, and Kristen Svien, who covered music and the arts. I was surprised Kristen had plopped down next to me, although as usual, she was icy toward me and avoided any eye contact. She'd been Moura's friend and devoted fan. When I'd finally asked her point blank if she thought I had something to do with my sister's murder, she mumbled, "Of course not," but then backed away—as though getting too close might put her at risk for one of my homicidal rages. It hurt, even though I should have been used to it. When I first got back to school, so many kids avoided me that it was like parting the Red Sea when I walked down the hall.

Anyhow, CJ sat across from us, along with Wolfman and Rita D'Angelou. Rita, who loved to laugh and was the only person I knew who could sit on her hair because she'd never cut it, covered women's sports. When she got overloaded, I helped her out. That's how I'd met Jenny back in ninth grade. Already beating veterans on the tennis team as a freshman, she was a natural for our spotlight feature on students who were "making news or noise." I also frequently assisted CJ, who reported on school clubs.

We had *a lot* of clubs—biking, hiking, teaching, chess, astronomy, and the one I was super involved with, the Psychology Club.

"All right gang, before we get into brainstorming about the next issue, I have something I want to talk to you about," said Mr. Bradford. "This is confidential, and I want to remind all of you that what is said in here, stays in here. Understood?"

"Absolutely, sir," Tony said, nodding his head vigorously. Tony was so smooth and slick, especially around adults, that I always felt a little greasy around him.

The rest of us nodded, too.

"Okay then. What do we tell people about who writes *Since You Asked*?"

"We say it's confidential—that it could be one of us or all of us, and that we're honor bound not to reveal who writes it," said CJ.

"Right. Why's that?" asked Mr. B.

Wolfman cleared his throat. "Because someone might get pissed off at the advice we give and decide to engage in a little payback."

"True. And why else, given what you know about who currently works on the column?"

I shifted in my seat and looked down. Oh God.

No one said anything for a minute. Finally, Donny spoke up. "Because of what happened to Clara's sister. People who don't know Clara might believe the rumors and say she shouldn't be giving other people advice."

I winced, even as Donny put his hand on my shoulder

and gave it a comforting squeeze.

"Someone could also write in to accuse Clara, or bully her," added Rita.

"Exactly," said Mr. B. "And yesterday, Clara received an anonymous threatening email."

All eyes turned toward me as everyone said how sorry they were and bombarded me with questions. "What did it say?" "What did the address look like?" And on and on....

Fortunately, Mr. B. cut the questions off before I could pull myself together to answer. "We don't need to get into that. But whoever this was seems to know Clara is the column's writer ... But how? I want all of you to think back over your conversations ... Is there anything that could have slipped out that gave her away? Not intentionally, of course. You're not going to be punished. No one's going to be mad at you. We just need to know so we can figure out who might be behind this."

Mr. B. then went around calling on staffers, one by one. Everyone said they'd been really careful and couldn't remember ever spilling the beans, even unintentionally. Kristen's voice seemed a little higher than usual when she denied having said anything about me being the column's writer, and she leaned as far away from me as she could. Rita, on the other hand, reached her hand across the table toward mine. "I would never do anything to hurt you, especially after all you've been through."

Donny and Wolfman chimed in with their own words of support. They felt like balm on an open wound.

Then Tony turned to me and said, "This must be awful for you. We'd totally understand if you wanted to take a leave of absence from the paper until this gets cleared up. Even though, of course, we'd hate to lose you. Right, everyone?"

"Thank you, but no," I said before anyone else could respond. "I think that's just what this jerk wants, to intimidate me and mess up my life. And I'm not going to let that happen—or let you guys down."

"Well then. If it's okay with you, Mr. Bradford, let's move on to talking about the next issue."

After the meeting, I went back into the newspaper office. Dad texted to remind me to be home by seven for dinner. Since Moura's death, we'd had only a few sit-down meals together, but dinner used to be a big deal at our house. Unless Mom was teaching late at her violin studio, or my parents had a late orchestra rehearsal at the university, we'd all dine together, often by candlelight. Eyes sparkling, my mom would sit at one end of the table and quiz Moura on what pieces she was working on. Moura was only too happy to dissect them. At length.

Then Dad would get into the act as well. They'd discuss what competitions Moura should enter, where she should go for summer study, and what invitations she should accept as a guest performer. To be fair, Dad sometimes made an effort to include me. He'd ask me what was new at the newspaper or with the Psychology Club. I'd get about two sentences out before Mom would say, "Wonderful, dear," and turn back to Moura to discuss the advantages of attending the summer music festival at Aspen versus the one at Tanglewood.

Tonight we were not only sitting down together for dinner, but my parents were taking a stab at entertaining. Dr. Nadia Lewitsky and her husband, Joel Rasher, were coming over, and my parents wanted to talk to them about creating a music scholarship in Moura's memory. Dr. Lewitsky had been Moura's piano teacher and longtime mentor, and Mr. Rasher was the leading music critic and reviewer in the state. He'd done a huge feature on Moura a few months before she died. Funny. Even in death, Moura managed to remain the center of attention.

At least I could get some of my own work done first. I took a couple of deep breaths before checking the staff inbox and then sagged against the back of my chair with relief. Today, there was only one email from a student who wanted advice. Thank God.

Dear Since You Asked,

Over the summer, I played in a co-ed softball league. We all hung out together after games and became good friends.

Well, to make a long story short, "Bill," the catcher, and I became more than friendly. It started when my car broke down and he offered to pick me up for the games and take me home afterward. He was so great to talk to, so mature. I fell hard. He's completely different from any of the guys I've ever dated—sophisticated, considerate, and real old-fashioned in a nice way—like when he picks me up, he holds the car door open for me and helps me get in.

He says he's in love with me, too, and when I finish school, he wants to marry me.

But the problem is, he's twenty-eight, I'm seventeen, and he's already married and has a couple of little kids. He says his marriage has been dead for a while, and he just has to figure out a way to get divorced without losing his children.

Bill has asked me to be patient and wait for him. I love him so much. But my girlfriends say I'm crazy. Am I?

—In Love but Wondering

Dear In Love but Wondering,

Let's just say you've got excellent taste in girlfriends. It's your choice, but I'd advise hanging on to them and losing the guy.

Talk about a wolf in sheep's clothing—okay, substitute a catcher's uniform for the sheep getup. Here's the thing: Bill may seem like the most sophisticated, charming guy on the planet, but stop and think about his behavior. He's a married man and a father who spent the summer trolling for a love connection with a teenager. Call me crazy, but that doesn't sound especially mature or considerate to me—more like major league manipulation.

If you play the patient damsel-in-waiting game, I'm having trouble foreseeing a happy ending. You don't have to watch Lifetime to know that the world is littered with people who've wasted years of their lives waiting for their married lovers to shed their spouses. And let's suppose he defies the odds, divorces his wife, and marries you. Then you'll be spending a good portion of your time caring for two kids who resent the heck out of you. And what will you do when Bill announces he's signed up for more co-ed softball, and by the way, would you mind watching the kids?

Besides, you're too young! We all are. You deserve to spend the next few years growing and changing and figuring stuff out like who you are, and who you want to be with. Anybody who tries to take that away from you isn't really someone who cares about you—even if he does open the car door.

—Since You Asked

I hesitated before sending my reply to Mrs. Rivera. I could understand how flattering it felt when someone a lot older treated you like an adult instead of a dumb teenager. A couple of summers ago, my parents threw a barbeque for the music faculty and grad students. Moura was away at a music festival, but I was there. Randy Hack, a new doctoral student, flirted with me big time and told me all about his dreams of becoming a film composer. I felt so grown-up—until my dad rushed over and put his arm around Randy. "So nice of you to talk to our daughter Clara, and you'll have to meet Moura when she gets back. The girls just turned fifteen, and we're so proud of them," he said. "Now let me introduce you to Alyssa, another grad student in composition." Off they went, along with my fantasy of playing grown-up femme fatale at my parents' party.

Anyhow, I hoped I wasn't coming on too strong and making "forbidden love" that much more appealing. But I didn't think she would have reached out for advice unless she suspected she was getting played. Which she was.

Chapter Four

By the time I got home, I was famished. I hoped our guests couldn't hear my stomach growling as the aroma of my mother's signature coq au vin and wild rice filled the house. After five months of frozen dinners, I'd forgotten what a wonderful cook she was.

Dr. Lewitsky and Mr. Rasher sat in the living room with my parents, sipping white wine and snacking on some disgusting-looking stuffed mushrooms. They rose to greet me. I hadn't seen them since the funeral. Like my parents, they seemed to have aged in just a few months. The creases on her face had deepened, and dark shadows underlined his eyes.

She hugged me and exclaimed, "It's so lovely to see you, Clara. I only wish we were all here together under happier circumstances." Her eyes misted, as she grabbed my hands in hers. "Look at these lovely long fingers—just like Moura's." She held up my hands as though she were showing off the prize winner of a hand model contest at the state fair. "Don't you think so, Joel?"

He shrugged and looked uncomfortable, while she blathered on. "Well, it's just a shame that you don't play."

I pulled my hands from hers. "Not really. Believe me, if you'd heard me play, you'd know why Mrs. Edlemore was so relieved to lose me as a student."

I was already sorry they'd come, wishing I was back in my cocoon of a newspaper office instead of here. But this was a command performance. Even if it hadn't been, I would have shown up for my mom and dad—especially Mom. I'd do anything to help her find her way out of her grief-filled fog—even spend yet another evening on Moura talk. Hell, I'd had a lot of practice.

As though sensing my feelings, my dad, bless him, piped up with: "Clara has other talents. She's like you, Joel. She writes for her school newspaper and wants to study journalism in college."

Mr. Rasher smiled politely. "Music feeds the soul, but words on paper can sing, too, no?"

"Yes," I said, liking him a bit better tonight. I knew he was a big deal in the music writing business, but his work always seemed a bit over the top to me, almost like his philosophy was—why use a simple word like "sad" to describe a piece of music, when you could use "lugubrious"?

He and his wife were a super example of "opposites attract." Whereas she was perfectly put together with her coiffed frosted hair and navy tailored pantsuit, he seemed … well, wild. If his dusty blond hair wasn't pulled back into a ponytail like it was tonight, it spilled everywhere. And his clothes always looked like, "I had to throw something on, so this was it." Tonight he wore jeans, weathered cowboy boots, and an ancient-looking jacket over a T-shirt from last year's Stravinsky Festival.

The conversation shifted to the logistics of setting up Moura's memorial scholarship fund. Dad proposed offering college scholarships to disadvantaged aspiring pianists, while Mom insisted, "It's really too late for a concert career by that time. Moura would have wanted to help younger gifted students get the kind of quality piano training they need."

As far as I knew, Moura had never had the slightest interest in advancing anyone's music career other than her own. But hey, this was the most animated I'd seen my mother in weeks, so who was I to argue?

The discussion continued into dinner. Dr. Lewitsky went on and on about memorializing my sister—her prize student, who'd catapulted her own reputation as a master teacher into the stratosphere—but Mr. Rasher was strangely quiet. Likely his wife had pressured him to write the flattering puff piece about Moura for *Ohio Magazine*. Was he as weary as I was of all conversations revolving around the great Moura Seibert?

I was starting to feel a tinge of guilt for having such thoughts, when Dr. Lewitsky turned to me. "You know, Clara, you could be a big help. How about if you contact all the young people who were Moura's fans about raising money for the scholarship? She has a memorial site on Facebook where you could get in touch with them."

I swallowed hard.

"Actually, Clara steers clear of social media," Dad said. "There were some … unkind things said after Moura's death."

"Well," Dr. Lewitsky said with a sniff, "I'd be glad to do a little research for you. You know how it is—young people respond more to another young person."

"Honestly, I don't think her fans would respond well to me. It's no secret there were a lot of rumors...."

"All the more reason to show them what rubbish all that talk was, how much you care," she argued.

"I should think you'd want to do anything to help memorialize your sister," Mom said in a low voice. For the briefest of moments, our gazes locked.

"I'll think about it. And maybe I can get an article in the school paper."

"Great idea, honey," my dad said. "Now, how about if we form a planning committee?"

Dr. Lewitsky seemed enthusiastic about all the possible candidates, until Dad brought up asking Anne Hartsell. "I'd rather not if you don't mind," she said. "Alex and Moura were such competitors, and it might be, you know, uncomfortable."

My dad looked puzzled but smoothly steered the conversation elsewhere. I was puzzled, too. Alex Kwon was Mrs. Hartsell's student—also very gifted and ambitious. He and Moura had gone head-to-head in competitions since they were kids. She usually came out on top, but as far as I knew, they'd been friends. So had Dr. Lewitsky and Mrs. Hartsell.

I filed this away in my mental folder of "Strange Things About Music People I Will Never Understand." Since everyone seemed to be done with their main course, I offered to clear the table and bring out the dessert and coffee. Even kitchen duty was preferable to committee talk.

When I brought in dessert, however, conversation was blessedly interrupted by "oohs" and "ahs" over my mom's chocolate mousse topped with real whipped cream. She'd definitely brought her A-game to tonight's dinner, and she looked brighter and more alive than I'd seen her in weeks. Maybe doing something in Moura's honor would really help her heal and move on with her life. I sure hoped so.

As they lingered over coffee, my dad brought out his trusty yellow legal pad to jot down notes on their next steps. A classic Dad move. Mr. Rasher excused himself and headed for the bathroom, and I retreated to the kitchen and pantry to put away the dishes. I was getting out some Saran wrap to cover the leftovers when I glanced down the hallway that led to Moura's studio. Her door was slightly ajar and the light was on.

My whole body stiffened. I'd avoided Moura's studio since that night—too many ghosts, too many memories. The sickening sweet smell of my sister's blood, her glassy-eyed stare, my own screams.

I felt myself sliding. *No—not going to replay this. Not again.* What had the therapist said? Take three cleansing breaths and substitute the bad stuff with the memory where Moura was alive, happy, playing the music she loved so much.

The breaths helped, but my curiosity won over, and I crept down the hall to Moura's sanctuary.

The door creaked slightly as I opened it wider. Mr. Rasher turned around, a startled look on his face. He held a picture of Moura that had been shot during a guest appearance with the university orchestra. Her eyes were closed, and her head was thrown back in ecstasy as she played the final notes of a Bach concerto.

"This is my favorite picture of her," he said, his voice sounding unsteady. "Years of covering music, and I've never met anyone this young who played with such reverence for the music, such passion. She was remarkable, you know?"

"She was," I said. He looked so sad that I moved toward him and touched his arm. "I loved listening to her play, too."

For the first time that night, he smiled warmly. Then he surprised me by giving me a hug. He smelled of sandalwood and country air.

When he drew back, he said, "I'm so sorry, Clara. I know how difficult this is for you, even if you and Moura … you weren't close, were you? Moura just didn't understand you. You were like two shooting stars on totally different trajectories."

I was about to tell him that Moura had been the only star in my family when Dr. Lewitsky walked in. "Time to go, Joel." Her voice sounded brittle. Was it hard for her to be in Moura's studio, too?

"Yes, of course," he said, as he handed me Moura's picture. "It was nice talking with you. Take care." He touched my shoulder as he brushed past.

"You, too."

Dr. Lewitsky grabbed his arm as they moved down the hallway ahead of me.

Chapter Five

That night, I lay awake for a long time, replaying the look on my mother's face when she challenged me to work on Moura's memorial scholarship. No matter how hard I tried not to think about the argument I'd overheard three days after Moura's murder, it lingered.

I was on my way into the kitchen when I heard my dad's voice. "I can't believe you told Martino that Clara resented Moura. What were you thinking?"

I froze.

"It's true, isn't it? You know as well as I do they didn't get along." I heard the familiar sound of ice cubes clinking into a glass.

"Not the point."

"Clara was in the house. They were alone. I can't think of anyone else who'd want to harm Moura."

"You can't be serious," Dad said, his voice rising. "You're her mother. Surely you know she's not capable of such a thing. There's not a violent bone in that child's body."

"You're right," Mom said. "My mind is so jumbled right now."

Jumbled, huh? So jumbled you could actually think your own daughter was a murderer?

Could my mother's memory really be that short? Moura and I had been close once, and even as the distance between us continued to grow wider, I still loved her.

When we were little, we didn't care about playing with anyone else—we had each other. We spent hours making up stories starring our favorite dolls, Princess Mia and Princess Rose, who refused to marry the neighborhood princes unless they agreed to all live together in one castle. And whenever there were nighttime thunderstorms, Moura always climbed into my bed. She'd snuggle up against me, and I'd tell her my own version of "Little Red Riding Hood" in which the wolf was far more scared of Little Red Riding Hood than she was of him. This would strike her as funny, and she'd giggle before falling back to sleep.

And then, on our tenth birthday, Moura announced she didn't want to share a room with me anymore. "You talk too much when I'm trying to go to sleep," she complained, "and if you're not talking, you always want to leave the light on to read. It's so annoying."

Soon after, Mom told me she was fixing up the upstairs bedroom. "It'll be your own special place. You'll have so much more space and shelves to keep all your books."

It really was a nice space. I loved the sloping ceilings, the built-in bookcases, and bright yellow walls. I knew I should have been grateful. But mostly I felt banished— kicked out of my sister's room, my sister's life.

No matter what I tried, I couldn't seem to reach her,

and the piano became a huge boulder that stood between us. One night, right after our fourteenth birthday, Moura had given this amazing solo recital, and I'd gone to her room, hoping to somehow find a way to reconnect. I told her how great she'd played that night.

She tossed off a "thanks" and said, "It could have been the two of us, you know."

"What are you talking about?"

"If you'd just been willing to practice and stick with the piano, we could have performed as a duo. There are all kinds of music written for two pianos, and people love seeing twins on stage."

"That would have been great if I had an ounce of your talent, and more importantly, loved it like you do. But it just wasn't me."

She shrugged. "Your loss."

Tears sprang to my eyes. "I miss you."

"I'm right here."

"It's just—we never talk anymore, spend any time together. I miss 'us.'"

"There is no 'us.' We're not little kids anymore. We have the same parents, we look a lot alike, and that's about it."

She was right. But that didn't make the sting of her words hurt any less.

I'd always dreamed that someday we'd find our way back to each other. Now we'd never have the chance.

I was finally drifting off when my cell rang. I fumbled for it in the dark and murmured a sleepy "hello."

No sound. Again.

I let out a stream of swear words and threw the phone down.

The next day, it was a relief to focus on something else. A semi-famous writer, Dr. Ritterman, author of *Get Out! Don't Leave Me!*, was speaking at Psychology Club after school about the challenges of loving someone with borderline personality disorder. Since our club president was out with the flu and I was the vice president, I was giving the introduction when Ben Marchetta slipped into the back row and I stumbled over the title of Dr. Ritterman's book. Smooth.

I'd always thought it was dumb to crush on someone you hardly knew just because they were eye candy, but that's exactly what I'd been doing ever since Ben walked into my French class. Whenever we were paired up for conversation, I got all tongue-tied. I blamed it on his amazing smile and those dark eyes that looked at me so intently when we talked. But this guy was so far out of my league I'd be lucky to be on the cleanup crew for his ballpark. He'd just moved here and was already being pursued by Monica Levin and Emily Stills, the two most popular girls in our class. Besides, a lot of the kids at school saw me as damaged goods. Unless you were a sicko, who'd want to get involved with someone who might have offed her own sister?

I forced myself to focus on our speaker. He seemed like a cool guy, and by the time he finished describing his case study of "Gwen," I knew one thing for sure—this disorder was no picnic. One minute, Gwen was covering her husband with kisses and telling him he was so wonderful she couldn't imagine how she'd ever lived without him. Ten minutes later, she was swearing at him and ordering him to pack his bags. The hapless husband had no clue what he'd done to get the boot. And then, by the time he'd finished packing, Gwen was—surprise, surprise—begging him to stay.

Dr. Ritterman went on to say that a lot of therapists had been reluctant to treat folks with the disorder, because they rarely got better. Recently, however, some clinicians were reporting good progress in working with their borderline patients. When I asked about causes during the Q and A, he shrugged his shoulders and threw up his hands in mock despair. "That's the 64,000-dollar question. No one really knows for sure. It's been linked to experiencing severe abuse as a child, often sexual abuse. But most likely, genetic predisposition is involved as well."

Was I being paranoid or was everyone looking at me after I'd asked my question? No doubt they were still wondering if I was suffering from a disorder much worse than borderline— the homicidal kind. Living under this cloud of suspicion was getting old. Then again, if the real killer, not to mention my little email friend, wasn't found soon, that cloud over my head would be the least of my problems.

After the meeting, I stayed to thank Dr. Ritterman and help Mrs. Olivet put her classroom back together before heading to the newspaper office. I thought no one else was around until I felt a tap on my shoulder. I nearly jumped out of my skin.

"Hey, sorry. I didn't mean to scare you," Ben said with that smile that could melt every ice cube in my kitchen freezer.

"Didn't know anybody was still around." My heart hammered in my chest so loudly I worried he could hear it.

"What did you think of the talk?"

"Thought it was really interesting. I've never known anybody with this disorder. Doesn't sound like much fun."

"It's not. I'm almost positive one of my aunts had this. Fortunately, she found a therapist who was able to help her."

"That's great," I said, as I started to breathe easier. Nobody this good-looking should be this nice, but apparently, he was. And it seemed a lot easier to talk to him in English. My French accent was embarrassingly bad. And Ben's wasn't so hot either.

"You know," I said, "I think if you shake anybody's family tree, you're bound to find a bunch of RWIs."

"RWIs?"

"Relatives with issues."

He laughed and I couldn't help smiling. Wasn't laughter supposed to be the key to a man's heart? Or was it food? I was going with the laughter.

"Okay," he said, "so the next time we get paired up in French class, we can talk about our crazy families. Deal?"

My smile faded. Ben wanted to discuss our families? Sure, he was new this year, but he must have heard the rumors. Was he another curiosity seeker? I hated this! Would I ever be able to have a simple conversation with someone without questioning their motives?

He looked at me, eyebrows raised, and I realized I hadn't answered him. Finally, I said, "With my lousy French, and my family, we should probably just stick to the weather."

Back in the office, I sharpened every pencil in my desk drawer. Since I always wrote on my computer, this was ridiculous. But I was stalling for time. I hated what this creepy message sender had done to me. I'd always been eager to open my emails. But now, my stomach was in knots at the thought of looking at my inbox.

Plus, I was obsessing about the frown that crossed Ben's face when I blew him off for wanting to talk about our families. What was wrong with me? Tomorrow I'd tell him I was just kidding, and I'd love to talk with him about anything—well, almost anything.

I made myself type in my password and look at my inbox. No new messages, thank God.

I was finishing up my draft of a piece on Dr. Ritterman's talk when Tony popped in. He must have sprayed half a gallon of Stud Man cologne on, because the office immediately reeked. CJ insisted his cologne was sexy, but I thought it was a great example of how too much of a good thing can be totally gross.

He handed me a latte from Starbucks. "Figured you'd still be here and could use a pick-me-up."

"Just what I was starting to fantasize about. Thanks so much!" I pulled the lid off and brought the cup to my nose and took a big whiff. I glanced at the wall clock—already after five. "So what brings you here so late, other than rescuing me from my afternoon blahs?"

"We're still getting hammered about Donny's piece on cheating, and I wanted to get some work in on an editorial."

"Sounds good," I said. "I'll send you my draft of the article on the Psychology Club speaker before I head out."

But when I opened my email back up to send Tony my draft, there was another message:

How can you live with yourself?
Soon you won't have to.

My whole body started to shake. I must have groaned, because Tony cried, "Clara! What's wrong? Are you okay?"

"Nope." I bolted into Mr. Bradford's adjoining classroom. I was done playing Lone Ranger, and I'd made a promise.

By now, I was breathing hard. Damn. Mr. Bradford was on the phone, and I hadn't even knocked. But he took one look at me and said, "Let me call you back," and hung up.

"Another one?" he asked. His eyebrows were drawn tightly together, and he ran his hands through the few stray hairs left on the sides of his head.

"Yup."

"Let's take a look. But first, do you want some water? Can I get you anything?"

"N … n … no," I managed to say.

We sat there together staring at the screen.

"I hate that you're having to go through this." He lifted his hand as if to touch my arm but then awkwardly dropped it.

"Thanks."

"Do you want to call Detective Martino right now or just forward this to him?"

"Let's forward it. I can't deal right now. I'll call him tomorrow."

"Okay, but you need to tell your parents. Tonight."

I was pulling a pizza out of the freezer when Dad walked into the kitchen and grabbed a beer out of the fridge.

"Where's Mom?"

"Upstairs, resting." He flipped the top open on his Coors and took a big swallow. "You know, I thought the grief counseling sessions would help your mother." He sighed heavily and took another sip of his beer. "If I could just get her to eat more, get out a bit ..."

"She seemed better at dinner, talking about Moura's memorial fund. Maybe working on that will help."

"I really hope so.... Now tell me, how was your day?"

"It was fine until the end." My stomach did a major flip-flop. Maybe pizza wasn't such a great idea.

"What happened?"

I filled him in on the latest email and assured him that Mr. Bradford and I had already contacted Detective Martino.

"I'm so sorry, honey," Dad said. Then he pulled me into an awkward hug, and just as quickly, released me. He'd never been much of a hugger, but he was trying. "This is awful," he said, as he dragged his fingers through his thick hair, now almost totally gray.

"Yup."

"Maybe we should take you out of school until this gets cleared up."

"No way! This is my senior year." What I didn't say was that the thought of spending all my time in our tomb of a house with a mother who barely spoke to me—let alone looked at me—was more horrifying than dealing with my email stalker.

"I know, but we have to think about your safety, and—"

"I can't live my life locked up in this house. I can't do it. Period." My voice shook, and I tried to push back my tears, but they leaked out anyway. I swiped at them with my forearm, and Dad handed me a Kleenex.

"All right, all right. We have to think this through. I want to talk to Detective Martino. Now."

Just then, the doorbell rang. I flinched at the sudden noise. What a jumpy mess I'd become! "Were you expecting someone, Dad?"

"No. Let me see who it is."

Chapter Six

I followed behind Dad, wiping away the evidence of my meltdown. He peered through the peephole and then flung the door open. "Just the person we wanted to talk to."

Detective Martino lumbered in, wearing a misshapen black rain coat that was missing a couple of buttons, and took a seat in the living room. "I'm sure Clara has told you she got another message today."

He probably hoped I hadn't told my father, so he could demonstrate what a truly untrustworthy sort I was, but …

"We were just discussing what to do," Dad said. "Is there any way to figure out who's sending Clara these emails?"

"Unfortunately, it looks doubtful." Turning toward me, he said, "Do you do much shopping online?"

"No, not really." *What in the world does that have to do with anything?*

"What about your friends? Anyone you know who likes to shop online?"

"Detective," Dad interrupted, "just tell us what this is about."

"It looks like the messages are coming from one of those web businesses that offer temporary, disposable email addresses. Shoppers like them because they can avoid having their regular email accounts flooded with spam. Most of them are only for receiving emails, like a confirmation receipt for a purchase. But a few also allow you to send emails and don't require any registration process. The address you use automatically disappears within a matter of minutes."

Dad leaned forward, his eyes narrowing. "So you're telling us you have no way to trace who's sending these?"

"Unfortunately, that's what it comes down to. I'm sorry."

"And you asked me if my friends and I like to shop online, because you think I'm sending these messages to myself? Or my friends are?" I said, my voice rising. This was unbelievable.

"It's my job to ask questions, Clara. I have to investigate every possible angle, especially because these messages may be connected to your sister's murder."

I was tempted to grab him by his jowls and pull hard, but Dad, bless him, launched his own attack.

"How dare you insinuate that Clara sent these messages to herself! This is just more of the same from you people! Stop harassing my daughter, or so help me, I'll take legal action." The vein on his forehead throbbed, and my heart pounded triple time.

"I'm not trying to harass anybody. But I have to consider every possibility. I'm sorry if I've offended you. And Clara," he said, turning to me, "you must continue to keep me informed. I've alerted the security officer at your school about your situation. He'll help you stay safe."

I nodded, my heart slowing down a bit, even as I thought, *fat chance*. Leonard High's security officer, Bernie Pittman, spent most of his time flirting with the females in the office and sneaking cigarettes out by the back dumpsters. He was not what you'd call a promising candidate for protecting me.

Dad, however, seemed somewhat mollified. "Well, that's something. Is there any way you could assign some officers to watch Clara when she's not in school?"

"I wish we had the manpower to do that. I'm sorry to say, Dr. Seibert, insults and threats like the ones Clara's been dealing with since Moura's death have become epidemic in our country ... I know how upsetting this must be."

"This goes beyond upsetting! I have one daughter who's been murdered and another who's being threatened. Again. And what about Moura? Is there anything new in the investigation? *Anything?*" Now the vein in his neck kicked in.

"I wish there were, but we're not giving up. We're continuing to check out leads that come in."

"What leads?" Dad said, his face getting darker by the second. I hoped he'd remembered to take his blood pressure medication this morning.

"Nothing definitive right now. As soon as we have anything solid, I'll let you know." The detective stood up. "You have my word. I'll keep you informed."

As he headed for the door, he stopped and turned around as though he'd forgotten something. He gave me a long look. "I'd be very careful if I were you, Clara."

My mouth dropped open. I couldn't tell whether he was advising me to be safety-conscious, or whether he was warning me that if I didn't watch out, my identity as my sister's killer and email self-terrorizer would be unmasked.

Maybe that was the point.

I plodded through the next few days. No new messages from my email stalker, and no getting paired up in French class for cozy conversations with Ben Marchetta. Instead, Madame Auld paired me up with Kerry Sheffield, who was such a soft talker that I never had any idea what she was saying. It was like conversing with myself. Meanwhile, Ben had gotten assigned to talk with Emily Stills, who'd given me a withering look when she'd passed by my desk and was now giggling and batting her fake eyelashes so fast I hoped they'd fall off.

As usual, the column kept me going. Every time I was tempted to go into pity-party mode, somebody reminded me I was far from alone in having problems. Take today's email, for instance:

Dear Since You Asked,

First of all, thanks so much for not printing my last email to you, and please don't print this one, either.

You probably don't remember me, but I wrote to you last spring about my boyfriend. He's real popular, and I was super flattered when he wanted to be with me. I asked you how I could get him to trust me, because he was constantly grilling me on who I was with, and we'd get into these humongous fights if he didn't like the answers.

At first, I didn't like your answer, either. Instead of giving me advice on fixing the relationship, you told me I was in danger, and I needed to "grow a backbone and dump the jerk."

All I can say is—you were right. Two weeks after I wrote you that letter, the shoving started—then the slapping and the punching. I finally grew that backbone and broke up with him.

So you'd think that would have solved it, right? But guess what? He drives by my house, slowly, every night. At least I think it's him. And when my girlfriends and I go to the mall, he always just happens to be there, too—not too close, but there, watching me.

And my parents like him! They want me to get back together with him. They don't believe that "such a wonderful guy" could ever have acted this way. As far as they're concerned, I made a big mistake breaking things off with him.

Again, please don't print this. I don't want your readers to think there's no way out of a bad relationship. I'm still glad I broke up with him. I know I'm better off now than I was. But he just doesn't quit! How do I escape this?

—Took Your Advice, but …

I sat there for a long time, wondering what I could possibly say. We had a lot in common. She was still scared. And angry. Me, too. Finally, I wrote:

Dear Took Your Advice, but …,

My favorite fantasy is that we could push an "Eject" button and send the creeps in our lives hurtling into space, never to be heard from again. I can totally understand why you're so angry.

But I hope you also realize how awesome you are! You took back power over your own life. That's why this jerk is pushing back and trying so hard to get under your skin, even if it is from a distance.

I know every advice columnist always says the same thing— "get professional help," but there's a reason for that. No one can make it through something like this alone. I had a friend who went through this, and she found a really great support group for teens run by the Women's Project Center (425 West Helms Road, tel. 937-345-6203). I'd definitely check it out.

I'm really sorry your parents haven't been more supportive. Don't give up on them. And write everything down!

You've already done the really hard part. Hang in there— you are so worth it.

—Since You Asked

I didn't know whether I'd said anything remotely helpful, but this was all I had in the tank right now. I forwarded her email and my response to Mrs. Rivera before I opened my inbox. There it was. Another message.

The guilty must suffer
It's almost payback time.…

I closed my eyes, clutched my roiling stomach, and rocked back and forth. *Deep breaths, take deep breaths*, I told myself, but it was no use. Bile rose in my throat. I barely made it to the bathroom where I deposited all the remains of the chicken à la king from lunch. Yicht.

I splashed water on my face, stuffed a breath mint in my mouth, and geared myself up for the drill—talk to Mr. B., forward the email to Martino, tell my dad.

The trouble was, they couldn't help me.

What should I do? This email jerk hadn't come out directly and accused me of murdering Moura. But I'd bet a year's supply of Mellow Moose ice cream that if I didn't figure out who murdered her, this creep was going to come after me. Sooner rather than later. Solving my sister's murder wouldn't bring Moura back, but maybe it would give us some kind of relief, some kind of closure. She didn't deserve to die, and my family didn't deserve to be put through this hell. I had to do something. But what? Start my own investigation?

That was crazy, right? The sum total of what I knew about homicide investigations came from watching *Law & Order* reruns. And it could be dangerous. Moura's murderer was out there, and my nosing around could make him—or her—mighty nervous.

But what did I have to lose? I was already in danger. My family was in so much pain. Doing something— *anything*—had to be better than sitting around waiting to become the next casualty that could leave my parents totally destroyed. Wasn't I always advising the people

Chapter Seven |

"So," Jenny said, "you got another message and decided to play Nancy Drew? Have you lost your mind?"

"Possibly, but I'm done sitting around waiting for this idiot to make a move. The message today said, 'The guilty must suffer.' The jerk thinks I murdered Moura and wants revenge. If I can figure out who murdered my sister, it's like killing three birds with one stone. I get this creep off my back, bring her killer to justice, and give my family some relief from the pain of knowing her murderer is still alive, while my sister lies underground."

"I see your point, but let's pause for a moment. Can we discuss over leftovers? That new Italian place across the street makes a mean chicken cacciatore. I've got a carton full in my fridge."

Jenny wasn't kidding. The cacciatore was to die for, and my messed-up stomach had made a miraculous recovery.

"I really don't want to be a downer," she said as she put her fork down a few minutes later, "but how do you think you'll discover who killed your sister? The police have been investigating for months, and they haven't gotten anywhere."

"That's just it. How hard have they been looking? Martino zeroed in on me right away and still seems stuck on the idea. It's like he read the homicide statistics that indicate the murderer is most often a family member, and decided it had to be me. I was home, and Mom and Dad had eighty plus witnesses who placed them at the university orchestra rehearsal. And don't forget, half the Youth Orchestra heard me screaming at Moura two nights before she was murdered."

I paced back and forth, replaying that fight. Not exactly my finest moment. But I'd been so pissed. Mom and Dad had a faculty dinner and insisted I had to take Moura to rehearsal and pick her up two hours later. My sister, of course, had never bothered learning to drive, unwilling to take the time away from her daily practice schedule. Naturally, I'd been appointed her backup chauffeur. When I dropped her off, I begged her to find another ride home. "I've got three tests tomorrow. Text me and let me know ASAP if you've got a ride. And don't forget like you did the last time, and the time before that."

No text, of course, and when I got there, she was sitting around with Kristen and Alex. When she saw me, she looked surprised. "Oh, my God, Clara, I forgot to text you. We're going to Denny's. Kristen said she could drop me home."

She didn't even have the grace to apologize. I exploded. "I told you I have three tests tomorrow. You're always doing this to me. It takes three seconds to text someone, but no, I don't even deserve three seconds of your precious time.

You know what? I don't recognize you anymore. You may be a great pianist, but you've morphed into this totally self-centered bitch."

Moura's face turned white. Her friends looked away and seemed frozen in an awkward silence. Finally, Moura said, "You're overreacting. I said I was sorry—"

"No, you didn't. You never do."

"Well, I meant to. I just forgot. We have a big concert coming up—"

"That's just it! You always have a big concert coming up. It never occurs to you that maybe I have a life, too. I'm done, okay? From now on, find yourself another lackey to drive you around."

I stalked off, but not before I heard Moura mutter, "Can you believe her?" to her friends.

Jenny interrupted my trip down memory lane. "Look, sisters fight. And face it. She really was all about herself and nobody else."

I gave her a long look. It was one thing for me to call Moura a self-centered bitch, but I didn't like it when other people dissed her. Besides, she wasn't around anymore to defend herself.

Jenny immediately changed the subject. "Okay, back to this investigation thing. Martino must have interviewed everybody who might have known anything—the neighbors, her friends, her teachers. He must have searched her computer and cell phone for clues. What makes you think you can find out anything he didn't?"

"Maybe I can't, but I have to try. Somebody's got to

know something. There were no signs of forced entry. Nothing was taken—well, except for the bookend that the police think was the murder weapon. This was personal. I'm convinced of it."

"Agreed. She must have known and trusted this person to let them into her studio."

"My guess is she was playing something for the killer, and that's why there's no evidence she struggled—nothing under her fingernails, no defensive wounds on her arms or her face. You know how she went into the zone when she played. I think the murderer snuck up on her and hit her so hard that she lost consciousness instantly."

I flashed back to the way Moura had looked the night I'd found her, blood pooling all around her head, seeping into the piano keys, dripping onto the rug. So much blood. And that sickening smell. "Oh God," I cried, as I stumbled and fell onto the couch. I squeezed my eyes shut.

Jenny threw her arm around me. "It's okay, Clara. It's going to be okay."

I took deep breaths, then looked into Jenny's warm hazel eyes, so full of concern. "Sometimes I think nothing will ever be okay again."

"I know, and I worry about you. But what if you try talking to people and they get really mad, thinking you're trying to pin your sister's murder on them?"

"I'll try my hardest not to seem accusatory. I'll say I've been getting these threatening emails that are scaring me, and Moura's death has devastated my family. Not knowing who killed her has made it impossible for us to move on.

So I'm trying to talk to everyone I can think of who knew Moura well, or who might have seen something. If we all put our heads together, maybe something will occur to us that the police overlooked." I looked at Jenny expectantly. "So what do you think?"

"That's good. But suppose one of these folks you're trying so hard to enlist in your 'Let's find Moura's murderer team' is the killer and decides you're getting a little too nosy?"

"I'll just have to take my chances. Or maybe you'll be my bodyguard, tennis racquet in hand?"

"Tennis Mafia to the rescue!"

"There's a Tennis Mafia?"

"We do it all, baby," said Jenny with a wink.

"Yeah, right ... Oh, one more thing. Moura's piano teacher asked me to contact her fans about a memorial scholarship—see if they want to help. They're the last people I feel like talking to, but maybe they know something."

"Worth checking out."

I jumped up and fished out a yellow legal pad and a couple of pens from my backpack.

"Fall break's next week. Let's make a list of who I need to talk to."

Oh God. I had officially morphed into my dad.

The next day after school, I ran into Kristen as she came out of the newspaper office. Bingo. Kristen was on my list. Maybe I could get started with the investigation right now.

Of course, just looking at Kristen made my eyes hurt.

Every other week, she dyed her hair a different color. Today, it was fluorescent orange. Between her hair and her uniform of tie-dyed dresses and granny boots, her look screamed, "I hang with the artists." And she did.

"Hey, Kristen," I said with what I hoped passed for a super friendly smile. "Do you have any time to have coffee with me? I could really use your help on something."

"What do you need?" she asked, eyeing me warily.

"I want to talk about Moura."

Her eyes widened. "Why?"

"Moura really liked you."

She seemed to perk up a bit. Truthfully, I had no idea how Moura had felt about Kristen personally, but I was pretty sure she'd loved Kristen's gushing about her playing, especially in print. And Kristen was well connected to the music scene in Springbrook.

"I'm not sure if I'll be any help, but I'm willing to talk. I can't do it now, though. I'm covering the final rehearsal for the orchestra before they go off on their fall break trip. How about we meet at Starbucks later? Around five?"

I'd snagged a rear table at Starbucks, where we'd have some privacy. Their sound system was playing an ancient Ella Fitzgerald recording of "You Leave Me Breathless." An image of Ben Marchetta floated across my mind, but I quickly pushed it away. What an amazing voice Fitzgerald had had—it was like taking a bath in warm honey. I wasn't a regular at Starbucks just because of their mocha lattes. They also played my kind of music. Ever since my grandma, whose mom had been a nightclub singer, had introduced me to all the great Ladies of Jazz—Ella Fitzgerald, Sarah Vaughan, Billie Holiday, Lena Horne—I'd been hooked. I figured I was the only one at my high school who was more familiar with my great-grandmother's music than Beyoncé's latest.

Kristen showed up a few minutes past five, and I met her at the counter. "Thanks for coming. I've got seats for us back there," I said, gesturing toward the table I'd staked out. "My treat today. What would you like?"

"Tea would be great. How about a Chai Spice?"

After fetching her tea and my usual mocha latte, I told her how much I appreciated her talking to me and asked her to keep our conversation confidential. "I don't want to get in trouble for interfering with a police investigation, but they don't seem to be getting anywhere, my family is devastated, and now I'm getting these creepy emails."

"I'm sorry for you and your family. I really am. But what can I tell you that you don't know, or the police don't know?"

"Well, I'd really like to talk to everyone Moura was close to. Who would you say were her close friends?"

Kristen took a sip of her tea and frowned. "Honestly? Moura was not easy to get close to. For one thing, she wasn't around that much, especially after she started homeschooling. Even for those of us who loved her and loved her playing, she was a bit of a mystery. It was like she avoided getting too personal when she talked to you. It was always about the music. Maybe it was different with

Hannah. They were *very* close," she said. "And I guess you know she'd dated Richard. Have you talked to either of them yet?"

"Not yet. What about Alex? It's no secret he and Moura were very competitive. Any issues between them that you're aware of?"

Kristen looked down, fiddled with her stir stick, and then looked up at me. "Alex is a friend of mine. He's very upset about Moura and would never have done anything to her."

"Right—but they competed for years, and she came out on top a lot. Was there any resentment there?"

"Oh, come on. Didn't you resent her at times? The family superstar?"

"I've never denied that," I said evenly. "But I also didn't kill my sister."

"Well, I can't see Alex harming her, either."

We were quiet for a few moments, as I watched her shred her napkin into little pieces.

"Is there something you're not telling me?"

She blinked several times and finally brought her gaze to mine. "It's probably nothing, and I'm not even sure that what I saw was anything."

"What? Tell me!"

"Well, it kind of looked like they were arguing one night at a Youth Orchestra rehearsal. A few weeks before Moura ... you know ... the director gave the musicians a ten-minute break. When I came out of the restroom, I noticed Moura and Alex at the end of the hallway. I wasn't close enough to hear what they were saying, but Alex was gesturing a lot, and he pointed his finger at her and shook it. She said something back to him and then pushed past him and stormed down the hall. When she passed me, her face was all blotchy red, and she didn't even acknowledge me."

"So you have no idea what they were talking about?"

"No clue. I'd never seen them be anything but friendly toward each other. I've racked my brain about that rehearsal, and there was nothing unusual about it. They each had pieces where they were the featured pianist, and both played really well."

"Did you tell the police about this?"

She shrugged. "No, I mean, I couldn't even be sure they were arguing, and Alex is the farthest thing from a murderer. I've known him since we were in kindergarten. And anyway, the police mainly asked about you."

That figures. "So what did you tell them?" I asked, not sure I wanted to know.

"I had to tell them the truth—you know, about how you told her off in front of us after rehearsal that night—and how no one in Moura's world, including Moura, paid you much attention. She was on her way to stardom, and you were, well, you were not."

I winced. All those feelings of pathetic loserdom threatened to pull me under. Again. But I wouldn't let her get to me. "Well, thanks for your honesty. Just one more thing. Can you think of anyone else outside of the staff who might have known I was the writer for *Since You Asked*?"

"Oh, that," she said, lowering her gaze. "I probably

should have said something.... That night you yelled at Moura? Afterward, she told everybody who went to Denny's that you were 'always making mountains out of molehills, and you had no business giving anybody advice in that stupid newspaper column of yours.'"

I froze. I couldn't believe Moura had outed me. Then again, she probably couldn't believe I'd told her off in front of her friends.

"Oh, my God," I said, burying my face in my hands.

"I tried to do some damage control—told everyone not to say anything because we didn't want anybody to know who wrote the column. At the time, I didn't think it was that big a deal. Alex was the only one at Denny's who went to our school. But he wouldn't have blabbed."

"Were Hannah and Richard there?"

"Yeah, sure. We all still hung out, even though Richard and Moura weren't together anymore."

Great. Just great. Moura's inner circle had apparently all known I wrote the column. Moura might as well have pasted a bull's-eye on my chest.

"I'm really sorry Moura told," Jenny said, when I'd stopped by her apartment to fill her in. "But I was pretty sure other folks outside the paper must have known. And obviously, you've got to talk to Alex."

"No kidding, but I'll probably have to wait until after break. I called his house on my way over here, and his mom said they were leaving tomorrow morning for a bunch of visits to conservatories. First stop, Juilliard. I guess we know they have at least one opening with Moura dead."

"But it's hard to imagine Alex killing anyone. He always seems so buttoned-down, so mild-mannered," Jenny said.

"Are you forgetting all those Nick at Night episodes we watched of the old *Superman* show? That's exactly what they said about him when he was pretending to be Clark Kent."

"Alex doesn't strike me as the Superman type," she said.

"No? Guess again, Wonder Woman! Alex is a black belt."

"You're kidding. A pianist who does karate? Isn't he worried about protecting his hands?"

"Apparently not."

"When does he have the time? The guy gets straight As and practices piano a zillion hours a day."

"I interviewed him once for a psychology research project on time management. This guy gets more done in a day than I do in a month," I said.

"He just doesn't seem like the type, though, to get violent."

"That's what neighbors always say when they discover they're living next door to a serial killer: 'Such a nice guy, so friendly, we had no idea.'"

"Point taken. So if Alex isn't available, are you going to try to talk to Hannah and Richard this week?"

"That's the plan. Also want to call Dr. Lewitsky—see if she's got any contact info for fans I can go talk to."

"You want company?"

"No, but thanks. I think they'd be more likely to clam

up if two of us showed up. It would seem too much like an interrogation. For sure, though, I want to keep running everything by you. It helps."

"Okay. You hungry?" Jenny stood up.

"Always. What have you got in mind?"

"How about Chinese?"

"Is this about seeing Mr. Hottie Deliveryman again?"

"Nah. I stood close to him last week, and he reeked."

"Of what?"

"Cigarettes. You know I can't stand the smell, not to mention the stupidity of anybody who smokes."

"Remind me never to take up smoking."

"Clara, no offense, but you seem to be doing a great job of risking your life without smoking a single cigarette."

Chapter Eight

Hannah lived across town in a small bungalow set far back from the street. As I knocked on her door around eleven on Monday morning, I could hear the strains of a violin, probably Hannah practicing. Her playing had helped her snag a scholarship to a Catholic high school in town. I'd lucked out that they were on fall break, too.

Moura's longtime best friend was wearing an old pair of gray sweats and an oversized long-sleeved T-shirt when she let me in. Her appearance startled me. With her blonde curls, sparkling blue eyes, and peach complexion, she'd always reminded me of a commercial for farm-fresh milk. But today, her hair hung limply about her washed-out face.

"Thanks for seeing me," I said, as she gestured for me to take a seat in the cramped living room.

"No problem. My mom's at work and my little brother's at the Y, so this is a good time to talk." She picked up a pile of newspapers on the armchair across from me and chucked them on the floor before sinking into the lumpy seat. "So what can I help you with?"

"The police don't seem to be getting anywhere with

Moura's murder, and now I'm getting threats, and—"

"You're getting threats? That's awful!" She looked genuinely horrified. "What's going on?"

"Just some jerk emailing me. Probably nothing, but he thinks I killed Moura. I've got to figure out who did. I'm trying to touch base with everyone who was close to her to see if we can come up with any ideas about who might have wanted to hurt her."

"I can't imagine anyone wanting to hurt Moura. She had scores of admirers, not enemies. And she was my dearest friend in the world." Tears welled up in her eyes and spilled down her cheeks.

"I know. I know how much you miss her."

"It's just ha … hard," she said, between sobs. "We'll never spend another Sunday afternoon playing duets together."

I swallowed, feeling guilty. I'd raked all this up for her again. "I hope it helps to know that you were one of the few people Moura really felt close to."

"I guess—it's just … no one in my family understands how I feel about music. If it's not fishing or NASCAR racing, they're not interested. It's like I dropped down from another planet into their lives. But … but … Moura—she *got* me. I *got* her. From that first day we landed in music camp together, two geeky seventh graders, there was that connection. You know?"

"I do know. We actually have something in common. Your family doesn't get you because you love to make music, and my family doesn't get me because I don't."

"Yeah, Moura used to wonder where you came from." She gave me a half-smile.

"She wasn't alone.... Was there anything different about Moura in the last few weeks before she died? Any problems she was having? Things she was worried about?"

Fresh tears dripped down her face, and she wiped them away with the sleeve of her sweatshirt. "I ... I don't know. That's part of what's been so awful for me. We'd always told each other everything, but in that last month or two, it was like she closed up. She started canceling out on our Sunday afternoons. I kept asking her to talk to me, tell me what was going on. I knew something was bothering her, but she denied it over and over."

"You have no idea what it was?"

"None. I knew she'd broken things off with Richard, but she insisted it was no big deal. She told me she thought his pride was probably a little wounded, since he's used to doing the dumping, not being the dumped. But she was sure he'd waste no time moving on. Richard's always been a player, and I don't mean just music."

"I believe it," I said, thinking about his Adonis-like good looks when he'd appeared at the door to pick up Moura. Even when I idly made conversation with him about the weather while we waited for my sister to descend, his eyes checked me out. Richard's autopilot seemed permanently set on semi-seduction mode.

"What about Moura's relationship with Alex? Were there any problems or issues between them?"

Hannah blinked hard, then shrugged. "I thought it was

pretty amazing they got along as well as they did. They always seemed to be going after the same things, you know? And they were both so good, in different ways."

"But did he resent her? The last few years, he was more often the runner-up, and she was the winner when they went head-to-head."

"I'm sure it was hard for him, but he always said Moura made him work that much harder to become a better pianist. She said the same thing about him. We hung out with him. We were all friends."

"What did she think of him?"

"Moura really respected Alex—his work ethic, his determination, his technical prowess. She felt that he was actually stronger technically, but he had more trouble tapping into the emotional nuances of the music. Underneath it all, he's a passionate guy, especially about music, but his parents are real reserved. We used to wonder if he held back when he played because he'd been raised to think it wasn't cool to let your emotions hang out all over the place."

"Hmm, interesting." And it was, but a trickle of resentment riffled through me, as I recalled Moura making fun of me for speculating about what made people tick. Apparently, it was fine for her to do that with her BFF—just not with me.

"Yeah. Alex has always been so self-contained, so disciplined. Moura and I went to one of his karate exhibitions once. Guess what his nickname is at the studio where he trains?"

"What?"

"The Silent Killer."

"You're kidding." Every hair follicle on my body stood on alert. I had to press on. "Did you pick up that there were more tensions between Alex and Moura in the last few months before she died? Did she ever mention them arguing about anything?"

She paused and rested her chin on her hands. "Now that I think about it, the last time the three of us went to Denny's after a concert, he was needling her a little. I remember he lifted his soda glass and clinked it against ours and said something like, 'Let's toast Moura Seibert—the most beautiful, gifted up-and-coming pianist in the kingdom. And the most manipulative girl I know.'"

"What did he mean?"

"No clue."

"How did Moura respond?"

"For a minute, she didn't say anything. Then it was like she decided to laugh it off and not even respond—well, except that she tore open the wrapper on her straw and blew it at him."

"And she never mentioned anything else about them arguing? Maybe at an orchestra rehearsal?"

"No ... well, actually, yes. She did say he was pissed about the Joel Rasher article about her. Alex thought the piece was going to be about both of them, and it ended up being a solo deal for Moura. He was pretty sure Rasher was focusing on Moura, since she was his wife's student. But Moura insisted it was a stupid misunderstanding, that

Mr. Rasher was planning a whole series of articles on rising music stars. Alex was next on his list."

"So did she clear things up with Alex?"

"No, not that I picked up. But she didn't say much to me those last weeks—it was all superficial. It was like she put up this wall. I knew something major had to be going on for her, but she wouldn't talk about it."

"That must have been hard. I know how close the two of you were.... To tell you the truth, I used to be so jealous of you. I'd peek into the studio sometimes on Sundays, and you and Moura would look so happy together playing—like you were in your own world, and I was always going to be an outsider."

"Sorry. For Moura, everything was about music, and you weren't into that. But," she said, her lower lip trembling, "those last weeks, you had nothing to be jealous about. I'd already lost her, at least the closeness we had.... And now she's gone forever." She brought her hands to her lap, clasping and unclasping them over and over. The skin on her knuckles was rubbed raw.

We were all rubbed raw, I thought, as I thanked her and slipped out the door.

One murder. So many victims.

Chapter Nine |

After meeting Hannah, I was so wrung out I felt like I needed a blood transfusion. But I stopped at Mickey D's instead and texted Richard, Moura's ex, to ask if he'd be willing to meet me.

He called me back immediately, sounding very intrigued and as usual, in Richard flirtation mode. "How could I possibly say 'no' to meeting with you, Clara? But before I get my hopes up that you're hitting on me, tell me what this is about."

"I want to talk about Moura."

His voice dropped. "Not my favorite topic of conversation."

"It's important." I went through my spiel, and he did sound genuinely sympathetic when I told him about the creepy emails.

"If some psycho's after you, then, of course, I'll help you any way I can. Let's do lunch tomorrow at the Bagel Café."

"You're on."

After that, I called Dad to get Dr. Lewitsky's number.

"I'm so glad you decided to help with this, honey."

"I realized it's important."

Dr. Lewitsky sounded genuinely pleased when I called her. "I'm so delighted you're willing to take this on." She promised to text me the number of the girl, Leslie Hall, who organized the memorial site.

The Bagel Café was one of my favorite places to eat in Springbrook. It always smelled like a combination of baked bread and freshly brewed coffee. Yum.

When I walked in at noon the next day, Richard was already camped out in a rear booth. He rushed over and gave me a hug. I had to admit he smelled good—sort of a sandalwood scent. "You look great," he enthused, as we headed back to the booth and slid into our seats. "I'm serious. You should be on the menu. You look good enough to eat."

"Cut the crap, Richard."

He laughed. "Sorry. I can't help myself sometimes."

"No kidding."

The waitress came over and recited the specials. Richard ordered the café's signature bagel burger, and I went with the chicken salad. I'd been eating so much chicken lately I was amazed I hadn't started clucking.

We spent a few minutes engaging in idle chitchat, mostly about Richard's favorite topic, which was Richard. A cellist, he jokingly admitted he was now working his way through every girl in the string section of the Youth Orchestra.

"So," I said, once our food had arrived, "tell me what drew you to Moura."

He pursed his lips and squeezed more ketchup on his burger before answering. "Maybe the challenge. I mean, your sister was hot, she was brilliant, but let's face it, she was not the easiest girl to get to know. You know what the guys in Youth Orchestra used to call her?"

"What?"

"The Ice Princess."

"Lovely," I said. "Did she blow anyone off who might have been angry enough to hurt her?"

"Nah. Her vibe kept guys away."

"But not you. What was up with that? Trying to melt the Ice Princess with your charm?"

He shrugged and cleared his throat. "Something like that ... Who knows? It was complicated."

"What do you mean?"

"Let's just say we were very different. I'm a pretty laid back guy. I like to party, joke around. Moura, on the other hand, was, well, serious with a capital S."

"True. Do you think that maybe it bothered Moura that you've never been able to resist flirting with every girl within a sixty-mile radius?"

"Hey, I only flirt with really cute girls—like you, by the way. And trust me, Moura couldn't have cared less what I did with my spare time."

"Are you sure about that? Word is she broke up with you, not the other way around. That must have been quite a shock to your system. From what I hear, your MO is to break hearts, not gets yours broken."

He lowered his chin and shot me a long, lazy look. "I

guess all those rumors that you and your sister weren't close are true, huh?"

"Yeah. So?"

"You really don't know, do you?"

"Know what?"

He leaned forward and whispered, "Moura took using people to a whole new level. I was her cover boyfriend, and when she didn't need me anymore, she showed me the door quicker than you could play a minute waltz."

"Cover for what?"

"Moura and Hannah were lovers."

My mouth must have been hanging open a mile or two, because Richard reached over and lifted my chin up to close it.

"You're kidding."

He shook his head.

"Are you sure about that?"

"Yeah. Saw it with my own eyes. Totally by accident."

"Tell me."

"It was the night Moura gave that benefit concert last winter at the Clark Theatre. After the concert, I went backstage to surprise her with some flowers, but the stage manager told me she'd already headed down to her dressing room. So I took the stairs behind the stage. That's when I saw them. Moura and Hannah were on the landing, going at it hot and heavy. I freaked. I dropped the flowers and ran back up the stairs and out of the theatre."

"Did Moura know you'd seen her?"

"Yeah. She called me that night, begged me not to say

anything to anyone. She said she was just experimenting and it wasn't serious. But I'm not that stupid. I saw how they were together."

"But you kept seeing her after that?"

Color flooded his face, and he gave me a sheepish grin. "I know it was stupid."

I shook my head—typical Richard—and pressed on. "So how did that work out for you?"

"Well, obviously, not well. A few weeks later, she dumped me."

"I'm sorry." And I meant it. Regardless of the circumstances, breakups were no fun when they weren't your idea.

He took an enormous bite out of his burger. Moura's rejection clearly hadn't affected his appetite. When he finished swallowing, he said, "No biggie. I think we were both sick of all the play-acting. And though Moura was a great pianist, she was lousy at pretending she was into me."

"What did you mean about her no longer needing you as a cover? Wasn't she still with Hannah?"

"I don't think so. I got the impression she and Hannah were on the outs. Moura wouldn't say, but I was pretty sure she'd moved on." He leaned forward. "If I were you, I'd talk to Ms. Steinberg."

"The Youth Orchestra conductor?"

"Yup. Moura hung out in her office. A lot."

Chapter Ten |

As I sat in the parking lot of the Bagel Café, my head was spinning from Richard's big reveal. I'd promised Jenny I'd come over to the Springbrook Tennis Club for her opening match of Leonard High's fall tennis tournament. But what I really felt like doing was running onto the court, grabbing her, and saying, "We have to talk. NOW!"

Like that was a possibility. I thrust my key into the ignition.

By the time I got to the club, a crowd was gathering to watch Jenny's match with Anna, last year's runner-up to Miss Teen Ohio. Jenny might be the top seed, but there was no question that Anna was the main attraction for most of these gawkers. She was beyond gorgeous, with doe-like brown eyes, long blonde hair pulled back in a jeweled ponytail holder, and a figure whose dimensions were the closest match to a classic Barbie doll that I'd ever seen on an actual human being.

I stood by the fence, preferring to be close to the action. I called out words of encouragement to Jenny, but they probably didn't even register. Jenny blocked everything out when she played. Anna put up a great fight, but she was clearly outclassed by Jenny, whose serve was on and whose ground strokes were deep and sent Anna from corner to corner until sheer exhaustion caused her to mis-hit the ball and send it into the net or sailing out of bounds.

I was surprised when Dave Levy slipped in beside me to watch. His shirt was still drenched in sweat from his doubles match. He and his doubles partner, Tim, were an odd couple. Dave claimed to be 5' 8", wore his long hair in a ponytail, and was so warm and friendly that his opponents complained he could lull you into thinking he was your friend while cleaning your clock. His partner, Tim, on the other hand, was about 6' 5", with hawkish features, a crew cut that screamed Army ROTC, and a perpetually somber look on his face.

"Heard you had a great match," I said. Unable to resist teasing him, I added, "Checking out the beauty queen, huh?"

"She's a goddess."

Certain he was talking about our visiting Barbie clone, I prepared to roll my eyes and make a snarky comment. But when I turned to Dave, I realized he wasn't looking at Anna. He was staring intently at Jenny, a look of sheer adoration on his face.

So much for my BFF's insistence that short guys were never interested in her. Did she have any idea Dave was crushing on her? And he was hot—and really nice.

I couldn't help it. My matchmaker instincts went into full alert.

The minute Jenny's match was over, I grabbed her for an emergency conference at the Mellow Moose. "You know what makes this Hannah thing feel so awful?" I said, after filling her in on my meeting with Richard.

"What?"

"Moura didn't trust me enough to tell me. It's just one more reminder of how so *not* close we were. There I was, writing all those articles supporting the Gay-Straight Student Alliance, and my own twin didn't bother to tell me she was with Hannah. Why did she shut me out? I would have been more than supportive."

Jenny squeezed my arm. "It wasn't you. She was so into being the great Moura Seibert that her whole life became a performance. She didn't want anyone to see who was really behind the curtain."

I lifted my hands up in the air, then let them drop. "But the arts are full of people who are gay. What difference would it have made to her career?"

"Probably nothing. But there are plenty of haters out there. Look at all the kids we know who are still in the closet. Who wants to bring out the name-callers and have your love life be the hot topic everybody's tweeting about? Or risk your parents getting all bent out of shape?"

"My parents would have been okay. At least I think so. Maybe a little surprised, but it's not like they don't have gay friends at the university. I guess I'll just never know what Moura was thinking. Or feeling, for that matter. But I'm going to have to talk to Hannah again."

I scraped the bottom of my bowl to scoop up the last

drops of my chocolate raspberry truffle, the best comfort food on the planet—or at least, in Springbrook, Ohio. "Anyhow, let's talk about something else … like what do you think of Dave Levy?"

Jenny bit her lip and a pinkish hue spread across her face. "Well, you've seen him play. He's super smart, quick, deadly at the net."

"Yeah, yeah, so he's a good tennis player. Not what I'm asking. What do you think of him as a guy?"

The pinkish hue morphed into a deep rose while she hesitated. "Truth? Total mini-hunk. Super friendly to everyone, and the only person who can make dour Tim, his doubles partner, crack a smile. If I were your height, I'd be knocking on his door and begging him to date me."

"So a handful of inches, and you nix the idea of ever going out with Mr. Mini-Hunk with the amazing personality?"

"Get real! Can you picture Dave and me together? Would you want to be with a girl who outweighs you by fifty pounds and when you go to hug her, your nose is smashed into her breastbone?"

"I don't know. He could adjust his nose slightly and enjoy the scenery down there."

"You're impossible," she said, throwing her wadded-up napkin at me.

"Just sayin'. Today, he came over to watch your match, and the way he was looking at you, I detected a major crush in progress."

"You have lost your mind. The guy hardly speaks to

me. If he's in a group and I come over, he suddenly stops talking and won't even look at me. I've been wondering whether I did something to him in a past life."

"And it never occurred to you that he's interested but doesn't know how to approach you, get things started?"

"You're hallucinating."

"He called you a goddess, dummy."

She clutched my arm and nearly cut off my circulation. "Really?"

"Really." Her eyes sparkled, and if I could have freeze-framed that moment, I would have. Jenny deserved a great guy in her life. And it was a whole lot more fun to think about her finding him than it was to deal with my own life.

The next morning, I pulled up to Hannah's house around eleven. I hadn't called ahead of time. I wanted to see her reaction with no forewarning.

Hannah answered the door wearing a faded blue sweatshirt and jeans with more holes than pockets. She looked resigned rather than surprised to see me again.

"Can I come in?"

"I figured you'd be back," she said, her voice sounding wooden.

I followed her inside, moved an empty Oreo cookie bag over, and took a seat on the plaid couch, which had stuffing leaking out of one arm. The air in the cluttered room smelled stale, like no one had opened any windows for a long time.

"Is anyone else around?"

"No, we're good. I can talk."

"So I met with Richard and—"

"And he told you about Moura and me," she said, gazing at me steadily, as though daring me to look away.

"Yes," I said, staring right back at her. "And I guess I'm confused about why you didn't think that was worth mentioning to me."

"Why do you think? Look around you. What neighborhood do you think you're in right now? This isn't your liberal university enclave. You're in God Squad territory. My mom is convinced that homosexuality is a sin that will send you straight to hell. She would have kicked me out of the house if she had any idea. And Moura wanted people to be interested in her music, not her private life. It was nobody's business but ours."

"I respect your privacy, I really do. But I have to figure out what was going on with Moura when she was killed. I need your help."

She blinked several times and picked at the cuticle on her left index finger, then looked up at me. "If I could help you, I would. But I told you the truth the other day. Moura shut me out those last few weeks. Like I said, I knew something was going on, but she wasn't talking, especially not to me."

"Did she break things off with you?"

"Romantically, yes." Her voice quavered. "She said she still wanted to be friends, but she didn't love me anymore in that way." Tears spilled down her cheeks, and I felt guilty all over again for poking at her tender wounds.

"I'm really sorry. Do you think there was someone else?"

"She didn't say, but I think there must have been."

"But you have no idea who?"

"No. I mean, I know she didn't give a shit about Richard, and I can't think of anyone else we even knew or hung out with that she ever seemed interested in."

"Richard told me she was spending a lot of time with Ms. Steinberg."

Hannah's mouth dropped open. She didn't say a word for several seconds. "I guess anything's possible. Ms. Steinberg's … one of us, but I'm pretty sure she's been with somebody for a long time. But now that I think about it, she did spend a lot of time talking to Moura."

"Were you very angry with Moura?"

She snorted. "Subtle, Clara. You want to know if I killed her in a fit of rage because she dumped me?"

Heat rushed to my face. I dug my nails into the scratchy seat fabric. "Look, I would have been pretty pissed off if I'd been as close as you two were for years, and suddenly she said, 'Never mind.'"

"Well, of course, I was angry. Moura was everything to me! But I would never have hurt her. Ever! And I thought she'd come back to me. But now, I'll never know." She hung her head and her shoulders shook as she sobbed.

I didn't have a clue what to do or say, but I had to do something. I put my arms around her.

She lifted her tear-streaked face and shoved me away. "Get out. Just get out."

That night, I lost count of how many times I relived those awful moments in Hannah's living room. I felt like a first-class jerk.

Funny how when Moura was alive, I'd always thought of myself as Moura's sole victim, her throwaway twin. But I was far from alone in having gotten hurt by the great Moura Seibert.

Nothing to do but keep going. I picked up my phone.

Leslie Hall picked up on the third ring.

After I identified myself, her voice was so chilly I wanted to grab my coat.

"Moura's twin, huh? Why are you calling me?"

I explained about the scholarship and asked if she'd be willing to meet about getting the fans on her site involved.

"Hmmm, I'm not sure. I gotta be honest with you—a lot of us don't trust you. We still wonder about that night. It could have been you. Hell, a lot of us think it should have been you."

I nearly dropped the phone. *It should have been you.* Had she really just said that? I took a deep breath and plunged ahead. "Seems to be a common sentiment. But I didn't kill my sister, and I already feel guilty enough that I'm still alive."

Her tone softened. "Sorry. It's just … you're not doing this to pull suspicion away from yourself, are you? You know, like OJ did when he offered a reward for finding his wife's killer?"

"No! Dr. Lewitsky asked me to contact you, and I agreed. Moura and I had our issues, but I loved her. And her playing. I honestly think the scholarship is a good way to honor her memory."

"Okay. There are three of us who do a lot with the site. Let me check and see if we all agree it's a good idea to meet with you."

Two nights later, I dropped by the Youth Orchestra rehearsal as they were finishing up. It was weird. I kept expecting to see my sister, hear her.

Richard dashed over when he saw me. "What brings you here, gorgeous?"

I rolled my eyes. "Was hoping to catch Ms. Steinberg."

He clutched my arm. "Please don't tell her I said anything," he whispered. "I like being first chair."

I held three fingers up. "Scout's honor."

I continued threading my way through the musicians toward the front of the auditorium where Ms. Steinberg was talking to a clarinetist. Several gave me those raised eyebrow "What are you doing here?" looks, but I ignored them.

Now she was headed for the side door. "Ms. Steinberg," I called out.

She turned around and looked startled to see me. "Clara?" she said, sounding uncertain. "You looked so much like Moura for a minute …"

"I know. I'm sorry. Could I speak with you?"

She nodded. "Let's go down to the office."

"So," she said, once we were seated with the door closed, "what can I do for you?"

After I told her about the threats, she looked appalled. "I can't believe someone would do such a thing."

"Me either … I know you spent time with Moura outside of rehearsals. Did she confide in you about anyone she was having problems with?"

She leaned her chin against her hand. "Not really. She liked talking to me about Juilliard. She was very appreciative of my letter of recommendation and seemed convinced it had helped her get admitted a year early. I graduated from there and still have quite a few contacts."

"That was really nice of you."

"Truthfully, your sister didn't need me. Her playing was what got her in. And she worked hard to finish up her high school credits early."

"Moura was very determined."

"She was," she said with a sad smile. "And what a reader! We used to swap books all the time from our music collections."

"Her favorites were the biographies," I murmured.

"Mine, too."

I was getting nowhere fast. "Would you say you were closer to Moura than you were to the other musicians in the orchestra?"

Her eyebrows knitted together. "Moura was … mature for her age. We shared a lot of interests. You're not asking if there was anything more going on, are you?"

"Should I be?"

"Of course not. Where is this coming from?"

"A couple of orchestra members mentioned that the

two of you were spending a lot of time together, that maybe you were developing a … a special relationship."

"That's absurd! I'm in a long-term relationship, and even if I weren't, I certainly wouldn't get involved with my students." Blotches of red had erupted on her face and neck.

I stood up. "I'm sorry. I'm just trying to figure out who killed my sister."

She shook her head. "The answer's not here."

I lay in bed that night mulling over my conversation with Ms. Steinberg. She couldn't have been more than thirty—and pretty, with a thick mane of strawberry blonde hair. It was certainly possible my sister had been attracted to her. But I couldn't imagine Ms. Steinberg crossing a line that way. Then again, it had never crossed my mind that Moura and Hannah had been a couple, so I wasn't counting on my powers of observation. Or intuition.

Too wired to sleep, I flung my covers off, heaved myself out of bed, and crept downstairs to the second floor. Maybe Moura had left some clue in her bedroom, something the police had overlooked.

I moved past my parents' bedroom, paused to listen to my father's even breathing as he slept, and scared myself each time one of the floorboards creaked. As I drew closer to my sister's room, I was startled by the light spilling out from beneath her door.

Carefully, I eased the door open and peeked in. The old rocking chair that usually sat in the corner had been pulled over beside Moura's bed and moved back and forth rhythmically. A tired hinge softly groaned, and as I drew closer, I heard the whispers of a familiar singsong voice. "And when the prince heard her play songs of love and longing on her lute, he declared it was the most beautiful sound he'd ever heard. She became princess of the kingdom and promised to play her lute every day for all to hear. The End."

I sank down on the edge of the bed and murmured, "You used to tell us that story when we were little. I loved your stories."

Mom looked up, then looked down at her hands, clutched in a tight fold in her lap. "Lately, I've been thinking a lot about when you girls were small—how all three of us would snuggle into this chair and I'd read to you or make up stories. Those were happy days, weren't they?"

"They were," I said, my voice catching. In those early years, Moura and I had both loved the stories our mom would weave for us. And we'd spent hours playing dress-up and making up stories of our own.

"I feel closer to your sister when I come in here. Your father thinks it's morbid, so I wait until he's asleep. He wants us to move, you know. Sell the house, get a fresh start. But this is all I have of her—her room, the lingering scent on her pillow. I can't let go. I just can't."

"I know," I said, touching my mom's hand tentatively. It looked so tiny now, so frail, like the rest of her. "You just have to give yourself time. And it's great that you're working on the memorial project. I decided to help, too.

I've contacted the girl who organized the memorial site."

"That's wonderful, dear," she said, her voice sounding far away. "So what are you doing here?"

"I was having trouble sleeping, and then I saw the light on in here." Okay, so half of that was true.

"Well, you should get back to bed. She paused, then added, "I think I'll stay here for a few more minutes, though."

"I can stay if you want company."

"No, thanks. I'd rather just be by myself right now."

"Right." I tasted my own bitterness, my own confusion. My mother didn't want me around, didn't even know me well enough to recognize that I would never have hurt my sister. I loved her, ached for her, even the tiny sliver of her that had been mine before my sister's death. But I couldn't reach her, couldn't help her. Her grief had swallowed her whole. It was as though she were gone.

Just like Moura.

Chapter Eleven |

The next morning, I felt like a flattened compost heap. It hadn't helped that I'd gotten another one of those annoying "nobody there" calls at two in the morning. It took three cups of coffee to revive me, as my thoughts drifted to what I'd face in my column inbox when I got back to school. Mr. B. had made me promise to take the week off and assured me he'd let me know if anything came in.

I was pulling out my list of people to talk to when Leslie called.

"No promises, but we'll meet with you," she said tersely. She gave me her address, and we agreed to meet at two.

Leslie lived at the end of a cul-de-sac in one of those new antiseptic subdivisions where all the houses look the same and the trees are three feet high.

But inside, her house was beautiful. Thick oriental rugs covered the floors, and a gorgeous harp sat in the corner of the living room beside a grand piano.

Considering the home's formality, Leslie seemed under-dressed in her crimson sweats. She didn't smile as she introduced me to Brayden, a gangly guy who had to be at least 6' 6", and Wendy, who was short and round. Brayden and Wendy didn't smile, either. Friendly group.

At least they listened politely as I launched into my song and dance about the scholarship. "This is definitely legit," I said as I wound down my pitch. "If you have any questions, I know Dr. Lewitsky, or my parents, would be glad to talk with you."

Leslie glanced around the room. Brayden looked up at the ceiling, but Wendy nodded slightly. "We'd be willing to publicize it on our site," Leslie announced. "Actually, we've been talking about organizing a memorial concert. Maybe we could do it as a benefit to raise money for the scholarship fund."

"That'd be great!"

"You can tell Dr. Lewitsky we'll be getting in touch with her about details." Leslie started to stand up, but I wasn't ready to be dismissed.

"Actually, there's something else."

Leslie sat back down, and I definitely had their attention as I described the threats I'd been getting. "The first one used the exact same phrase you did the other day, Leslie— *It should have been you.*"

She held her hands up. "Whoa! You can't think I'm your cyberstalker. Sure, we've had our doubts about you, made a few comments here and there. But threaten your life? No way! We're not part of some Music Mafia out to get revenge."

I bit back a smile. Tennis Mafia, Music Mafia, whatever

it takes. "Okay, but you know a lot of music people. Can you think of anyone who might be convinced I killed Moura and wants to make me pay?"

"Lots of people think you might have killed Moura," Wendy broke in, "but I don't know anybody who's totally convinced—or nuts enough to think the solution to losing Moura is to get rid of you."

"Reassuring. So what about anyone who might have had a beef with Moura? Been angry with her?"

Wendy looked around the group. "Should we tell her about Fred?"

"Who's Fred?"

"This guy we kicked off the site," Leslie said. "He kept posting these rants abut Moura—how she wasn't really that great, was an arrogant twit, that kind of thing. We told him our site was about celebrating Moura, not dissing her. And we all defriended him."

"Sounds like someone I need to talk to."

"He's annoying as hell, but he's harmless," Leslie said.

"Just to be on the safe side, how about giving me his contact info?"

The next morning, Fred's mother informed me that he was out of town on vacation, but she'd give him the message that I wanted to get a hold of him.

Time to move on to more adults. I glanced at the phone numbers posted on the fridge. There it was—the home phone for Dr. Lewitsky and Mr. Rasher.

Nervously, I punched in their number. He answered on

the third ring. When I stumbled through my explanation of why I wanted to talk to each of them about Moura, he said she was at the university teaching, but he could see me that afternoon. "Do you mind driving out here? I'm on deadline. But I'm happy to take a break and talk with you." He gave me directions to their old farmhouse which was about twenty miles outside of town, and we agreed I'd come around two.

The thought of driving by myself to some secluded farmhouse in the boonies to meet an adult guy creeped me out. I punched in Jenny's number. "Hey, any chance you could come with me to go see Joel Rasher this afternoon?"

"Earth to Clara! I've got my semifinal match this afternoon."

I hit my forehead. "Geez, how stupid can I be! I knew that. I'm sorry, Jenny. I completely blanked."

"No problem. Want to come over for dinner and fill me in?"

"You know I do! Good luck today. Prepare to give me a complete rundown, okay?"

"Blow-by-blow, baby, unless I get upset, in which case, we will never speak of this again."

If I hadn't been so anxious about talking to Mr. Rasher, the drive down the narrow country road would have been perfect. We were having one of those awesome autumn days where the air smelled like apples and dry twigs, and the leaves were bathed in every shade of gold, tangerine, and amber. When they made a canopy above as I drove through patches of heavily wooded areas, I got chills. It was like being in a magical chapel. I'd always loved this time of year. When Moura and I were little, we'd dive into the piles of leaves Dad raked up and bury ourselves in them. We'd roll around and giggle before poking our fingers and toes up, and finally our noses when it got too hard to breathe. And now Moura really was buried and would never know another autumn.

I took some deep breaths and made myself focus on what I could do right now to make things better for Moura—and for me.

When I got to the farmhouse, I was struck by how homey and inviting it looked. Set back from the road, nestled in a forest of trees, the place was painted white, with hanging baskets and wicker furniture adorning a wrap-around porch. I pulled my Bug up behind a slate-colored Mini Cooper, which I figured must be Mr. Rasher's car.

He flung open the door. I was about to tell him how much I loved Mini Coopers when a strange look on his face stopped me from saying anything. He was silent for several moments, before exclaiming, "My God, Clara, I had to do a double take. Standing there, you looked so much like Moura."

"Some days, people say we look nothing alike, and other times, they tell me I look so much like her it's eerie. I suppose it's an illusion."

"You're right. Well, come in, come in. It's good to see you."

"Thanks, and thanks for seeing me on such short notice."

He led me past the living room dominated by a mahogany grand piano and a great fireplace and back into their country kitchen. "I made some coffee."

He poured us both cups, set the pot down, and gestured for me to take a seat at their gnarled oak kitchen table. I glanced down at a sheaf of papers. A big sloping scrawl, with words crossed out and arrows going everywhere, covered the top one.

"Is this the draft of one of your articles?"

"Yes. I'm doing a piece on the orchestra's upcoming season."

"So you write in longhand? I do all my writing on the computer."

"A lot of writers tell me that they can't imagine working off screen. But for some reason, I can create more easily when I'm writing longhand. Then, after I've got my first draft, I usually transfer over and work on my computer." He smiled and cocked his head. "I guess everybody's process is different. My philosophy is to do whatever works."

"Agreed," I said. He seemed so friendly and unassuming sitting there barefoot in his old jeans and Mozart sweatshirt I couldn't imagine why I'd felt so nervous about talking to him.

"But you're not here to talk about our writing processes. What did you want to ask me about Moura?"

"Well, when I talked with a few of her friends, they mentioned she seemed distracted the last few weeks of her life—like something major was going on, maybe someone new she cared about romantically. Did you get that impression? Did she say anything to you?"

"Not really. We mainly talked about her music, a little about her family. You saw the article. It was all about her passion for music, her development as an emerging artist, her desire to go to Juilliard, her dreams of a concert career—that sort of thing."

"But did you notice that she seemed distracted, maybe agitated in some way?"

"Well, I was aware she was moving toward a big change in her life. Even the changes we look forward to can be stressful, right?"

I nodded. "You mean, her early acceptance to Juilliard and anticipation about the move to NYC?"

He took a sip of his coffee and set it down. "Definitely. Her whole life as she knew it was ending, and an entirely new one was about to begin. I'm sure leaving Nadia, who'd become practically a second mother to her, was going to be hard. She knew the competition would be fierce."

"But she and Alex had been big rivals for years. She always seemed to relish the competition."

"I think they both did. But she knew that at Juilliard, there would be tons of pianists like Alex and her, some even more driven and determined—as hard as that is to imagine," he said with a chuckle.

I poured myself some more coffee. "Speaking of Alex, were you aware that he was upset about the feature you did on Moura? A friend told me that he thought your piece was going to be about both of them."

"Just a misunderstanding that got cleared up quickly.

Initially, my plan was to do a piece featuring both of them, but then I convinced my editor to let me do a whole series on up-and-coming gifted musicians in the region. Alex's feature is coming out next month."

"Oh, okay…. Do you think there's any possibility that Alex and Moura had gotten involved romantically?"

"Those two? They were like brother and sister. I can't imagine that. But she probably had lots of suitors. She was a very appealing young woman, after all."

"Yes, she was. Which leads me to ask—and I wish I didn't have to—was there anything going on between you and Moura?"

His eyes widened, and he drew back. After a few seconds of uncomfortable silence, he said in a low voice, "I admired your sister tremendously. She was fascinating to interview, and I'll always believe she had a brilliant career ahead of her. But I'm a thirty-two-year-old married man. Your sister was a teenager."

His cell broke into Mozart's *Requiem.* He reached for it and eyed the caller ID. "I need to take this call from my editor. Is there anything else?"

"No," I said, standing up and moving toward the door. "Thanks so much, and please tell your wife I'll call her about getting together to talk."

On the drive home, I was so busy replaying our conversation in my head that I didn't pay much attention to the occasional passing cars and pickup trucks on the narrow country road. But as I rounded a curve, I spotted a black van in the opposite lane that was weaving slightly, drifting dangerously close to my lane. Was the driver drunk? Asleep?

I gripped the steering wheel. My heart caught in my throat. I laid on my horn, but instead of moving back over, the van was now in my lane. It was headed straight toward me.

I screamed, swerved, and my car careened off the road, hurtling down an embankment. A wooden fence loomed before me. I hit the brakes. Nothing. *Please, God. No, no.*

Then came the sounds. Wood splintered into a thousand pieces. My chest slammed into the steering wheel. My head bonked into the side window. Hard.

Finally, a shuddering stop. So dizzy. Everything around me swam in a murky green. I leaned against the backrest of my seat and closed my eyes.

Chapter Twelve

Hours later, I lay in a hospital bed at Springbrook General. I felt so groggy from the pain meds that I poked my own lips to make sure they were still there.

I'd struggled to explain the accident to the police who had taken my report in the emergency room. It hadn't really been a hit and run—more like a scare and run.

I knew I was very lucky. They'd done a mess of tests. Despite the baseball-sized bump on the side of my head, I had only a slight concussion plus a couple of bruised ribs. Still, the ER physician had recommended the hospital keep me overnight for observation. I was already itching to get out of there.

Dad sat by my bed, his face ashen gray, as he held my hand. And surprise, surprise, my mother was MIA. "Not feeling well," Dad explained, "but she sends her love."

Sure she does. I didn't say a word.

"That's some bump you've got there, honey."

"I know."

"Tell me what happened."

"A black van was swerving around, then it got in my

lane and headed straight toward me. I thought it was going to kill me! I panicked, turned my steering wheel too sharply to try to get out of its way, and lost control."

"Did it seem like the driver was intentionally trying to hit you?"

I shivered. "I think so. Either that, or scare me half to death. It looked a lot like the van that was hovering in the parking lot the night I went to talk to the police."

"What? You never told me about that!"

Shit. This was the trouble with these stupid pain meds. I'd let my guard down. I took a deep breath, then immediately regretted the aggravation to my ribs. "I'm sorry! You were already so upset with me that night about not telling you about the email. And I wasn't sure whether it was someone trying to spook me, or just someone who'd paused in the parking lot to make a phone call."

"Tell me exactly what happened that night."

I described the van stopping near me, like it was waiting, and then my freak-out when I couldn't find my car keys.

"Why didn't you have your keys already out from unlocking your door?" In less than a minute, Dad had gone from sympathetic to furious.

"Honestly? I think I was so upset that when I got to the station to make a report, I flew out of the car and forgot to lock it."

"Are you serious? After all the talks we've had about safety precautions? This is totally unacceptable! Are you deliberately trying to get yourself killed?"

I struggled to avoid breathing too deeply. Taking deep

breaths was murder on my ribs, but it was tough to keep calm when Dad was in attack mode. "No! I'm sorry, okay? It was stupid. I wasn't thinking clearly. Please stop yelling at me! I can't take it right now." My voice shook, as I pushed back my tears.

"All right, all right. I'm sorry for yelling. But you need to use good judgment, be careful."

"I'm trying. And I really did think maybe I was just overreacting that night in the parking lot."

He glowered at me. "You absolutely must tell me what's going on, even if you're not sure it's anything. Let me, let the police, be the judge of that."

"You're right."

"Okay then ... so today, what were you doing out there anyway?"

I swallowed hard. "I went to see Joel Rasher."

"Why?"

"I wanted to talk about Moura. He spent a lot of time with her when he was working on the article, and I've been having a hard time dealing with her being ... gone." I was beginning to wonder if this was my new specialization, telling half-truths. But admitting I'd been doing some sleuthing on my own would send my dad right over the edge and get me grounded. Indefinitely.

Apparently, I was getting good at this skirting-around-the-truth stuff, because Dad's face softened, and he squeezed my hand. "I'm glad she lived long enough to see the wonderful piece he wrote about her."

A couple of hours after Dad left, there was a knock at my door, and Detective Martino poked his head in. I was watching a rerun of an episode of *Law & Order* and muted the sound as he moved into the room.

"You okay?"

"Why Detective Martino, I didn't know you cared," I said, dryly.

"I'm concerned, Clara." He opened his notebook and pulled a pencil from behind his ear. Then he had me go through my story. Again, and then again, as he jotted down notes.

"So who knew you were going out there today?"

"No one, as far as I know." I wasn't about to tell him Jenny had known and risk her spilling the beans to him about my investigation. Jenny was incurably open and honest.

"Okay, well, this isn't much to go on, but we'll work on it. Anything else?"

My cell rang.

"Want me to get that?"

"Sure."

He listened for a moment, then hung up. "Nobody there."

"I've been getting a lot of those. No name—don't recognize the number."

"And you didn't think you should mention this to me?"

Shit. What was I thinking? "I should have—just, the email messages have been so much scarier. The calls—they've been mainly annoying, and they started happening before the emails."

"And it didn't occur to you they could be connected?"

So much for my detective skills. "I … I guess I didn't think about that."

"Apparently. I'm taking your phone. I'll have my techs check it out."

He stood up and gestured toward the television. "You can get back to your show. I just wish it were as easy in real life to catch the bad guys."

Dad brought me home early the next morning. I sank into bleary-eyed couch-potato mode for the rest of the day. Jenny rescued me from watching my sixth *Law & Order* rerun when she dropped by after her finals match.

"Just so you know, I was nearly upset today. I had to fight off two match points before pulling my act together and taking the final set. I blame you for this near-debacle. Clearly, I was distracted worrying about you."

"A likely story!" I said, throwing a pillow at her and then groaning at the disturbance to my rib cage.

"Careful there. Patients need to remain calm, you know."

"Yeah, yeah, yeah. So was Dave hanging on the fence during your match and doing his drooling thing?"

That pinkish hue spread across her face. Again. "I don't know about the drooling, but—now that you mention it, he and his doubles partner were both there."

I grinned at her. "Why am I not surprised?"

The rest of the weekend was one giant slog. Alex and Fred were the next people I really wanted to talk to, but they weren't back in town yet. And with my car in the shop for at least a week, I had no wheels. Besides, I felt like crap. My ribs were sore, the pain meds made me sluggish, and the thought of spotting any black vans on the road made me mega-jumpy. Every time I closed my eyes, I saw that van headed straight toward me, and my pulse shot into overdrive. I'd heard about people claiming they saw their lives flash before their eyes in near-death experiences. But all I'd seen was that black van barreling toward me like an angel of death on speed.

At least I had my phone back. Martino had dropped by with it. Whoever had been calling me was using one of those temporary disposable phones. No way to trace it. Big surprise.

Getting back to school on Monday felt like a welcome distraction from my endless replaying of my un-accidental accident. Of course, I had to field a lot of questions about my appearance. It wasn't just the putrid-looking bump protruding from my head. I was moving so stiffly from the bruised ribs that I could have been a casting shoo-in for a zombie movie.

"So," Ben said to me as he plopped down in the seat next to me in French class, "what happened to the other guy?"

My stomach fluttered. "It was a clean knock-out," I said, praying he hadn't noticed my voice had just shot up two octaves higher than usual.

"Seriously, are you okay?"

"More or less. Had a little car accident on Thursday."

"What happened?"

"Long story."

"I'd love to hear it."

Just then, the bell rang and Madame Auld called us to attention. "Today, you may pick your own partners for conversation. I want you to imagine you have just met someone, a stranger you might like to get to know better. But at first, you are making very polite conversation. So avoid, what do you call it, TMI?" Scattered laughter erupted around the room.

Ben leaned over and whispered in my ear, "I came prepared, partner."

The hairs on the nape of my neck stood at rigid attention. "That makes one of us," I said, totally stressing over my inability to appear semi-relaxed and confident at the thought of conversing with Ben. In French.

He pulled out a paper and studied it. I glanced around and caught Emily glaring at me. A good sign. I turned back to Ben, feeling my confidence inch up. "You have a cheat sheet?" I teased.

"Yup. Okay, here goes." He paused dramatically, then reached over to shake my hand. His hand felt warm and strong. A surge of electricity passed through me, and I prayed the hair on my head wasn't standing straight up. *"Bonjour, Mademoiselle Clara. Bon de vous voir aujourd'hui? Comment vous sentez-vous?" (Hello, Clara. How are you today? How are you feeling?)*

Okay, I could handle this. Let's see, how did I feel? Excited, nervous, amazed—but definitely better, now that Ben was, well … flirting with me! *"Je me sens beaucoup mieux aujourd'hui. Merci de m'avoir posé la question."* *(I feel a lot better today. Thanks for asking.)*

"De rien." (You're welcome.) He glanced at his paper, knitted his brows, and then carefully read, *"Depuis que vous avez suggéré que nous parlons de la météo, je ensoleillé veux vous poser une question. Comment est la météo près de chez vous?" (Since you suggested we talk about the weather, I have a question for you. How's the weather in your neck of the woods?)*

I laughed, grabbed my ribs and groaned, and then couldn't help but laugh some more. I looked out the window. *"Le temps est ensoleillé. Une belle journée d'automne." (The weather is sunny. It's a glorious fall day.)*

"C'est excellent," (Great.) Ben said with a wink. He studied his paper again. *"Mais demain, il pourrait être nuageux avec une chance de boulettes de viande italiennes?" (But tomorrow, will it be cloudy with a chance of Italian meatballs?)*

I giggled again. *"Est-ce que vous avez dit boulettes?" (Did you say meatballs?)*

"J'ai essayé de vous tromper," (I was just testing you.) he said with a mischievous smile.

"J'aurais dû savoir," (I should have known.) I said, poking him in the arm.

Studying his list of phrases, he read, *"Ce week-end, la météo sera exceptionnellement chaude. Vous souhaitez venir avec moi à Blakeley's Farm à choisir les citrouilles?" (This weekend, the temperature will be unseasonably warm.*

Would you like to go with me to Blakeley's Farm to pick some pumpkins?) He looked up, and his dark gaze held mine. Could he hear my heart beating triple time?

OMG. Had Ben asked me to go to Blakeley's pumpkin farm with him this weekend? My body temperature had to have risen by twenty degrees. *"J'aimerais bien," (I'd love to.)* I managed to squeak out.

He leaned forward and whispered, *"Mon français est terrible. Vous avez dit 'oui,' n'est-ce pas?" (My French is terrible. You did say 'yes,' didn't you?)*

"Mais oui." (I did.)

A huge smile lit up his face. *"Super. Je vais vous chercher vers midi le samedi. Nous pouvons obtenir un déjeuner et ensuite aller à la ferme." (Super. I'll pick you up around noon on Saturday. We'll grab some lunch and then head out to the farm.)*

A whole afternoon with Ben. I couldn't believe it. *"Ce sera merveilleux." (Sounds wonderful.)*

I floated through the rest of the school day—well, as much as you can float anywhere with a couple of bruised ribs. But hey, who cared about a little soreness? I decided I was officially in love with the French language. And I'd never again discount the wonders of conversations about the weather.

But when I got to the newspaper office and booted up my computer, the weight of my fear bore down on me again. Damn this jerk! Opening my email for the column used to be a huge highlight of my day. Now it was more like an exercise in anticipatory self-torture.

Shit. There it was. My hands shook as I pressed "Open."

Getting a little accident-prone, are we?
Next time you won't survive.
I do love the holidays, don't you?

I wanted to get away from the message, the office, into the safety of Mr. B.'s room. Dizzy, so dizzy. I stumbled backward. Just as I felt myself sinking to the floor, a pair of arms grabbed me and held me up.

"It's okay," Tony said. "I've got you."

"Thanks. I … I didn't even hear you come in," I mumbled, inhaling his cologne and praying I wouldn't pass out, as he guided me into the closest chair.

"I gather you were preoccupied. Was it another threat?"

I nodded. "Can you go get Mr. B. for me?"

"I'm on it."

Mr. B. came rushing in moments later, looking more disheveled than usual, his glasses nearly toppling off the bridge of his nose. "I'm so sorry, Clara. I've been checking, too. Tony, can you give us a minute?"

Tony stiffened, then grabbed his stuff and made a quick exit. I was pretty sure he was frustrated that Mr. B. was kicking him out in the middle of Drama City at our little newspaper office, but I knew Mr. B. was trying to protect whatever tiny morsel of privacy I had left.

Mr. B. studied the message, and I studied him. "So what do you think?"

"He's given you a time frame. The earliest would be

Thanksgiving, so what does that mean? Four weeks, five weeks?"

"Five and a half." I swallowed hard and shivered, unable to think. Cold, I was so cold.

"You don't have to keep putting yourself through opening these, you know," Mr. B. said.

He took a handkerchief out of his pocket and wiped his creased forehead, shiny with perspiration. "I'm happy to open them and give you reports if you like—or just forward them on," Mr. B. continued.

"Thanks, but I think I'd feel worse not seeing them myself."

"Okay then. I'm calling your dad to come pick you up. And let's forward this to Detective Martino."

Two hours later, Detective Martino was in our living room.

"Our first priority is keeping Clara safe," Dad said. "I'll take her out of school if I have to. And I'm getting her out of here for the holidays—someplace where no one can find her or get to her."

"Dad, how's that going to be a solution? This jerk has figured out a way to know where I am. I can't escape!" My voice rose as I dug my fingernails into the afghan and picked at a loose thread.

"Unfortunately, Dr. Seibert, I think Clara may be right. But she's made me think of something. Where's the car being repaired?"

"Al's Auto Shop," my dad said.

"Excuse me for a minute." He stood up, fished his cell

phone out of his pocket, and moved out into the hallway.

Dad paced, and I plucked at more loose threads, as Detective Martino's absence turned into ten minutes, and then ten more. If he didn't return soon, I'd be well on my way to unraveling the afghan.

When he finally strode back in, his face was flushed. "Al located a GPS tracking device on the underside of Clara's car. Sergeant Driscoll is on the way over to the shop right now to check for prints and bag the device for evidence. We'll try to trace where it was purchased and who bought it."

So it hadn't been my imagination. Someone had been tracking me like prey before the kill. A chunk of icy fear lodged in my gut.

"What are the chances you can trace it, Detective?" Dad asked.

"I don't know, but I'll take any lead we can get." He stood up, as if poised to go. "Clara, when your car is ready, give Sergeant Driscoll a call. He'll meet you at Al's and show you how to check your car for any new tracking devices."

I nodded, as Dad said, "But what's our next move here? I can't sit around and wait for someone to go after my daughter!"

"I know this is very hard. I'll talk to the police chief and weigh our options. I'd love to figure out a way to flush this perp out." Detective Martino shifted his gaze to mine and said, "But for that, I may need your help, Clara."

Just as I was about to cry, *"I'm in! I'll do whatever it takes to catch this creep!"* Dad tersely announced, "I categorically forbid any plan which involves putting my daughter at risk."

"But Dad, we need to get this jerk!" I said.

"I've already lost one daughter, and I'm not going to risk losing another. This is not up for discussion."

I shrank back into the sofa and gritted my teeth. There was no reasoning with Dad! He didn't get it. I was at much greater risk waiting around to be target practice.

"I understand," Detective Martino said, solemnly. He extended his hand to shake Dad's, and then mine. "I'll be in touch."

As I lay in bed that night, the words, "five and a half weeks," marched across the video screen inside my mind. Over and over.

Sleep seemed out of the question. I glanced at the clock. It was after eleven. On the chance that Alex might still be up, I hoisted myself out of bed and texted him. Apparently, he was a night owl, too, because he texted right back. We agreed to meet at the Starbucks close to school the next day around four.

Wednesday hit, and I could barely keep my eyes open. On the positive side, my ribs were a lot less sore, and I was so tired, my body was incapable of holding on to any excess pockets of tension. Of course, when Ben whispered to me in French class that he was really looking forward to Saturday, my energy level got a kick start. And I was looking forward to talking with Alex.

After school, Mr. B. met me at the door of the newspaper office. "I know you don't want a babysitter, but I thought I'd hang out while you open your inbox. I don't want to put you through another unwelcome surprise by yourself."

"Thanks." A month ago, I would have been irritated that Mr. Bradford wanted to look over my shoulder while I checked my column inbox. Now it was a relief.

He pulled a chair up next to mine, and we booted up my computer. Anxiously, I scanned the entries. An email for the column, but nothing from the jerk. Yay!

"Looks clear." Mr. B. stood up. A warm smile spread across his craggy face. "Come get me if you need anything, okay?"

"Will do." I wasted no time reading the email.

Dear Since You Asked,

I never thought I'd be writing to you, but I could really use some advice. It's about this girl. She's beautiful and smart and really nice. We're both good at sports, and well, I can't stop thinking about her.

But I think she'd be embarrassed to go out with me. I'd probably even embarrass her if I asked her out. And she's so nice she might say "yes" to a pity date, because she wouldn't want to hurt my feelings. And then, her friends and my friends would think the whole thing was hilarious, and we'd be the new joke of the school.

I'm not big on humiliating myself or the girl of my dreams.

But how do I stop thinking about her? Any advice?

—Guy Who'll Never Get the Girl

Okay, I'd bet my Ella Fitzgerald vinyl collection that this was Dave. I rolled my pencil between my palms and debated what to say. Finally, I wrote:

Dear Guy Who's Already Decided He'll Never Get the Girl,

You're absolutely right about one thing. We're in high school. Gossip and teasing are year-round recreational sports.

So what? You and your dream girl are good at sports. I'm assuming that means you actually play them. And as you well know, when you play, sometimes you lose, and sometimes you win. Any guesses on the one sure way you'll never win?

Besides, there are always annoying hecklers in the stands. Why let them get into your head and take you out of your game?

And how about letting your dream girl have the chance to say yea or nay to a date? What makes you so sure she's not as interested in you as you are in her? I assume fortune-telling isn't one of your skill sets. At least you didn't mention it.

You asked me for advice on how to stop thinking about her. But in my opinion, that's the wrong question.

It's up to you, of course, but if it were me, I'd be swinging for the fences. You never know.

—Since You Asked

I said a silent prayer that not only would Mrs. Rivera like my answer, but that Dave, and Jenny, would read it.

I smiled. Here I'd always thought I wanted to be a journalist or a psychologist, but I might have some potential in the matchmaking department.

If I lived long enough.

Chapter Thirteen

Alex Kwon dashed into Starbucks at five minutes past four, and I waved him back to my favorite corner table.

"Sorry I'm late," he said. He gave me a quick hug. "I'm glad to see you."

"Alex, you smell like my father. Is that Old Spice you're wearing?" I teased.

"Guilty. It's my dad's. He wanted me to wear it for good luck at the auditions last week, and now the stuff has grown on me. So what do you think?"

"You'd be perfect for a 'young and on the rise' ad campaign. I can see it now—'The smell of success, starring up-and-coming concert pianist Alex Kwon.'"

He laughed, and I realized I missed this guy. I couldn't imagine him hurting Moura. How many concerts and competitions had the two done together? Dozens and dozens. I could still remember how serious he'd looked when we were in second grade, and he and Moura had played for a retired music teachers' association meeting. Decked out in his plaid sports jacket and clip-on bow tie, he'd tried very hard not to smile because of his missing front teeth. Ten years later, he had a great smile, courtesy of his orthodontist. And he'd switched out the bow tie for a classic necktie, which he wore to school every day along with a button-down shirt.

"So," I said, "first tell me about how your visits went."

"Your latte looks great. Let me get one, and then I'll tell you all about it." He waved me off when I offered to treat and returned a few minutes later with a supersized caramel torte latte loaded with whipped cream.

"Watching your weight, I see."

"Always," he said. "So overall, things went well. I really liked Eastman, loved Boston. And of course, Juilliard is Juilliard—my absolute first choice. I took a private class with one of the teachers—they recommend you do that before you audition. He was really encouraging. I guess it's going to come down to who says 'yes' and who gives me the most money. My parents want me to consider Oberlin, too. They'd love to see me stay in-state, but my heart says, *'City lights! New York! Boston! Here I come!'*"

His eyes shone, and a current of sadness swept through me. I was happy for Alex, but it was so hard knowing that Moura would never have the chance to follow her dream.

"So I hope you don't mind my asking, but what's with the bump on your head?"

I filled him in on the accident and the threats.

"How can I help?"

I hesitated, then dove in. "Someone saw you having an argument with Moura at a Youth Orchestra rehearsal, and I've heard there was tension between you in the last weeks of her life."

Alex's mouth dropped open. "Whoa! Like I didn't see you telling her where to get off that night at rehearsal? You didn't kill her, so why put me on your suspect list because she pissed me off, too?"

"I'm not accusing you. I'm trying to sort things out, and frankly, I'd like to save my own life, as well as get to the bottom of my sister's murder. You asked me how you could help. So please tell me everything you know."

He lifted his chin and leaned toward me. "I did not kill your sister. That doesn't mean there weren't times when I wanted to strangle her."

I winced.

His face colored. "Poor choice of words. I'm sorry."

"It's okay. Things like that come out of my mouth, too, and then I feel like I've stabbed myself. So what was the argument about?"

"Well, I was pretty pissed about the Joel Rasher feature. Moura charmed the pants off the guy, and suddenly an article that was supposed to be about both of us turned into a solo puff piece starring Moura."

"But I thought that was because he decided to do a whole series of features on young gifted musicians in the region, and you were next."

"He came up with that plan later on. And I'm grateful for that—the piece he did on me is coming out next month. But the point is, Moura always had to be first. She had no interest in sharing the spotlight. And that wasn't the only issue anyhow."

"What else?"

"She always wanted the advantage, no matter what. Example—she knew that I'd been working on the Bach concerto the university orchestra was slated to play last season. I was dying to do it. The concerto was perfectly suited to my technical strengths, and Bach is my passion. So what would you guess Moura did?"

I took a sip of my latte for strength, then said, "I'm afraid to guess. Tell me."

"The minute Moura found out the concerto was on the season's docket, she got her dibs in with your dad to play it. He had no idea I'd been working on the piece for months." His long tapered fingers gripped his mug, the heat of his anger at the memory palpable.

I gulped. The awful thing was I could totally imagine Moura doing that. "I'm so sorry. If it's any consolation, I remember you playing the Beethoven brilliantly the night you guested."

"Thanks—not really the point, though, is it?"

"No."

"You want to know something, though?"

"What?"

"Manipulative as she was, and irritating as she was, I miss her. She pushed me to become a better musician, a better artist, and I know I pushed her, too. In a strange way, we were good for each other."

"I think you're right. But I have to ask ... was there anything going on between you and Moura romantically?"

He held his hands up. "No way! Never! No offense, but if I ever find time for a girlfriend, I'd definitely be in the market for one I could trust."

I winced again at his brutal honesty. I'd always felt so badly about the distance between Moura and me, but maybe that wasn't such a terrible loss after all. "Any ideas then who she might have been involved with at the end of her life?"

"None. Hannah was pretty convinced there was someone new, but Moura wasn't exactly the confiding type. A few rumors floated around about Ms. Steinberg and her. They were always talking music, loaning each other books. But I never got the vibe there was anything more to it."

"What about Dr. Lewitsky's other students?"

"Moura was her only student who wasn't at the university. Dr. Lewitsky took her on because she was so talented—and frankly, because she works with your dad. I don't think any of her college students really knew Moura personally. The only time we ever saw them was when we guested with the orchestra." He took a final swig of his latte and set it down. "I wish I could be more help."

"Is there anything else you can think of? Anything different Moura said or did in those last few weeks?"

He paused, his brow furrowed. "Now that you mention it, I thought this was odd. A few weeks before she died, she called me and asked me a bunch of questions about Mrs. Hartsell. What was her approach like? Did I feel she really pushed and challenged me? That kind of thing. Finally, I said to her, 'What's going on? Are you shopping for a new teacher?' She laughed, and said, 'Oh no, I was just curious.'"

"You think maybe Moura was considering jumping ship?"

"I have no idea. But she wasn't in the habit of calling me out of the blue to interview me about my piano teacher."

Jenny picked me up from Starbucks in her father's sleek Mercedes instead of her Corolla.

"How'd you score the fancy wheels?"

"My reward for winning the tournament. Dad said we could trade cars for the week. You know my dad—it's all about winning. I'd probably be taking the bus this week if I'd lost." She shrugged and tried for one of her "no biggie" smiles. I didn't buy it for a nanosecond.

"No offense, but I didn't even know he was aware that you played tennis."

"Very funny. We actually had a family dinner last night—first one in weeks. In between all the shop talk about their latest cases, my parents asked me a total of three questions: How was my game coming along? What colleges were courting me for tennis scholarships? And let's see. Was I keeping my grades up? How's that for showering me with their parental warmth and concern?"

"My suck-o-meter reads eleven on a ten-point scale. But you're stuck with me as your BFF, and I could give a holy crap about your win-loss record or your GPA. Besides, once my car's out of the shop, you won't be in danger of having to take the bus. Of course, there's that small stalker problem you might have to deal with when you're riding with me."

She squeezed my arm. "We'll keep my tennis racquets handy to defend ourselves. Speaking of your stalker, did you learn anything new from talking to Alex?"

"I'm not sure. He pretty much confirmed a lot of things I'd heard from other people. Yes, he was pissed at Moura for maneuvering to keep the spotlight on her and not him. No, he didn't kill her. And no, he wasn't involved with her, and he doesn't know who was."

"Same old same old," Jenny said, her voice sounding flat.

"Yeah, but there was one thing he threw out at the end."

"What?" she said, as she turned in to my driveway, cut the engine, and faced me.

"Moura called him a few weeks before she died and asked him a bunch of questions about Mrs. Hartsell, his piano teacher."

"Wow. Weird. Didn't you tell me she and Dr. Lewitsky were pretty much joined at the hip?"

"That's how it always was, so this is really strange.... You want to come in? We can raid my freezer for something for dinner."

"As long as it's not another of those frozen pizzas you fed me the last time. I was belching for hours afterward."

"How very unladylike of you. Come on."

We headed inside and found a couple of Cokes and Lean Cuisines we thought we could stomach. Dad was at an orchestra rehearsal, and Mom was nowhere in sight. Probably in her bedroom. Or in Moura's room, whispering fairy tales to her dead daughter, while ignoring her living one. I shook myself, wishing I could shrug off my bitterness.

"So," Jenny said, as we got our entrees out of the microwave and sat down at the kitchen counter, "loved the news you texted about Ben. Now give me a blow-by-blow of the big ask-out."

I told her all about how he'd remembered that I'd said we should just talk about the weather the next time we got paired up and how he'd segued from the weather to asking me out, in French no less. "He was so adorable looking at his cheat sheet."

"I'm jealous! Nothing that romantic has ever happened to me, in or out of French class."

"You take Spanish."

"Even so."

"As a matter of fact, I have great faith that your time is coming. Be sure to read my next column."

"I always read your columns, silly. You're a great writer."

"Thanks. This one is written especially for you."

"What are you talking about?"

"Wait and see. You'll figure it out." I took a sip of my Coke and then grinned at her over the rim.

"Spill it right this minute! You know I hate surprises."

"You're not going to hate this one."

"So you're really not going to tell me?" She set her fork down and glared at me.

"Nope."

"Clara Seibert, there are times I find you incredibly annoying."

"I know, but you love me anyhow."

She groaned. "All right, you win. So what's your next move on the investigation?"

"I want to talk to Mrs. Hartsell and see if Moura contacted her. And I'm going to try to meet Fred, the guy the fan group defriended."

"Maybe I should go with you to see Fred. He could be dangerous."

"You've got enough to do. I'll take my Mace."

"You sure?"

I nodded.

"How's your chicken?"

"Let's just say it's a good thing we have Dove Bars to look forward to."

"I'm feeling better already."

That night, I finally connected with Fred. His bass voice was so deep he could have been an announcer on the mystery channel.

"You're Moura Seibert's sister? I was not a fan. Why on earth would you want to talk to me?"

"I'm trying to touch base with everyone. It's a long story, but I need your help."

"My help? You're kidding, right?"

I swallowed hard. "Please," I begged. "I'm getting threats. I need to talk to anyone who knew anything about my sister."

Dead silence. Just when I was wondering if he'd hung up, he said, "All right, I suppose I can spare you a few minutes. I work at Mel's Doo-Wop Shop on Fourth Street. I could meet you on my break tomorrow at the McDonald's across the street around five thirty."

"Great. Thank you."

"What do you look like?"

"Moura."

Chapter Fourteen

"You weren't kidding about looking like your sister," Fred said, inspecting me as though looking for signs of possible contamination.

"So they say. But that's pretty much where the similarities end."

"Yeah?" He dipped a fistful of fries into his ketchup. I wasn't surprised he'd ordered a Big Mac meal. He was huge, like somebody who'd once played football and never bothered to change his eating habits after hanging up his cleats.

"So Leslie told me you were posting negative stuff about my sister."

"Damn right. Don't mean to offend you, but it drove me crazy that after she died, everyone acted like she'd been some perfect saint, the greatest pianist ever. Sure, she was good, but that kid Alex Kwon was just as talented and a whole lot nicer. She was a royal bitch."

My chin jutted out. I'd thought that myself. Many times. But I still felt defensive when anyone else attacked her. "What do you mean?"

"My coworker's kid Ricky had cancer. The family had no health insurance, so last winter, I decided to organize a benefit concert to raise money for their medical bills. I thought if we could have all kinds of music—from country to classical, we could pull in a big crowd and raise some serious cash."

"Sounds like a good idea to me. I'm into jazz myself."

"Too bad Moura didn't agree with you. When I went backstage last year after one of her concerts, I told her how much I admired her playing and explained how sick Ricky was and how much her performing in the benefit would help his family. You know what she said to me?"

"What?"

"She told me she didn't see how it would help her career to perform with a bunch of people into 'popular drivel.' Said, 'I'm a classical artist, not an act for an amateur talent show.'"

"She was a bit of a musical snob," I admitted.

"A bit? Hah! There's a lot of great music that's not classical. But what really got to me was how she didn't care a hoot that a little boy was dying and his family was on the brink of going under financially. I even showed her a picture of him, and all she said was, 'Cute. You can leave now.'"

"Ouch. So were you able to do the concert?"

"Yeah—had it down at the American Legion Hall. A lot of people came out. Oh, and Alex Kwon played. Now there's a class act."

"I've always liked Alex. So what happened to Ricky?"

"He died a month later."

"I'm so sorry." And I was.

He shrugged. "So you said you were getting threats?"

I told him about the emails and starting my own investigation of Moura's murder.

He swallowed an enormous bite of his burger. "Let me guess. You're wondering if I killed your sister?"

"Did you?"

He burst out laughing. "Sorry," he said, when he was finally able to talk, "homicide's not my thing. My idea of violence is posting nasty comments online."

"Seems to be the weapon of choice these days.... Do you know anybody else my sister pissed off?"

"Not personally. But I can't believe I was the only one she'd blown off. That kid Brayden who hangs out with Leslie? He was nuts about her—always writing this sappy poetry and posting it on her fan site."

"Wow. Didn't know that.... Anyone you're aware of who might be convinced I killed my sister and want revenge?"

He leaned forward. "There was a lot of nasty gossip and rumors at first, but all that has really quieted down. There must be people who still think you did it, but as far as I know, they're not talking."

And that's the problem.

I thanked him and started to give him my number in case he thought of something else.

"Don't need it. I have it."

"You have my number?"

We stared at each other.

"Duh—you called me, remember?"

That night, I went over everything with Jenny on the phone. "Funny how people who were in love with Moura never seem to think that might be worth mentioning—first Hannah, now Brayden."

"Can you blame them? They don't want their names starred on your suspect list."

"Yeah, so now I need to talk with Brayden again."

"Duh."

"You're the second person to 'duh' me today. I'm starting to feel really stupid."

"You're not. Sorry."

The next afternoon, there were no new emails from my stalker buddy. But the new email that had come in had me wringing my hands. Literally.

Dear Since You Asked,

Please don't print this.

I wrote to you a few weeks ago about how after I broke up with my abusive boyfriend, he was still bothering me.

Well, you're not going to believe this, but I think he's really changed, and I'm even thinking of getting back together with him. I know this sounds crazy, but right after I wrote to you, he sent me a long letter apologizing for everything he'd done and telling me it was no excuse, but he'd never been so desperately in love with anyone before. He said he's getting counseling, and he promised that if I'd give him another chance, he'd never treat me bad again.

When we talk, he's so sweet. And he gives me flowers and writes me love letters nearly every day.

People can change, right? And everybody deserves a second chance, don't they?

—Wondering

I pressed my fingers to my forehead. I could feel a headache coming on. This guy's shtick was straight out of the Abuser's Playbook. But how could I help her see that, without making her so angry or defensive she'd run straight back into his clutches?

Finally, I came up with:

Dear Wondering,

I'm really glad you wrote to me again. It must have felt so good to get a letter of apology from your ex. And what's not to like about flowers and love notes?

But I know you wouldn't have written to me if you didn't have doubts. I really hope you'll listen to them—and to your gut.

I have a friend who went to the teen support group meetings at the Women's Project Center. She brought me a pamphlet she picked up about the "Cycle of Abuse." The way your ex is acting sounds suspiciously like the "honeymoon stage." After abusers have gone off on their victims and want to hold on to them, they start showering them with flowers, romance, and promises that the abuse will never happen again. But it almost always does, and it doesn't get better. Each time it happens, the abuse gets worse.

I really, really don't want that to happen to you. You sound like a very nice person who wants to be fair and caring by giving your ex a second chance. But in this case, being nice may be dangerous. Think back to when you were desperate to get out of this relationship, and how tough it was to actually make the break. Ask yourself if you're ready to risk a rerun, only with the violent scenes ramped up.

IMO, you deserve better. I'm in your corner!

—Since You Asked

I shivered as I thought about this grease ball. He had to be one ultra-smooth operator to have wormed his way so convincingly back into her life.

Nothing to do but pray she'd find that wonderful backbone of hers. Again.

Camped out in my bedroom that night conjugating French verbs and daydreaming about Ben, I was feeling better. That is, until Detective Martino called with more bad news. No identifiable prints on the tracking device, and the serial number had been shaved off, so tracing it was a no go. He sounded as frustrated as I felt.

And I couldn't get a hold of Mrs. Hartsell. I wasn't surprised. She was a busy lady, and I also suspected she might be reluctant to talk to me. I left another voice mail, and then called Alex. My car was due back tomorrow, and I was determined to make contact.

Miracle of miracles, he answered his phone. "Taking a practice break," he said. "What's up?"

"First off, thanks a lot for meeting me yesterday. I've got to pick up my car from the shop tomorrow, but after that … well, I'd like to drop by your teacher's studio and see if I can talk with her. Do you know when she's finished giving lessons?"

"I'm her only lesson on Fridays. Get there around five, and you'll catch her." He gave me directions to her studio and invited me to come a few minutes early to hear him play. He was working on a new Brahms piece he was really excited about.

I hesitated. "You know I love hearing you play. But it's still … a little painful for me—a lot of memories. I'll try, though."

After school on Friday, Dad drove me to Al's to pick up my car, and Sergeant Driscoll taught us how to look for devices. He was a super skinny guy with a bushel of red hair, a booming voice, and a friendly smile. "Don't forget to check every time you get into your car, you hear?"

"Believe me, I won't," I assured him.

"Meet you back at home, honey?" Dad asked me as we got ready to take off.

"Actually, I promised Jenny I'd drop by." Not exactly the whole truth, but explaining that first I was planning to pay a visit to Mrs. Hartsell wasn't an option.

"Be very careful. Understood?"

"Absolutely," I said, as I gave him a quick kiss on the cheek and gingerly got into my beloved VW. I felt giddy as I started the car and cradled the steering wheel in my hands. It was like getting an old friend back.

But as I drove out of Al's lot, pinpricks of guilt punctured my bubbly mood when I looked in my rearview mirror. Dad stood there watching me, looking solemn and gray.

I pulled into the narrow parking lot a few minutes before five and sat in my car, admiring the historic mansion where Mrs. Hartsell had her studio. It looked like something out of a Victorian fairy tale. I loved its arched doorways, stained glass windows, and the twin turrets that topped the stately home. It was located in "Olde Towne," my favorite neighborhood in Springbrook. Its heyday had been at the turn of the last century when wealthy families had been intent upon showcasing their success with their fabulous downtown dwellings.

I thought about waiting until five to go in, but then decided I needed to face down my memories. I couldn't spend the rest of my life avoiding listening to piano music because Moura was gone. And I knew it would mean something to Alex for me to hear him play.

After locking up my car, I scrambled up the stone outer steps and three flights of stairs to Mrs. Hartsell's studio. Time to get into better shape. I took in big gulps of air, nearly overwhelmed by the building's faintly musty smell mixed with the stronger scent of furniture polish.

I wondered if all the other tenants had begun their Friday happy hour early, because the building seemed deserted, until I got close to the third-floor studio where the strains of piano music wafted through the air. The waiting room door was ajar, but I stood outside until Alex finished the run-through of the Brahms. I'd gotten there in time for a powerful climax and then a shift downward in mood and energy to a quiet, contemplative ending.

"Yes!" Mrs. Hartsell shouted. "Beautiful resolution there at the end. Now this go-round, try for a more gradual build to the climax."

The door to the waiting room outside the studio creaked as I opened it wider to enter. They both looked up. Mrs. Hartsell seemed startled to see me, and Alex gave me a friendly wave.

"I didn't mean to interrupt," I said. "My apologies. Is it all right if I sit here and listen to Alex for a few minutes?"

She hesitated. "Is that all right with you, Alex?"

"Sure. Clara mentioned to me she wanted to drop by to talk to you after our lesson, and I invited her to come early to hear the Brahms."

"Well, come on in then. Why don't you take a seat in here with us?" She ushered me to a cozy gingham love seat in the corner of the studio. I sniffed the yummy scent of cinnamon and nutmeg from the teapot that sat next to me on the side table.

"This is Brahms's Intermezzo no. 2 in B-flat minor. Alex has only been working on it for a few weeks, but it's really coming along," she said. She took a seat next to Alex and leaned forward intently, as he began to play.

I was stunned. This was not the Alex I remembered whose expressiveness had never matched his technical prowess. It was as though he had finally found the key to imbuing the notes with every bit of the emotion and passion that had been curiously missing from his playing.

When he'd finished, I sat there for a moment, unable to speak. Mrs. Hartsell gave him a few notes on passages she wanted him to refine but effusively praised his interpretation.

"So," he said, turning to me, "what did you think?" His eyes eagerly sought mine, and I realized that my opinion, for whatever reason—maybe just because I was Moura's sister—mattered to him.

"That is absolutely the best I've ever heard you play! I'm so thrilled for you!" I reached my arms up for his inspection. "See these goose bumps? They're from hearing you play!"

"Wow, thanks," he said, giving me a hug. "Coming from you, that means a lot to me."

Tears came to my eyes, and I didn't try to stop them. "I've missed that, Alex—hearing someone play so movingly that I got chills."

I meant what I said. But dark shadows of doubt also nudged at me. Alex had told me that having Moura as a competitor had pushed him to get better as a musician. Yet, her death seemed to have released something in him, an emotional power in his playing that he'd never been able to access while Moura was alive. Was that a coincidence, or did it mean something?

He pulled away from our hug and squeezed my shoulder. "Thanks for coming to hear me. And now I'll get out of here, so you two can talk."

He gathered his things and slipped out the door. I turned to Mrs. Hartsell. "I apologize again for barging in like this. I really needed to talk with you."

"I understand. I'm sorry I missed your calls." She moved over to the love seat and gestured for me to join her. "Would you like some tea?"

"No, I'm fine, thanks." I sat down and faced her. She had a round, kind face, framed by stray tendrils that had escaped from the mass of thick gray hair piled high on top of her head.

"Well, let me tell you again how very sorry I am about your sister. She was a very gifted and special young woman."

"Thank you."

"What did you want to talk with me about?"

I went through the condensed version of why I was trying to get a bead on my sister's life the weeks before her death. "Alex mentioned that Moura had called him, asking lots of questions about you as a teacher."

"They were friends. My guess is they compared notes all the time about their music."

"Did Moura ever contact you?"

She shifted in her seat. "Probably best for you to talk directly with Dr. Lewitsky. I have nothing but admiration for the work she did with Moura."

"I agree, but you haven't really answered my question."

She stood up and extended her hand. Clearly a dismissal. "I advise you to let Moura rest in peace."

When I dropped by Jenny's, she said, "Sure, it's frustrating that she wouldn't talk to you. But she told you without telling you. If Moura hadn't contacted her, she would have said so, instead of refusing to discuss it with you."

"Yeah. I had the feeling she's not sure whether Dr. Lewitsky knew about Moura's possible defection. And if she didn't know, Mrs. Hartsell would rather keep it that way." I rubbed the back of my neck.

"Why do I get the feeling something else is bothering you?"

"It's Alex. It was eerie. He played with such emotion. It felt like Moura's death unlocked something for him— almost like being free of her allowed him to play with a whole new abandon."

"Like maybe he offed her because he felt stifled by her somehow?"

"My gut tells me 'no,' that Alex would never have hurt her, but hearing him today really made me wonder."

"So he's still on your suspect list. What's your next move?"

"For starters, I've got to follow up with Dr. Lewitsky. I'm not looking forward to that, but I don't see any alternative. Plus, I need to get hold of Brayden." I pointed to the "pink passion" polish Jenny was neatly applying to her nails as we talked. "That color looks really good."

"You want some? You need to look smashing tomorrow, right?"

"Definitely. Hand it over when you're done."

"Did you decide what you're gonna wear?"

"Let's talk possibilities."

And we did. I tried not to think about how weird it was that Jenny and I could move from talking about my "life and possible death" investigation one minute to talking about my hot date tomorrow in the next—all while doing our nails. It was official: I'd become the new Queen of Living in the Moment. What other choice did I have?

Chapter Fifteen

"You look great!" Ben said when he came to pick me up. "And I can hardly see the bump on your forehead."

"The joys of CoverGirl. And you don't look so bad yourself." Ben was wearing a chocolate brown sweater that matched his amazing eyes.

The day was indeed "unseasonably warm," just like Ben had predicted in our French class conversation. Our feet crunched on the dappled yellow and amber autumn leaves, as a handful of clouds drifted lazily past.

Ben opened the car door for me, and I tried not to wince as I gingerly lowered myself into the seat. His musky scent mingled with the car's leather aroma and the whiff of something that smelled like Italian food. Yum.

"So," I said, "where are we going for lunch?"

"Look in the back seat."

I turned around. An enormous wicker basket lay on the floor. "A picnic—Yes! What a great idea."

"Glad you approve. I hope you like Italian deli food, because that's what I brought."

"Perfect."

"How are your ribs feeling?"

"Still sore, but so much better. I may even be able to bend over to pick a pumpkin. I was worried I'd have to play 'helpless female' and ask you to haul up whatever pumpkin I chose."

"Well, you might still have to do that if you decide you can't live without a giant pumpkin. Then I get to try to impress you by flexing my muscles."

His lopsided grin made my heart flutter and my face burn. I couldn't help smiling. The farther we got from town, the farther away my fears seemed. Riding with Ben, I felt warm and hopeful. And almost safe.

When we pulled up to the farm half an hour later, the parking lot was already three-quarters full. I eyed every dark van we passed as we searched for a parking spot. I clamped my mouth shut and closed my eyes. *Damn it! Do not let your fears ruin this day.* I took a deep breath, determinedly opened my eyes, and stole a glance at Ben.

His eyebrows had shot up at least an inch. "Are you okay?"

"Yeah, sorry. Just thinking about something ... I don't mind walking. Let's park way out."

Ben pulled into a spot on the farthest edge of the lot. As we passed one of the dreaded black vans, a man wearing a baseball cap jumped out of the driver's seat. He was walking straight toward us! Oh God—that night in the police parking lot, the guy had been wearing a baseball cap.

My breath came in jagged bursts. I clung to Ben and

dug my fingers into his arm.

"Clara, what is it?"

My stomach churned. I couldn't speak, couldn't move. But when I blinked again, the man in the baseball cap was no longer headed in our direction. He'd veered around to the other side of the van and was helping let out a pretty blonde-haired woman and a boy who looked to be around seven or so.

He glanced over at the two of us, seemingly rooted to our spot. Then he waved, and said, "Beautiful day, isn't it?"

"It is," called Ben. He pulled me away. "What was that about?" he whispered.

"Mistaken identity." I managed to release my death grip on his arm and practiced breathing like a normal person.

"You've got some 'splainin' to do."

"I know.… What's with the accent?"

He laughed. "My uncle has every episode ever made of the old *I Love Lucy* show. That's Ricky Ricardo's line to his goofball wife, Lucy."

"Goofball, huh?" I poked him in the ribs.

"Yup."

We continued walking for what felt like at least a mile and finally reached the picnic area. Couples and young families swarmed like bees in a rose garden. Not a free table in sight.

"No problem," Ben said. He pulled out an old army blanket from his backpack.

"Talk about being prepared. Were you a Boy Scout?" I teased.

"I was, until my friend's dad wasn't allowed to lead our troop because he's gay. That was the end of Scouts for me."

I squeezed his arm. "You do realize a guy with principles is totally irresistible."

"I bet you say that to all ex-Boy Scouts."

"Always."

We picked a spot beneath a tangy-smelling, gnarled apple tree on the lawn behind the tables and spread out our blanket. I hesitated, trying to figure out the best way to sit down without inflaming my bruised ribs or clinging to Ben. Again. Finally, I went for my best version of the dancer's sit I'd learned in a modern dance class in eighth grade. You put all your weight on one foot, fold the other behind you, and lower yourself with as straight a back as you can muster. That went well until I fell over like a drunken duck, with my face squarely in Ben's lap.

"Sorry," I murmured. I was sure my face looked like a scorched tomato, as Ben guided me back to a sitting position.

"Next time, you can just ask me if you want to do a lap dance." He snorted and handed me a cream soda.

"Ha, ha." I pulled my stash of ibuprofen out of my jeans pocket and swallowed a handful with a swig of cream soda. My ribs didn't even hurt that bad yet, but we'd be doing a lot more walking later on.

"You okay?"

"Yeah, just taking precautions in case my ribs flare up this afternoon."

He nodded, and fished two thickly wrapped footlong

packages out of the picnic basket. "Okay, you've got an important decision to make. Italian sub—or, let's see— Italian sub?"

I breathed in the scent of oregano and freshly baked bread, amazed that the knots in my stomach from the parking lot scare had loosened enough for me to eat. "Hmm … That's a tough one. How about the sub?"

We ate in silence for several minutes. I searched my brain for something to say and came up empty. It had been so long since I'd gone out with anyone it was like I'd forgotten how to do it. Just as I was about to launch into major panic mode that I was the world's most boring date, Ben said, "So are you going to tell me what's going on?"

No small talk for this guy. I took another sip of the cream soda to buy some time. Finally, I said, "What have you heard about me? About my situation?"

He brushed a newly fallen leaf off the blanket and looked up at me. "I know that you've been through a lot— that your twin was murdered last spring, that the two of you weren't close, and that some people at the time suspected you of being involved."

"At the time? Actually, there are still plenty of folks around who think I offed my sister," I said, unable to quash the bitterness in my voice. "And now there's some creep who's decided he needs to get revenge—and soon."

"What do you mean?" Those beautiful eyebrows of his inched up again.

I filled him in on all the grisly details. His eyes got

wider and wider.

"Wow. I had no idea. This totally sucks. But should you really be doing your own investigating? Isn't this something the police should handle?"

"They're working on it, but they've gotten nowhere with my sister's case. And as long as this creep thinks I killed my sister, he seems bent on destroying me. I don't want to be the last bowling pin standing and wait for this guy to knock me down. Permanently." I dug my fingernails into my jeans.

"What can I do to help?"

"I'm not sure anybody can help me at this point. Mostly, I'm running around talking to people who were close to Moura … But you deserve to know what you might be getting into by going anywhere with me."

"I'm glad you told me, even though now you're not going to be the only one freaking out every time we come across a dark van."

He was such a nice guy. Worry lines creased his beautiful face. I swallowed hard. I had to give him an out. "Honestly, maybe it's not a good idea for you to hang with me right now. It's not exactly going to do wonders for your reputation—not to mention your safety—to be my friend."

He laced his fingers through mine. "You're not going to scare me off *that* easily."

His gaze held mine, and a surge of electricity passed between us. I couldn't deny the attraction. But could I trust him? How could I trust anybody at this point?

"Please tell me you're not somebody who gets a charge out of dating dangerous girls. I've had more than my fill of disgusting come-ons from guys who want to 'get it on with the killer chick.'"

He shook his head. Then he winked at me. "I don't want to hurt your feelings, but you look about as dangerous as my best friend's grandmother. I peg you as one of those people who capture a bug inside their house and take it outside rather than kill it."

"How did you know that?"

"It's my intuition."

I gave him a playful punch in the arm. "Smart Ass Alert!"

"Guilty," he said, as he picked up one of the jumbo chocolate chip cookies he'd brought for dessert and took a humongous bite.

"So just to clarify, why did you ask me out if you don't think I'm an exciting homicidal maniac?"

"Fishing for compliments?"

"Yup."

He stared at me for several seconds, his brow furrowed, as though I'd just assigned him a complicated physics problem. Maybe he was having second thoughts about asking me out.

"Sorry," I mumbled. "That was a stupid question."

"No! I was thinking that's hard. Why is anybody attracted to anybody? I don't know. I mean, yeah, you're really cute, even when you're all banged up. But there's more, you know—maybe something familiar."

He leaned in and brushed a stray curl off my cheek and tucked it behind my ear. There was something so intimate about the gesture, so sweet. My cheek tingled where he'd touched it, and for some odd reason, tears gathered behind my eyelids.

"Familiar?" I wondered if he could hear the slight tremor in my voice.

"This is going to sound nuts, but I see the pain in your eyes and how hard you're working not to give in to it."

We hardly knew each other, but it was like he could see inside me. How was that even possible? Yet, hadn't I sensed the same thing about him? Tentatively, I reached over and touched his hand. "Why familiar? Tell me?"

He didn't say anything for several seconds—just took my hand and buried it in the warmth of his. Finally, he cleared his throat. "My mom and I were really tight. We sort of grew up together. My dad was never in the picture. Anyhow, she died of breast cancer this summer. That's how I moved here. I'm living with my uncle, my mom's brother."

I bit my lip as I thought about what Ben had gone through. Was going through. I'd lost Moura, but it wasn't the same. No way would I ever have described our relationship as "tight." I took a deep breath. "I am so sorry. I had no idea … Does it help to talk about it?"

"It helps to know you want to listen. And because of what you've gone through, you can understand." He squeezed my hand. "You know, when you're the new kid at school, you spend a lot of time getting the lay of the land, just watching. I didn't know you well, but I felt a connection almost right away. Maybe it's because I knew you were having a tough time, too. Besides, a lot of girls—and guys, for that matter—try to impress you, get your attention. But that's not you. Like at that Psychology Club meeting. You were so into it, asking all those questions, instead of trying to impress all those psychology buffs with what you knew."

"Thanks. I feel like my head must be getting bigger talking to you."

"Now that you mention it—it does look like a giant pumpkin!"

I swatted him. "Speaking of my insatiable curiosity, what were you doing at that meeting?"

"Other than scoping you out, you mean?"

A fresh wave of heat washed over my face. "Other than that."

"My uncle's wife was borderline. They finally got divorced a couple of years ago, but he went through hell and high water with my aunt. He loved her, but it was really tough for him."

"I bet he's glad to have you around."

"We have our moments, but I think it's been good for him to have some company."

"What's he like?"

"Definitely a conversation for another day." He stood up. "You ready for some pumpkin-hunting?"

"You're on."

The rest of the afternoon passed in a delicious blur. The meds had kicked in, and I was able to tromp through acres of pumpkin fields with Ben almost pain free. He teased me mercilessly about the asymmetrical pumpkins I insisted on picking. "Who wants perfection?" I asked him. "Boring!"

We took lots of pictures. It was a definite competition to see who could make the most ridiculous face as we posed with our pumpkins. We even convinced a passerby to take a picture of us with our haul.

Still, when we headed back to our car, I scanned the parking lot for any more black vans.

I loved that there weren't any.

By the time Ben dropped me off, I was exhausted, my hair was a wind-blown mess, and I couldn't have cared less. Ben helped me haul the pumpkins up the steps to the porch.

"I wish I didn't have to go to work," he said. "I'd love to stay and help you carve these."

"Where do you work?"

"My cousin's deli—where all that great food we scarfed came from."

"Tell your cousin the subs were fantastic!"

"Will do." He grabbed my shoulders and leaned his face in close to mine.

I breathed in his musky scent and then boldly cupped my hands around his face and kissed him. His lips were soft and tasted so sweet.

"Geez, now I really don't want to leave," he said, his

breathing sounding jagged. He buried his face in my neck and whispered, "Promise you'll wait to carve these pumpkins until I can do it with you?"

"I promise."

I spent most of Sunday daydreaming about Ben—and worrying about why he hadn't called. When I wasn't stressing about Ben, I stressed about calling Dr. Lewitsky. After writing and rewriting my pitch to her, I finally dialed her home number. Mr. Rasher picked up. When I asked to speak to his wife, he hesitated. "Hang on for a minute, and let me see if she can come to the phone."

He must have covered the phone's mouthpiece because a flurry of muffled voices rose and fell. At one point, I thought I heard Dr. Lewitsky raise her voice by several decibels. Didn't sound promising.

But a minute later, she came on the line. "Just the person I wanted to talk to! I can't thank you enough for meeting with Moura's fan group. Leslie Hall phoned me and said they're totally on board with helping out. They even want to organize a benefit concert."

"That's wonderful. I'm glad I could help."

"Oh, you have. And I really want to talk to you about publicity, since you write for your school paper. Do you have some time next week to drop by my office to talk?"

This was too good to be true. "Be glad to." We made arrangements to meet after school on Tuesday during her office hours.

Since I was on a roll, I decided to try to track down

Brayden. I called Leslie and asked for his number.

"What do you need it for?" Her tone let me know she still wasn't ready to let me into the Moura fan fold, even if they were willing to work on the scholarship.

"Dr. Lewitsky wants to talk to me about publicity. I heard he was a good writer and thought maybe we could collaborate."

"Oh. Well, okay. I'll see if he wants to talk to you. He'll call you if he does."

Chapter Sixteen

Monday morning, I steeled myself for a major letdown with Ben. The way my life had been going lately, I figured he'd spent Sunday having second thoughts about getting involved with me. Ben was a lot of things, but he wasn't stupid.

Well, maybe he was a little stupid. Just as I was about to walk in the door to French class, I felt a tap on my shoulder. I whirled around and there he stood, a goofy grin on his face.

"You forgot something very important on Saturday," he said.

"What?"

"You never gave me your cell phone number. And your landline's unlisted."

"True. But you didn't ask, and you didn't give me your number, so we're even."

"Okay, truce. I'm sorry. Being with you was, well … a little distracting."

"I'm glad." I willed my heart to stop thumping like a metronome on allegro, but it wasn't cooperating.

He took out his phone and we exchanged numbers. "You didn't forget your promise, did you?"

"The pumpkins and I are waiting."

"Good." He leaned closer and my breath caught in my throat. "I'm off tomorrow night. Can I come over around seven?"

"Perfect," I said, as the bell rang and we dashed in to take our seats.

A few hours later, I was on my way to lunch when a muscular arm reached out of the girls' bathroom door and yanked me inside.

"What the—"

Jenny clamped a hand over my mouth. "I saw it," she said. "I don't know whether to kill you or hug you. Do you think it's him?" Her eyes blazed. I'd read my share of novels where people's eyes blazed, but this was the first time I'd seen someone's eyes do this in real life.

I carefully removed her hand from my mouth. "My guess is 'yes,' but even if it's not, I think he'll relate to the situation. I've seen the way he looks at you. He's so into you he'd probably miss every shot if you ever took him on in a match."

A crimson hue crept up her neck to her face. "You really think so? But what if he never makes a move? I don't want to be that old lady in a Lifetime movie who still pines for the guy who got away forty years ago."

I hesitated, then decided that, oh, well, I'd come this far. Surely, meddling for a good cause was a forgivable sin.

"He's seen you on the court. He knows you're strong, gutsy, and he obviously digs that about you. Just because you're not into baseball doesn't mean that you shouldn't also be swinging for the fences."

"Are you saying you think I should ask him out? Have you lost your mind?"

"Possibly. But what have you got to lose?"

"How about my pride when he turns me down? Not to mention my reputation when he tells his friends the giant tennis girl came on to him. Just because I could be Buffy the Vampire Slayer's double on the court doesn't mean that I don't have my wimpy tendencies in real life."

I grinned. Jenny was a bit of a marshmallow off the court. "Time's a-wastin'," I said.

"Easy for you to say."

Not really, I thought. Time might be running out for me.

After school, my fingers shook as I checked my inbox. Mr. B. hovered in the doorway until I gave him the all clear and read my one email from an actual reader:

Dear Since You Asked,

Thought you deserved an update. When I got your last reply, I was pissed that you advised against giving my ex a second chance.

Then last week, I'd stayed late after school for some tutoring, and he was waiting for me by my locker. He pulled me into a hug and whispered that he couldn't wait for me to be "his" again. He was holding on to me so tight, I thought I was going to suffocate. I knew then, for sure. I pushed him away as gently as I could, told him I was really sorry, but I didn't want to go back with him.

He stood there for a minute and didn't say anything. His eyes got darker and darker—and suddenly he grabbed my hair and yanked my head back and slammed me against my locker. I thought he was going to kill me. Thank God some guy I recognized from tutoring showed up to get something out of his locker. He asked me if I was okay.

My ex laughed and said, "Just a little lover's quarrel." Then he turned to me and said in this syrupy sweet voice, "Gotta go. Sorry I got upset."

That is so typical! He acts like Mr. Perfect around everyone. I'm still kicking myself for almost falling for his BS a second time. How could I have been so stupid?

Anyhow, you were right. And I hope you'll write about this more, because girls need to know that if their Prince Charming seems too good to be true, well, maybe he is.

Thanks again for not printing my emails.

—Not Much Older, but a Whole Lot Wiser

I pushed my seat back and flung my hands down on my lap. I was glad "Not Much Older" hadn't gone back with this jerk, but I knew she wasn't out of the woods yet.

I chipped away at more of my nail polish as I thought about what to write back. Finally, I pushed "Reply" and wrote:

Dear Not Much Older, but a Whole Lot Wiser,

I'm so sorry your ex hurt you. But at least now you know for sure. You made the right call, twice, and you'll never again need to second-guess yourself about this guy.

"Mr. Perfect" doesn't sound like someone who wants to take "no" for an answer, and you deserve to live your life fully without being harassed or feeling unsafe. I know I sound like a broken record, but please, please talk to the folks at the Women's Project Center. They'll know more about your legal options, and my friend swears by their support group for teens.

Anyhow, I really appreciate your updating me. And congrats on all you've done to take care of yourself. That takes a lot of courage.

—Since You Asked

I kneaded my forehead with my fingers. I was scared for this girl. Her ex had to be furious that his "I'm a changed guy" ploy hadn't worked. Was he really going to let this go? I doubted it.

And my telling her she deserved to be safe? I might as well have been writing to myself. But deserving something and getting it were two different things.

The sound of shuffling footsteps grew closer. I opened my eyes to find Rita in the doorway. "Can you cover the women's basketball game at five? I've got a huge chem test tomorrow, and I'm freaking."

"Sure." Any excuse to delay going home was fine with

me. The other staffers thought it was weird I wanted to stay late at school every day and write in the office instead of at home or wherever. But our little broom closet of a newspaper office was my own little cocoon. If I could have moved in a cot and set up full-time shop here, I probably would have.

"Everything okay?" Rita asked. "You look like you're a million miles away."

"I'm hanging in there.… Can I ask you something?"

"Shoot."

"Have you ever known anyone our age who's hooked up with a boyfriend who turned out to be big trouble—you know, someone who's gotten physical?"

Rita looked down for a few seconds, then back up at me. "My older sister."

"You're kidding. Is she okay?"

"Yeah. She finally moved away. We don't talk about where. I miss her."

"I'm really sorry," I said and stood up to give her a hug. "That totally sucks."

"Tell me about it." She hugged me back and then quickly released me. Rita wasn't the touchy-feely type.

"Somebody wrote to the column and challenged me to write more about this. What do you think about my pitching an in-depth feature on dating violence at Wednesday's staff meeting?"

"Good idea."

Tuesday after school, I drove to the university in less than twenty minutes and parked as close as I could to the music building where Dr. Lewitsky, as well as my dad, had their offices. I walked down one hallway, then another. Chattering students, a bunch of them loaded down with instruments, passed by. One or two walked alone, their phones jammed next to their ears. Strange to think this might be me next year—a university student walking down a hallway chatting with friends between classes. If I lived long enough.

I hovered at Dr. Lewitsky's closed door that muffled the voices inside. I sat down in an empty chair across from her door to wait my turn.

Ten minutes later, the door opened, and a guy with saggy pants and stubble on his cheeks emerged. I took a deep breath, and tapped on Dr. Lewitsky's door.

"Come in," she called. When she looked up from her desk and saw me, her face lit up with a smile.

I took a seat and tried not to be too obvious about checking her out for any telltale signs that she might have something to hide. Mostly, what I saw was a woman who, as my mother used to say in the days when she was talking to me, "took pains with her appearance." Today, she wore a jet black pants suit, a perfect match for the sleek ebony grand piano in the corner and a dramatic contrast to her frosted blonde hair which seemed frozen in place. Her makeup was impeccable, and the word 'handsome' flitted across my brain. She was a handsome woman.

I gazed around the office, which matched her appearance. Even her desk looked spotless, with her papers carefully arranged. My dad claimed having a neat office stifled his creativity, and the piles of papers and books strewn all over his floor were a necessity to his productivity. Apparently, Dr. Lewitsky didn't have that problem.

What their offices did share, however, was a wall of windows that looked out on the woods behind campus. Deepening shadows sprawled amidst the towering pines.

"Your view is amazing."

"It is." She leaned forward and clasped her hands. "Let's talk publicity."

"We have an arts writer, Kristen, who was a huge admirer of Moura's. I was thinking she could do a splashy cover article about the fund and especially about the benefit concert. There could be an accompanying piece about Moura with lots of pictures. And we could organize a table at lunch to sell concert tickets."

"Sounds great. What about the other area high schools?"

"I can reach out to them, too. Moura's friend Hannah goes to the Catholic girls' school, and I can work through the Youth Orchestra to distribute publicity to other schools."

"Wonderful. This means so much to me to be able to remember Moura this way." Her eyes misted over, as she went on about missing working with Moura.

I finally decided to cut in. "Actually, there is something else I wanted to talk to you about."

I went through my spiel, sure it sounded as over-rehearsed as it was.

When I got to the part about my stalker, she said, "How awful for you! But I don't know how I can help." She unclasped her hands and grabbed on to her chair's armrests, rubbing her fingers back and forth across the fabric.

"A couple of Moura's friends told me she seemed distracted in those last weeks. They thought maybe she'd gotten involved with someone new, someone she felt very intensely about. Were you aware of anything like that?"

She chuckled. "Do you talk to your teachers about your love life?"

"Not if I can help it."

"Exactly. Moura's conversations with me were about her music, her goals for her career. Her romantic life was the sort of thing she might have talked about with her girlfriends. But Moura was rather private, you know."

No kidding. I switched subjects. "Did she ever mention anyone who might have been obsessed with her? Someone who might want to hurt me if they were convinced I'd killed my sister?"

"Hmmm, not really. You and I both know she had lots of fans. But I can't think of anyone who would be that crazy. Or deluded."

"Right. But did you notice any changes in her behavior? Did she seem anxious to you, different in any way?"

"I've thought about that, wondered. But all I come up with is that she was a bit tense about leaving, about going off to Juilliard, where the competition would be stiff and unrelenting. Plus, she'd worked with me for years, and now she'd have all new teachers. It's natural to be nervous, don't you think?"

I took a deep breath. Time for the plunge. "Were you

aware that Moura may have been considering switching teachers before she left?"

Color drained from her face. "Who told you that?"

"That's not important. I wanted your take on what was going on."

She leaned forward and stared at me, her eyes narrowed into dark slits. "That is absolutely not true. Moura was totally committed to our working relationship. She was fully aware and appreciative of all I had done to help her prepare for Juilliard and a concert career." Her hands shook slightly as she took a swig from the water bottle on her desk.

I started to mumble an apology, but she waved me off. "Look, I can understand how someone might have gotten that impression. Moura and I had been talking about how nervous she felt about starting with all new teachers at Juilliard, how it would be a hard adjustment after so many years together. I encouraged her to take a lesson or two with other teachers before she left, to ease her mind, let her see she'd be fine."

"Oh, okay." I bit my lip. "Well, that clears that up."

"Glad I could help." The lines on her face softened, and she leaned back in her seat.

"Is there anything else you can think of? Anyone who might have had an issue with Moura?"

She shrugged. "Not really. She and Alex were die-hard competitors, but they were also friends. I'm sure they got annoyed with each other from time to time, but Alex is a sweet boy. I don't think their issues were ever anything serious." She glanced at the clock above the doorway. "If there's nothing else, I should get out of here and go home. My husband's promised me his signature pasta primavera."

Dismissed in favor of a gourmet dinner.

As I slipped out the door, a familiar deep voice behind me boomed out, "Clara!"

Chapter Seventeen

Dad barreled down the hall toward me, his face flushed. "I've been looking everywhere for you. What are you doing here? And why did you turn off your phone?"

Before I could summon a response, Dr. Lewitsky emerged from her office. "Raymond," she called out. She flew toward us like a carrier pigeon eager to finish her route and clutched my father's arm. "Clara was just filling me in on the awful threats she's been getting. I feel badly I couldn't be of more help. She's so brave to be undertaking her own investigation."

Thank you, Dr. Lewitsky. My dad's mouth gaped open. "Been a brutal year for us," he finally murmured. "We appreciate your concern."

We said our goodbyes, and then Dad gripped my arm like I was a "person of interest" he needed to interrogate who might bolt at any second. He steered me back down the hall toward his office. "You have some explaining to do," he said.

Lately, I'd been doing a lot of that.

The moment Dad shut the door, he started yelling.

"Your own investigation? What the hell do you think you're doing, Clara? Are you out of your mind? Are you determined to get yourself killed?" The vein in his forehead throbbed as though it might explode.

"No! I'm trying to save my life, not sit around waiting for some jerk to take it away because he thinks I killed my sister!"

"And you didn't think you should clear snooping around with me first?"

"I'm sorry! I knew what your reaction would be. But I had to do something. Otherwise, I might as well hang a sign around my neck: 'Hey, El Creepo, come and get me.'" My eyes pleaded with his for understanding, but Dad was in no mood.

"You lied to me, didn't you? Telling me you went to see Joel Rasher because you were having a hard time with Moura's death. Ha! You went to see him because you wanted information. And you nearly got yourself killed going out there."

Tears spilled down my cheeks. I didn't bother wiping them away. "I *am* having a hard time with Moura's death—just like you and Mom are. I wasn't lying about that! I didn't tell you I was also asking questions, because I knew you wouldn't approve." Okay, so that was splitting hairs, but I hated being accused—even if I was guilty.

"Well, at least you have that right! I don't approve. And you will stop this so-called investigation immediately. Is that clear?"

I nodded, feeling lower than low. Now my dad didn't

trust me, and what had I accomplished anyway? I'd talked to practically everyone I could think of and was no closer to solving Moura's murder—or saving my own butt.

Dad sank down on the couch, his anger seemingly spent, and gestured for me to join him.

I sat.

"Now that we're clear on what I expect, I want you to know that I've already spoken with Detective Martino about this latest email. He's agreed to assign a couple of his men to watch our house over the Thanksgiving holidays. I promised him you'd stick close to home for the break—just in case."

Great. A prisoner on house arrest. There went my fantasies about romantic dates with Ben over the holiday weekend. Of course, hanging at home, even our tomb of a home, beat getting whacked by some psycho.

"There's something else I need to tell you." His voice had dropped another octave, and its tone made the hairs on my neck spring to alert.

"What?"

"It's your mother. I checked her into Pinehaven this afternoon. I fear she … she was planning to end her own life."

Oh, no, please God, no. "What? What happened?"

"Suzanne called me this morning to tell me your mother had dropped by and tried to give away her violin and favorite pieces of music. Suzanne refused to take them, but your mother kept insisting she wouldn't need them anymore." Dad's voice shook. I grabbed his hand and clung to it as he continued. "I rushed home and she was writing me a letter. There were pills, so many pills lined up on her bedside table."

My head pounded. My vision blurred. I couldn't believe this! My mother hadn't even wanted to go on living without her precious Moura. How could she? I was her daughter, too, for God's sake. And what about Dad? He'd tried so hard. I had to pull myself together for him. I squeezed his hand, wishing there was something, anything, I could do to make this all go away. "I'm so sorry. But she really wasn't getting any better at home. Maybe the doctors at Pinehaven can help her."

"I hope so. She's been wasting away. I can't seem to reach her."

"Me neither. You've done everything you could. And now you've made sure she's getting help."

His shoulders sagged, and lines of fatigue matted his face. "You've tried, too. We can only hope for the best …The hospital said we could visit her for a few minutes tonight. I thought we'd go grab a bite and then head there."

Shit. Tonight was my pumpkin-carving date with Ben. Nothing to do but call him.

He sounded out of breath when he picked up. "Jogging home," he said, in between huffs, accompanied by the sound of his sneakers slapping the pavement. "Ran to the store to get some flowers for a very cute girl with a really bad French accent."

Could he be any sweeter? I swallowed hard. "I'm so sorry I have to cancel tonight. My mom's in the hospital."

"Oh, no! Is she okay? What happened?"

"Let me call you later, and I'll explain. And I want to reschedule—please?" My voice broke, and I hoped I didn't sound as pathetic and lost as I felt.

"Of course.... Call me as soon as you can. I'll be waiting."

The chicken quesadillas at the Cottage Café failed to perk up Dad's and my spirits, and the hospital visit didn't help much, either. Mom looked so frail in her hospital gown, and her eyes seemed oddly vacant as we tried, unsuccessfully, to engage her in conversation. Dad kept repeating that we loved her and needed her and wanted her to realize she had so much to live for. I chimed in, too, if half-heartedly. I wasn't under any illusion that the argument that her surviving daughter "needed" her was going to matter much. It never had.

After we'd been there for half an hour or so, Dad was called in to speak with Dr. Abok, Chief of Psychiatric Services, and Mom and I were left alone.

I stared at the clock by her bedside. Were those seconds going forward or backward? How was it that silence could feel like a heavy weight pulling me down to a place where I couldn't breathe? I searched my brain for something, anything that would bring me back up to the surface. What could I talk about that would possibly interest my mother? Finally, I went with, "I bet your violin students will be glad when you come back."

She shrugged. "I doubt it. Suzanne seems to be doing fine filling in for me."

"I'm sure she is, but I bet your students miss you a lot."

She glanced at me for a nanosecond and then looked away.

"You don't like to look at me, do you?" I blurted out.

She closed her eyes and shook her head. "I'm sorry," she whispered.

"What is it that you see when you look at me?"

For several seconds, she said nothing. Her eyes remained closed, and I wondered if she'd drifted off to sleep. But then a lone tear slid down her cheek. "I see Moura, but then I realize it's you, and … and … Moura is gone forever. It's like a hideous dream that I can't seem to wake up from."

"I'm sorry," I managed to say. "I'll let you rest." I slipped out the door, slumped into a chair in the hallway, and buried my face in my hands. Her words reverberated in my mind—cutting and slicing through all my vulnerable places.

Wow. That may have been the most honest thing my mother had ever said to me. Too bad it didn't occur to her she wasn't the only one locked in a nightmare.

I'd pulled myself together by the time Dad returned from his talk with Dr. Abok. One person falling apart on him was more than enough.

On the drive home, he filled me in. Dr. Abok thought Mom might have to stay for several weeks while they addressed her "severe depression and grief issues." *Good luck with that*, I thought.

When Dad and I pulled into the driveway, I glanced up

at our porch. Something lay at our front door. In the dim light, I couldn't tell what it was.

Dad must have noticed, too, because he inhaled sharply. "You'd better let me check this out." His voice sounded grim. He pulled a flashlight out of the glove compartment and started for the porch.

A mess of horrifying scenes from *Law & Order* reruns flashed across my brain. I jumped out of the car and grabbed at the back of my dad's jacket to stop him. "Shouldn't we call the police? What if it's a bomb or something?"

Dad shook me off. "I'll just have a peek. You stay back here."

I nodded, nervously shifting my weight from one foot to the other.

Dad inspected the object without touching it. Then he turned to me, his head cocked. "Were you expecting flowers?"

Ben! I sprinted up the steps and peered at the envelope addressed to "the girl who makes French my favorite subject." I turned to Dad. "We're okay—I know who these are from."

I ripped the envelope open and Dad handed me the flashlight, so I could read the card:

Beautiful flowers for a beautiful girl …
I can't stop thinking about you.

Ben

I clutched the card to my chest and then bent down to swoop up the bouquet of lilies and asters, inhaling their delicate scent and sighing happily.

"I take it these are from the boy you went out with on Saturday?"

"Ben. His name is Ben," I said. *And he thinks I'm beautiful.*

I called Ben the minute I got inside to thank him for the flowers. "The best part is that they weren't a bomb. My dad and I freaked when we saw that someone had left something on our porch."

"Didn't mean to scare you."

"It sort of fit in with the day. It was ... I don't even know where to start."

"Tell me. I really want to know what's been going on with you."

So I did. I broke down talking about my mom. "I'm really sorry for unloading on you like this," I said.

"Hey, I want to be the guy you unload on. I just wish there was something I could do to make things better."

"You've already made things better."

"Really?"

"Really."

"I'm glad. Hey, my uncle just got back from Costco, and I need to help him unload stuff."

"Late shopping trip, huh?"

"Yeah, he works late a lot, so he doesn't get to the stores until late."

"You still haven't told me much about your uncle. I can't wait to meet him."

For a couple of seconds, Ben didn't say anything. "Yeah, well, you're a lot more interesting to talk about. See you tomorrow, okay?"

Chapter Eighteen

The next day, I was walking by the girls' locker room at school when a familiar muscular arm once again yanked me inside. The place reeked of sweat and hair spray. "We really need to stop meeting this way," I said between coughs.

Jenny's eyes gleamed, and she jiggled up and down like a figurine on springs. "You're never going to believe this," she squealed.

"You got a full tennis scholarship to Duke?"

"Better! Guess who's coming over to my house Friday night bringing movies and popcorn?"

"Dave?"

"Yes! Isn't it amazing? I was trying to screw up the courage to call him last night when he called me!" She did a victory jig.

"I'm so happy for you!" I pulled her into a fierce hug. Everything else might be going to shit, but at least Jenny's and my love lives were on the upswing.

"You know what he said? 'I'm bringing a Tom Cruise movie. He and I have something major in common— thankfully, not the Scientology thing.'"

"Dave has at least an inch on Tom Cruise," I assured her.

She giggled, and then her face suddenly fell. "Here I am going on and on about this, and not even asking you how you're doing. Some friend, huh?"

"You know you're the best! And it's much more fun to think about this than about my mother or any of the other crap going on in my life."

"Yeah, I get that … Anything else new?"

"You're not the only one with a hot date Friday night, although I'll be knee-deep in pumpkin goo, while you're snuggling on the couch with Mr. Mini-Hunk."

"You're such a schmaltz you'll probably carve a heart into one of the pumpkins."

"You know me too well."

Ben stopped by my locker after school. He pushed his wavy hair out of those dark chocolate eyes of his and leaned toward me. "I forgot to ask you where you put the flowers."

"Right by my bedside."

"I'm jealous."

A heat wave rolled through my entire body, as I tried to think what to say and came up empty. I was hopelessly out of practice with this flirting thing.

"You're cute when you blush, you know that?" he said.

"Umm, really?" How lame could I get?

He leaned in and nuzzled my neck. "Hmmm … so warm and soft. And why is it I always have to go to work when I'd much rather watch you try not to get flustered?"

My neck was on fire, but we both had work to get to. I

playfully pushed him away. "Go, you need to earn money. Those flowers won't last forever, you know. I'll need another delivery."

"Aren't you demanding?"

"Yup."

He laughed, then gave me a quick hug. "I'll call you on my break tonight, okay?"

"More than okay."

A couple of minutes before our staff meeting, I got a surprise call from Brayden. "Leslie said you wanted to talk to me about publicity," he said, sounding gruff.

"I do. Have you got any time this week to get together?"

We made arrangements to meet at Denny's on Friday after school, and I hustled into the newspaper meeting, sliding in between Rita and CJ. Tony strode in at the last moment and took his customary seat at the head of the table opposite Mr. B. What had he done—spilled a whole bottle of cologne on himself? He'd make a terrible criminal. People would be able to ID him from the scent alone. I wondered why he did that, when his looks alone attracted so much attention. Today, he was wearing skintight jeans and a baby blue polo shirt that matched his eyes. I glanced at CJ, who was practically salivating.

"We've been getting great feedback on the latest issue," he said. "Donny, people are asking for a follow-up piece on the cheating scandal. Are you up for it?"

Donny grinned so wide his whole face crinkled up. "You bet."

"Super. How about the rest of you? Any ideas for stories you want to pitch?"

Before I'd even had a chance to raise my hand, CJ announced she wanted to do a feel-good roundup piece on the various holiday toy drives and charity stuff our school clubs and teams were doing.

"Great," said Tony enthusiastically. "We need lots of pictures. The ones you got last year of the football team helping the Boys' Club kids pick out toys were golden."

We all nodded in agreement. Then I started in on my pitch. "I've been hearing from a reader who's been in an abusive relationship, and I'd like to write a feature story about dating violence. It's a big problem that doesn't get talked about nearly as much as it should."

Rita, bless her, agreed. "It's like the cheating issue," she said. "We can't pretend this isn't going on, because it is, and we need to do what we can to raise awareness."

Wolfman frowned. "I don't know—seems like kind of a downer. Doesn't really put me in the holiday spirit."

Tony chimed in. "Yeah, I'm not sure this is right for us. Maybe we should table it until after the New Year."

"I disagree," I said. "Violence can get even worse around the holidays with emotions running so high. We have to build awareness right now. Kids going through this need to know they're not alone."

"Point taken," Mr. B. said. "What do the rest of you think?"

"I like the idea," CJ piped up. "But will you have trouble getting people to talk? I mean, I'm just wondering. Don't a lot of abuse victims feel ashamed or scared to say anything?"

"That's what abusers count on," I said. "But if I can guarantee anonymity and change enough of the details to protect everyone's privacy, I think this can work."

"I don't know," Tony said. "All we need is a lawsuit on our hands when some informant falsely accuses a guy, and he gets recognized in your article and goes ballistic."

"I'm the last person who'd want to get involved in slinging false accusations at anyone," I said evenly.

Tony's face reddened. "Of course," he mumbled. "Sorry."

"Well," Mr. B. said, "Wolfman and Tony have some reservations, and some of you think it's a good idea. So let's put it to a vote, shall we?" He tore a sheet of paper into small pieces and passed them around. "Write 'yea' or 'nay' on going forward with this idea," he instructed.

Five minutes later, Mr. B. announced that the "yeas" had won five votes to three. One other person had obviously voted with Wolfman and Tony, but I didn't care. This was a project I could hardly wait to start on.

That night, I begged off going to the hospital with my dad. "Two tests tomorrow," I told him. "I'm really fried and overwhelmed."

But the truth was I was feeling pretty well-prepared for my tests. I just didn't want to go through another scene with Mommie Dearest refusing to look at me. I knew I should be more sympathetic. My mother was in so much pain she'd wanted to end her own life. But last night in her hospital room, I'd felt something come apart inside me. The connection between my mom and me had always been frayed around the edges. But now it felt torn beyond repair. For so long, I'd wanted my mother to see me, notice me, love me. And last night, I'd realized I was looking for something from her that she just was never going to offer.

It hurt. My insides felt like someone had taken a scouring pad and rubbed them raw. For a long time that night, I wrapped my arms around myself and rocked back and forth, the way I had when I'd been a little kid.

The next day, my tests went okay, but I felt like a slug on Valium. Of course, I did perk up in French class with Ben. Still, I was so wiped after school that I ran to Starbucks and picked up a mocha latte before heading to the office. I poked my head into Mr. B.'s classroom, and he followed me into the office for our daily check. My breath quickened and my fingers twitched as I booted up the computer and typed in my password. Not today, I prayed, closing my eyes for a moment.

But when I opened my eyes, there it was. Another one.

You and I both know what you've done....
Now you'll pay the ultimate price
I'm really feeling that holiday spirit, aren't you?
Over the River and Through the Woods

Frantically, I pushed "Reply" and typed:

I DID NOT KILL MY SISTER
PLEASE!
STOP THREATENING ME!

Fat lot of good that did. The same stupid automatic message came up. I slammed my fist into the desk. Bile rose up in my throat, and I tried to sit very still until the nausea passed. But my legs refused to stop shaking.

"This is getting old," said Mr. B. "It's hard to combat an enemy we can't see, can't respond to, isn't it?"

I nodded and choked back a sob.

"I'm so sorry. I wish there was more we could do.... How about I forward this to your dad and Detective Martino?"

I shook my head and brushed the tears streaming down my cheeks with the back of my hand.

"I have to let them know. That was our agreement," he said, sounding apologetic.

"I know. Can we just tell Detective Martino right now? My dad's going through so much. My mom, she … she's in the hospital. She was going to kill herself, but my dad found her just in time."

"Oh, Clara, what you've all been through is more than anyone should have to endure."

"Yeah. Tell me about it.… You know what I feel really guilty about?"

"What?"

"I'm kind of relieved she's in the hospital. It's been so … so awful at home with her." I couldn't believe I was telling Mr. B. this, but he'd always had that effect on me. One look at those eyes so full of concern, and I started unloading.

"I think it's natural to feel that way," he said. "It's hard to live with someone consumed by grief."

"She … she doesn't like to look at me. She says I look too much like Moura, but I'm not Moura, and she can't stand it."

Talk about TMI. What was wrong with me, spilling all this stuff to Mr. Bradford? But he didn't look irritated or even embarrassed. He looked sad.

"I'm sorry for your mother, but I'm most concerned for you. All I can say is that as one of your teachers and mentors, what I see when I look at you is a caring, gutsy young woman who's already one heck of a writer."

Was that a tremor in his voice? I realized there were tears in his eyes. I had no idea what I'd done to deserve such a caring teacher in my corner, but I wasn't asking any questions. "Have I told you lately that you're the best?"

"I believe that's come up," he said with a shaky grin that lit up his craggy face. "And I know the timing couldn't be worse, but we do have to tell your dad about this latest email. That was the deal we made."

"Even after I told you how great you were and unburdened my heart to you?"

"Even after that."

"Well, shoot. I've gotta go. I want to drop by the Women's Project Center."

But as I was pulling out of the parking lot, my cell rang. "Clara," said that familiar deep gravelly voice, "Mr. Bradford just sent me the latest email. Can you drop by the station on your way home?"

The center would have to wait.

Chapter Nineteen

It seemed like years since I'd last sat in Detective Martino's office, though it had only been a few weeks. His office seemed frozen in time—same piles of paper and dirty coffee cups that looked like candidates for some kid's "grow your own scum and mold" science project.

"So," he said, his heavy-lidded dark eyes staring at me so intently that I had to look away. "I thought we should discuss this latest email."

"It seems like more of the same to me. He's obviously planning something for Thanksgiving. Dad told me you're assigning some officers to our house over the holidays, and I really appreciate it. I'm … I'm really scared."

"That's understandable.… But I wanted to ask you about this one sentence in the message you got today. 'You and I both know what you've done.' What do you think he means?"

"It means what it's always meant. The jerk thinks I killed my sister, and he's decided to get revenge."

He leaned forward and gripped the edge of his desk. "What does he know, Clara? What is it that has this guy convinced that you killed your sister?"

"Are we back to this again?" I said through gritted teeth. "There is nothing to know! Nothing I know, and nothing this jerk knows. For the millionth time, I had nothing to do with my sister's murder. But lack of evidence has never stopped you—or this creep—from being convinced I must have offed my own twin."

"Now, now. All I'm saying is, if there's anything you haven't mentioned, even something that might have looked suspicious to someone else, but we could easily clear up—you need to tell me."

"I have told you! This is complete crap."

"I'm sorry if I've upset you, but I had to ask. That's my job."

I glared at him. "Your job is to find my sister's killer—and oh, by the way, save my life before some other homicidal maniac kills my parents' remaining daughter." Not that my mother would even notice, but he didn't need to know that.

"I'm working on it."

Apparently not hard enough, I thought, wishing I could spit the bitterness out of my mouth, out of my life.

"Do you believe this jerk Martino?" I complained to Ben that night on the phone. "He still thinks I must have had something to do with my sister's murder—or that at the very least, I must know something I haven't told him! There's not one iota of evidence I was involved, but never mind the facts."

For several seconds, Ben was silent. Just when I was starting to wonder if I'd lost the connection, he said, "He's probably really frustrated he hasn't been able to crack the case."

"Are you defending him?" I snapped.

"I'm saying that nine times out of ten, homicides are committed by someone close to the victim. You can't blame the guy for being suspicious of everyone who was close to your sister."

"Well, that puts me in the clear, because trust me—Moura and I were anything but close."

"I'm sorry. This totally sucks, and I wish I could make all this go away for you. What can I do to make things better?"

I took a deep breath and willed myself to calm down. "Let's see. How about staying to watch a movie with me Friday night after we're done carving? I'm up for some heavy-duty escapist entertainment."

Thursday night, I sat on Jenny's bed and watched her try on not four, not five, but eleven possible outfits for her date with Dave. By the time she settled on a wild multi-colored tunic and black tights that showed off her long shapely legs, my eyes were bleary.

Not so bleary, though, that I couldn't admire how great she looked. "In my next life, I want legs just like yours."

"All you have to do is spend three hours a day on a tennis court, and they're yours."

"If only."

"Why am I so nervous? It's not like this is the first date I've ever had."

"Could it be … I don't know … that you really like this guy?"

"I do," she wailed. "But what if it's really uncomfortable? I mean, he is six inches shorter. I can't spend the whole night stooping down."

"Go with just the opposite, girlfriend. Stand tall, and let him know that the height difference doesn't faze you."

"Easy for you to say, little one."

"I'm not that little, and anyhow, Dave is foaming at the mouth over you, big stuff. So flaunt it!"

Jenny threw a pillow at me. I threw one back.

"You really think so, oh great wise big shot advice columnist?"

"You're the one who hits the big shots, but yeah, I really think so."

I was munching on an English muffin wondering if Brayden was going to show when he walked into Denny's twenty minutes late. He barely acknowledged me as he slid into the seat across from mine. He ordered coffee and leaned back as far away from me as he could.

"You want a bite?" I asked, holding up the uneaten half of my muffin.

"Not really interested in breaking bread with you. I've thought about it, and I don't want to work with you. Hell, I don't want anything to do with you."

"Hey! What have I done?"

"You know what you did."

My chest tightened. "What did you just say?"

"Leslie can talk all she wants about how none of us know what happened to Moura, but I do. It had to be you. You were so jealous you couldn't stand it."

"I take it total lack of evidence doesn't bother you."

"I didn't say you weren't smart."

"Gee, thanks. But since we're throwing out theories, maybe *you* killed my sister."

"What the hell are you talking about? I worshipped Moura." His hand shook slightly as he brought his mug to his lips.

"So I hear. You used to post love poems for her."

He glared at me. "What's your point?"

"If I know my sister, she ignored you, blew you off. That had to hurt."

"I understood. She didn't have time to get involved with anyone. She was totally dedicated to her music, to sharing her gift with the world."

I didn't have the heart to tell him she'd managed to fit romance into her busy schedule—just not with him. "So I'm the one you'd love to see get what's coming to me?"

He smiled.

"Are you my cyberstalker?"

"What if I am?"

"Detective Martino will be very interested in talking to you. The cops take terroristic threatening pretty seriously. You're looking at some serious jail time."

The cocky smile disappeared. "Okay, okay. I was just

yanking your chain. I'm not your stalker."

"Why should I believe you?"

"God will take care of punishing you. He doesn't need me to intervene."

"Good to know he's on the job," I said dryly. "I just wish I could figure out who else is."

I was determined not to let Brayden's hostility and accusations ruin my date with Ben. He arrived promptly at seven that night, looking impossibly cute, his hair slicked back and damp after what had obviously been a recent shower. He pulled me toward him for a quick hug and smelled like Irish Spring soap. Odd choice for a nice Italian boy, but he smelled divine.

Of course, the overalls and cowboy boots he was wearing were a bit over the top. "What, you're auditioning for *Duck Dynasty*?"

"Hey, no making fun of my pumpkin-carving outfit. I'm trying to get in the spirit here."

"You've definitely succeeded," I said, just as I heard my dad clear his throat behind me. I turned and gave my dad the lifted eyebrows "Please do not embarrass me" look. It rarely worked, but I had to try. I turned back to Ben. "I want you to meet my dad."

Ben extended his hand. "Ben Marchetta. So glad to meet you, sir."

My dad grasped his hand and smiled. He loved it when young people exhibited "old-fashioned good manners." Ben had already put points up on my father's scoreboard. Of course, that didn't mean my dad could resist interrogating him about his interests and plans.

"I'm hoping to head to Ohio State next year," Ben told him. "I'm a history buff, so I'm planning to double major in history and education and become a high school teacher. So many kids think history's boring, but it doesn't have to be."

Dad looked impressed, and I felt … well, embarrassed. I'd been so wrapped up in my own problems I hadn't even asked Ben what he wanted to do after graduation.

"Wow," I said to Ben, after my dad had excused himself to go visit Mom and we'd gone back out to the porch. "That's really cool that you love history and want to teach. I feel bad that I never asked you about what you wanted to do."

"You've had a little bit on your mind, and we have lots of time to talk about what we want to do with our lives."

Lots of time? I sure hoped so.

While we worked on our pumpkins, Ben asked me about my stalled investigation. He wanted to know all about who I'd talked to and what came up. "Maybe together, we'll notice something more worth looking into," he said.

So I did. I went through all my various interviews and then speculated about who remained in the running as suspects. "Ms. Steinberg flatly denied the rumors about Moura and herself—said she was in a long-term relationship. Now Brayden readily admitted he was crazy about Moura, but he understood her lack of time for romance. Oh, and he thinks I killed her, but he's not my stalker, because God's going to punish me."

"Sounds like a real winner."

"No kidding. Then there's Fred who flat out detested her for not being willing to help with the cancer benefit. And I can't count out Hannah. She truly loved Moura and was devastated when she broke things off. Richard was one of Moura's rejects as well. He has an ego the size of Texas, so he had to be annoyed that Moura had played him. He was more or less her cover boyfriend while she and Hannah were hot and heavy."

"No offense, but your sister doesn't sound anything like you," Ben said, ripping through his pumpkin with a jagged knife.

"We were pretty different. Moura was intense, incredibly gifted, and very private. She didn't have a lot of time for anyone who wasn't into music. And even then, she could be difficult—like with Alex. He got very sick of her manipulating situations to her competitive advantage." I picked up my next pumpkin and studied it, before making my first stab at my heart design.

"Would Moura have let all these people into the house, no questions asked?"

I searched my brain for what I might have missed in all my interviews. "I think so."

"What did everybody say when you asked them where they were the night of the murder?"

"I couldn't ask them that! The minute I'd have opened my mouth and said, 'And where were you?' my entire cover would have been blown."

"Yeah, I get that."

"Of course, I did accuse Brayden. For all I know, he's already called the cops to make a complaint. Martino would like nothing better than to file charges against me for harassment. At last, he'd have some evidence I'd actually done something, so he could lock me up!"

"Oh, come on, he's not the enemy. It's this creep who's threatening you, not to mention your sister's murderer."

"Why are you defending him?" I sputtered. "You have no idea what he's put me through, and he's gotten exactly nowhere on my sister's case."

"I have a lot of family in law enforcement, so I know how hard they work, and how upset they get when they can't crack a case. They lean on everybody to try to catch a break. It's not personal. Besides," he said with a wink, "how could anybody suspect my girl, savior of bugs and all other living things?"

My girl? My heart launched into a drum riff inside my rib cage. Just when I was about to let Ben have it for defending Martino, he disarmed me. "I need to hire you as my publicist," I teased. "I could use some help rebranding my image. Lots of people would advise you not to sit next to me while I'm holding pumpkin-carving tools."

"They'd be wrong. My mom used to say, 'Opinions are like belly buttons. Everybody's got one.'"

I giggled. "I heard a much raunchier version of that saying."

"What can I tell you? My mom must have been protecting my tender ears."

"I need to check to see how tender they are." I set my carving knife down and planted a stream of kisses on his left ear. "Yup, very tender."

"I'd better check yours." And he did, leaving me with a major goose bump eruption.

"To be continued," he whispered. "But first, behold my pumpkin which I hereby dedicate to my favorite ear tester." With a flourish, he held up the pumpkin he'd been working on. Definitely a minimalist design—one giant eye carved on it. "Guess what this symbolizes?"

"I'm afraid to ask."

"For you to know that I've always had my eye on you."

OMG—a tall, dark, handsome boy on my porch who was as much of a cornball as I was—wearing overalls no less. I flicked some pumpkin goo off his cheek. "I plan to treasure this incredibly awesome pumpkin until it turns black and smelly." I whipped out my cell and snapped away, getting several shots of Ben with his one-eyed pumpkin.

After we finished carving our pumpkins, and I'd proved to Ben that I was as corny as he was by holding up my heart-decorated creation, we watched the movie he'd brought, *Pretty Woman*. "It was my mom's favorite," he said. "She'd be glad I was watching it with you."

That was it. He was officially the sweetest, most irresistible guy on the planet. "If you don't kiss me right now, Ben Marchetta, I may collapse into a puddle of despair."

"Can't have that," he murmured, before pulling me toward him.

The next morning, my cell went off at the ungodly hour of eight thirty. Since I'd lain awake for hours the night before thinking about Ben, I wasn't amused.

"What?" I said, groggily.

"Boula, Boulah! Boula, Boulah!" Jenny sang in a terrible imitation of a cheerleader's chant.

"I take it things went well with Dave?"

"Better than well! I can't believe it! I had to call you first thing and tell you. He's just the dreamiest."

"He can't be the dreamiest. Ben's the dreamiest."

"Well, he's my dreamiest. He's funny and sexy, and oh, my gosh, we had the best time, and guess what?"

"What?"

"You know how you said I have really long legs?"

"Yeah," I said, sitting up and blinking as I tried to focus my eyes.

"Well, they go with my relatively short torso. But Dave is just the opposite—long torso and short legs. So what do you think happens when we sit down?"

"My brain is not working this early. What?"

"It's like we're the same height! Isn't that amazing?"

"Obviously a match made in heaven," I said, dryly. Then I mentally kicked myself. Being sleep deprived was no excuse for being snarky to my deliriously happy BFF. "Seriously, that's great."

"And I take it things went well with Ben, too?"

"Yeah. It feels like he dropped out of the sky. It's like I begged God to give me some relief from the shit bucket hanging over my head, and he came up with Ben."

"I'm glad. And you know what? We deserve these great guys."

"Agreed. We also deserve sleep, so I'm hanging up now."

That afternoon, I headed downtown to the Women's Project Center, housed in a gray Gothic-style building surrounded by heavy gates. The place, which had once been a Catholic parish school, was imposing and had a definite "Don't mess with me" look. I figured the center could raise money by renting it out for a scary movie—maybe *Invasion of the Zombie Nuns*.

But once I was buzzed inside, the scary images in my head quickly dissipated. The walls were painted a cheerful yellow and were covered with posters of smiling kids and their moms.

After I explained what I was there for, the volunteer receptionist took me to the office of Lakesha Williams, the long-time director of the center. She was a striking woman with white hair pulled back into a chignon, high cheek bones, and skin the color of rich mahogany.

"I wondered when you'd come by." She gestured for me to take a seat and pulled her chair up next to mine. "Sam, Mr. Bradford, called me a couple of days ago and told me you wanted to do a story about teen dating violence. He speaks very highly of you." Her bracelets jangled, and I was fascinated by her graceful gestures as she spoke. "We used to teach together, and believe me, when Sam Bradford endorses you, that's high praise."

Bless Mr. B. for greasing the wheels for me. Once again,

I was learning the importance of who you knew in getting to the heart of a story. "Mr. Bradford's the best. And I really am eager to do this story. Would it be okay for me to sit in on the teen group meeting?"

"I'd need to ask the girls in the group for permission. And you'd also need to abide by our confidentiality rules. What's said in group stays in group."

"I understand, but I'm hoping to put a human face on the problem. It's one thing to read a bunch of statistics, and it's another to read somebody's story and think, 'That could have been me—or someone I care about.'"

"I agree, but there are privacy concerns and even more important, safety concerns for our clients. The most dangerous time in a violent relationship is when a survivor is thinking about leaving, or trying to leave. And a lot of support group members are on the cusp of making that decision. Do you understand?"

"I do." I sank back in my chair, preparing myself for disappointment. "I would never want to put anyone in danger."

She pursed her lips and seemed lost in thought for several seconds. Finally, she said, "If the support group members decide to let you sit in, and if any of them are willing to talk to you outside of group, you'd have to abide by our conditions. You print nothing without letting me, and them, see what you've written, and without our giving you permission to go ahead. We reserve the right to make you take things out or change things that any of us deem as too personal—or too dangerous. Would you be okay with that?"

"More than okay."

"All right then. We have a group meeting later this afternoon. I'll talk to them and let you know if they're willing to have you sit in next week. And Clara? I want to thank you for your interest in tackling this subject. Too many young people think this could never happen to them. But they're wrong."

Walking back to my car, I felt like someone had shone a sun lamp on my heart. What a rush to already be doing work that had the potential to help someone, to make a difference.

But as I drew closer to my car, my mouth fell open. I stumbled, clutching on to the parking meter to hold myself up. My tires hadn't only been slashed. They'd been mutilated beyond recognition.

Chapter Twenty

Two hours later, Detective Martino, Dad, and I sat in the living room, all of us drinking black coffee. Probably not the best thing for my nerves, but I needed something extra strong to hold me up.

"So tell me again what you were doing there," the detective said, notebook in hand.

"Like I said, I'm working on a story about dating violence. I went to see the director of the Women's Project Center about getting permission to sit in on their teen support group meetings."

"What made you want to research that? I would have thought you had enough violence going on in your own life, Clara." His dark, hooded eyes were doing that staring thing again. Somehow, no matter how many times I was a victim, I always ended up feeling like a suspect—his go-to whenever anything went wrong.

"I'm interested in preventing violence against anyone," I said evenly. "A reader who struggled with an abusive relationship challenged me to write more about this, and I took her up on it."

"That's laudable, Clara, but I don't think you understand the danger you're in. I have to be able to count on you to use good judgment." My dad's face was red, and the vein in his forehead was throbbing. Again. All I seemed to do lately was send his blood pressure up.

"I'm sorry. I really am! But I have to continue to live my life, Dad—we both do."

"Actually, your dad has a point," Detective Martino said. "There have been incidents like this before at the Women's Project Center. Boyfriends and husbands whose partners have gone to the center can get pretty upset."

"Okay, but why pick on my car?"

"I don't know. Of course, it's possible this isn't connected to the clients at the center, but was aimed specifically at you. You're sure you checked for a tracking device before you left?"

"Of course," I said, feeling defensive. As usual.

"The next time you go to the center, ask them if you can park your car in their lot behind the building. They've got 24-hour security back there."

"The next time she goes back? There's not going to be a next time, Clara! I will not have you deliberately putting yourself in harm's way!"

"But Dad! This story is really important! I'll be careful, I promise. You can even drive me there and back home. But please … don't make me give up my life."

"I want to save your life, not make you give it up." His face sagged. In a tired voice, he said, "Let's discuss this later." He turned to Martino. "Did you have any more questions for us?"

The detective closed his notebook and shoved it back into his shirt pocket. "Not right now," he said, hauling his beefy frame up to standing. "But we'll be in touch."

He lumbered toward the door and then turned around. "What concerns me, Clara, is the rage I see in this attack. Your tires weren't simply slashed. They were slashed over and over again. This really is a time when you need to be extra careful."

"I know."

That night after supper, I felt so nervous about being alone, and so guilty about adding to my dad's grief and stress, that I went with him to the hospital. It wasn't so bad. Mom actually looked a little brighter. Dad had brought over a bunch of her nightgowns, and she had a soft pink one on. Her color looked a little better, and the nurse said she'd started to eat. Definite progress. Of course, she still didn't look at me for more than a nanosecond, but hey, at least she was talking more with my dad. And anyway, I had a pumpkin on my porch with a giant eye carved on it to remind me that someone on the planet loved looking at me.

Ben called late that night after he got home from work, and I told him about my tires getting slashed.

"That's awful! Do you think it was the creep who's been emailing you?" His words tumbled out in a rush. I could tell he was freaking. Me, too.

"I don't know. I mean, it was outside the Women's Project Center, and Detective Martino said there have been incidents like this where clients' angry partners have damaged cars. But why my car?"

"Yeah. This seems personal. I hate this! I hate worrying about you."

"I know. I'm sorry. You got involved with the wrong girl." Hot tears burned my eyes. All I seemed to be doing lately was spreading collateral damage—worrying my dad, stressing Ben out—not to mention causing my mother distress at the very sight of me.

"You're not the wrong girl, dummy."

"Don't call me dummy."

"Well, don't say dumb stuff like that! You're not the wrong girl. What's wrong is the sucky situation you're in."

How was it this guy always knew what to say to make me feel better? "Thanks. Just cross your fingers for me that my dad doesn't decide to lock me in the house."

"Well then, I'll just have to throw a rope up and climb up to your window."

The next week felt like a reprieve. On the nights Ben didn't have to work, he came over to my house. Thursday night, we gave our tired pumpkins a memorial service after recycling them in the garden. Ben assured me, however, that he still had his eye on me. No new threatening emails, no annoying phone calls, and Ms. Williams had called with the good news that I was on for Saturday with the teen group at the Women's Project Center. Dad decreed I could go if he drove me and picked me up. No argument there.

Saturday's meeting at the center was powerful. Hair-raising, but powerful. I kept a low profile the entire time. I didn't say a word, and I didn't take any notes. After a few minutes, they all seemed to forget I was there. Belinda, a doughy, pale-faced girl, with dark shadows under her tired eyes, talked about the boy who claimed to love her so much that he forced her to down a Big Mac, fries, and a shake every day after school. He insisted on watching her eat—all of it. This way, he said, she'd be "a fat pig that no one else would ever want." If she tried to refuse to eat, he'd yank her head back and force-feed her. Or else he'd punch her in the stomach until she begged for mercy and agreed to take another bite. Nice guy.

The awful thing was several of the girls talked about how much they "loved" their boyfriends, how sweet they could be—until the next time, and the time after that.

The minute Dad and I got home, I sprinted to my computer and wrote down everything I could remember from the meeting, typing as fast as I could. Then I took a long, hot shower, wishing I could wash away some of the gruesome stories I'd heard.

That night, there was no Ben to distract me from all I'd seen and heard that day—and from all my other worries. He was working until close at the deli.

By Sunday afternoon, I could hardly wait to see him. He was picking me up after covering an extra morning shift. Ben was into rock climbing, and we were going to check out a gym over in Columbus. I was debating about what to wear when Dad, phone in hand, approached my door. "Two o'clock? I'm sure we can make it," he said before hanging up.

Oh, no. This did not sound good. Sure enough, he poked his head in. "There's a family support group meeting today at two at the hospital. Dr. Abok thinks it would be really helpful for us."

"But Dad, I have a date with Ben. He's coming in less than an hour! Can't we wait and go next week?" The last thing I felt like doing was breaking a date with Ben in favor of going to a meeting with a bunch of strangers whose families were as screwed up as ours.

"I really want us to go, honey. I know your Ben will understand." He handed me the portable phone. "Give him a call, and I'll be waiting downstairs for you."

I nodded bleakly and punched in Ben's cell phone number. Since caller ID wouldn't identify me on our unlisted home phone, I wondered if Ben would even answer.

On the fourth ring, someone did, but it wasn't Ben. The guy on the other end had a nasal voice with the remnants of what sounded like a Brooklyn accent. There was a lot of noise in the background.

"I'm sorry," I said, momentarily confused. "I was trying to reach Ben Marchetta."

"Oh, hey. I'm Vinny, Ben's cousin. He works with me at the deli. This is his phone all right. He left about half an hour ago, and he forgot it. He's probably home by now. Have you got that number?"

"I probably do on my cell, but I'm on our home phone right now. Can you give it to me?"

When I punched in the number moments later, a deep gravelly voice answered.

I froze, unable to say anything. "Can I help you?" the voice asked, sounding impatient.

I managed to get the words out to ask for Ben.

"Benito," he yelled, "someone on the phone for you."

My stomach lurched. The man who'd just called out to "Benito"?

I'd know his voice anywhere.

Chapter Twenty-One

"When were you planning to tell me?" I asked Ben the minute he came on the line.

"Tell you what?"

"You know very well 'what'! Your uncle is Detective Martino, isn't he?"

Ben said nothing.

"I take that as a 'yes,'" I said through clenched teeth.

"I'm sorry. I was going to tell you, honest."

"Honest! How can you even use the word? How could you do this to me? Is that what all those questions about the investigation were about? You were spying on me for your uncle?"

"No! He doesn't even know about us! I figured he'd have about the same reaction you're having."

"I'm sure. I don't believe this! I trusted you. You let me go on and on dissing your uncle. How could you?"

"Okay, I'm a jerk! I admit it. I wanted to tell you, but things were going so well between us. I didn't want to ruin it."

"Well, guess what? Now you have!"

"Can we talk about this when I pick you up?"

"No. That's why I'm calling. Dad insists we have to go to this family support group meeting at the hospital this afternoon, which is about the last thing I'm in the mood for. Definitely in keeping with this terrific day I'm having."

"Well, how about tonight, then? I can come over. Obviously, we need to talk."

I didn't say anything for several seconds. I willed myself not to cry, but tears slid down my cheeks anyway. "I can't do this right now. We're done."

"Please, Clara. I never meant to hurt you."

"I c ... c ... can't."

I didn't think the meeting would qualify as a pick-me-up, but in a strange way, it did. Dad and I sat around a big circle with three other families. The facilitator, Mrs. Margolies, was an earnest-looking woman with an enormous mop of frizzy hair and giant tinted glasses. She oozed sincerity. Even in my semi-numb state, it was impossible not to warm to her.

The family members who poured out their stories drew me in as well. A distraught mother named Marilyn talked about her teenage daughter who'd tried to slit her wrists: "I'm so angry! How could she do this to us? To her little sister? And then I feel guilty because I'm furious at her. And I'm so scared she'll try again."

The anger, the rage, and then the guilt—I could identify. I kept quiet, though. I didn't feel up to saying anything. Dad spoke, talking about how hard it was to lose a daughter to violence and have another daughter get threatened while watching your wife waste away before your eyes. His leg jiggled and his voice was unsteady as he spoke of "feeling like Sisyphus—I keep rolling the boulder up the hill, only to have it fall back down."

I held on tight to Dad's hand. Once again, I realized how wrapped up I'd been in my own problems—too wrapped up to be of much help to my dad. He was struggling to survive, too.

No cross talk was allowed during the meeting, but Mrs. Margolies did reassure us that our feelings were normal and not anything we should beat ourselves up about. And she talked about how suicidal depression was an illness that distorted perceptions so completely that a family member might truly believe he or she was doing his or her loved ones a favor by checking out. Listening to others talk about their anger somehow softened my own, and it distracted me from thinking about Ben.

After the meeting, Dad and I looked in on Mom, but she was sleeping. We went out for a quiet dinner at the Golden Phoenix, our favorite Chinese restaurant, and then headed home.

Back in my bedroom, I switched my phone back on—three phone calls and two texts from Ben. *Not going there.* I thought about calling Jenny to fill her in on the end of my romance with "Benito," but I was too down to talk. I turned off my phone, climbed into bed, and gathered myself up into a fetal position beneath my favorite afghan. Thankfully, I was so emotionally exhausted that sleep came quickly. Sweet oblivion.

The next morning, Dad drove me to school, since my car was in the shop getting its tires replaced. If I'd been a car, I would have needed my tires replaced, too. Talk about feeling totally flat. I dragged myself from class to class. The worst part was French. I could sense Ben's eyes on me for much of the class, but I couldn't bear to look at him.

At least after school, there were no new emails. Instead, there was a follow-up letter from one happy guy:

Dear Since You Asked,

Can't thank you enough for your advice to "swing for the fences." I took the chance and wow! I'm the luckiest guy I know. I'm going out with my dream girl, and I feel ... well, ten feet tall!

You rock. Thanks for encouraging me to give it a shot ... well, I mean a swing.

—The Guy Who's Now into Baseball

This had to be from Dave. Bless Jenny, because she'd kept my confidence. I was almost certain Dave had no idea he'd written a thank you note to her BFF! I really was happy for them, but pinpricks of jealousy traveled down my chest as well. Ben had made me feel so happy, so wanted. But it hadn't been real. He'd let me down big time. And down I'd gone.

I shook myself, determined to squelch my pity party. By the time Dad picked me up half an hour later, I had a smile firmly pasted on my face. I was getting pretty good at this "Smile While Your Heart is Breaking" stuff. I'd love to know the real story behind that old song.

Dad drove me to retrieve my car. Its spiffy replacement tires looked strangely out of place on my scruffy VW Bug, but hey, I was thrilled to have my wheels back.

I called Jenny when I got home. She and Dave had gone public that day with their relationship. "A few raised eyebrows and catcalls, but nothing we couldn't handle," she reported. "One jerk walked by us and started singing 'It's a Small World,' and Dave just laughed and gave him the finger. He says as long as I don't care about the teasing, he could give a flying you know what."

"He's flying all right. I've never seen a guy so happy and excited."

"I know. I am like ... so lucky. I wake up every day and think, 'Is this really me? Am I really going out with this amazing guy?'"

"I'm really happy for you. For both of you."

"So ... what's going on with your dream guy? I tried to call last night, but your phone was off."

No more putting off talking about it. I took a deep breath and launched into a full blow-by-blow of our final phone call.

Surprisingly, Jenny was not sympathetic. In fact, she was downright critical of me. "What do you mean, you refused to discuss it with him face to face, and you're not answering his phone calls or texts?"

"I can't deal right now. There's no excuse for not telling

me. How can I trust him? He was asking me a zillion questions about my investigation the night we were carving pumpkins. He denied he was spying on me for his uncle, but how can I know for sure? And even if he wasn't, he let me go on and on dissing his uncle. The whole thing is beyond humiliating! Nobody does this to somebody they care about!"

"Unfortunately, people do stupid things. Sometimes especially to someone they care about. At least give him a chance to explain."

"I'm too crazed right now with everything else. It's two and a half weeks until Thanksgiving! I can't cope with one more thing. Or one more person I'm not sure I can trust. I feel like I should be wearing a big sign over my heart: 'Broken. Closed for repairs.'"

"Look, I know you're hurt and this is an awful time. But I've seen the way he looks at you. You're throwing away something that could have been really special."

"Maybe so, but … right now, I can't handle this." My voice broke, as a fresh wave of tears weaved their way down my face. I was sick of crying, sick of myself, sick of my life.

"Do you want me to come over?"

"No! I'm okay. Just please don't rag on me about Ben. I feel awful enough already."

"Got it. And even when I think you've lost your mind, I have your back. Don't forget that."

"I never do."

That night, Dad was at rehearsal, and the house was deadly quiet. I sat on my bed, trying not to panic about the dwindling number of days until Thanksgiving while I pored over all my notes from my interviews about Moura. The big question mark that kept coming up was: Who was her mystery lover? Could it have been Ms. Steinberg? Why didn't anybody know for sure? Granted, Moura was private, but even Alex had found out about Hannah. And Moura had made no secret of dating Richard.

It didn't make sense, but then what about my sister's murder had ever made sense? I wondered if she'd left any clues behind, anything that would tell me who she'd been involved with, or what was going on. I knew the police had confiscated her computer and gone over all her files, all her emails. Ditto with her cell phone. But was there anything in the house they could have missed?

I tiptoed down to the second floor toward Moura's bedroom, which was ridiculous because no one else was at home to hear me. But snooping into my sister's private life seemed to call for stealth. Her bedroom door creaked slightly as I opened it and flipped on the overhead light. The air smelled stale, and it was like stepping into a museum, where everything was carefully preserved. Moura had loved periwinkle, and the room was awash in it—curtains, comforter, even the cushions on her rocking chair.

I started with her bureau, going through her neatly folded underwear, nightgowns, and tops to see if she'd left any stray notes, any clues. All my search revealed was that

Moura had been much neater than I was.

Next, I moved on to her jewelry. We'd both received musical jewelry boxes from our parents on our eighth birthday. Mine had a twirling ballerina, while Moura's, of course, featured a revolving grand piano. When you wound it up, it played "Für Elise." I was startled when I lifted the cover, and the opening notes filled the air. *My mother*, I thought. She must have kept it wound on all those nights she'd come in here to sit by Moura's bed.

I looked at my watch. Dad would be home in a few minutes. Hurriedly, I went through the drawers of my sister's bedside table, finding only evidence that she was totally obsessed with her music. She'd scribbled numerous notes to herself about particular sections of pieces she had a new idea for and wanted to rework.

Other than a mess of dust bunnies, there was nothing under her bed. And her desk top and drawers contained only textbooks and tons of course notes and assignments.

When I opened her closet, my throat tightened. There were Moura's favorite periwinkle sweaters, the long dark skirts she'd favored, and her formal concert dresses, encased in clear plastic garment bags. Even after all these months, a trace of the Vera Wang Princess perfume she'd worn permeated her sweaters.

I searched through any pockets I could find, but all I came across were scraps of Kleenex and a few packets of breath mints. As I worked my way toward the back of her closet, however, I stumbled upon another item I didn't recognize. Moura was not a jeans and sweatshirt kind of girl, but this was a large black sweatshirt with a picture of Pablo Casals, the famous cellist, on the front. I sniffed it and picked up the faintest whiff of sandalwood. This had to be Richard's. He was a cellist, and I had a vague recollection of his cologne smelling like sandalwood. But why had Moura kept it? Had he been more important to her than she'd let on? Or had she simply forgotten to return it?

Next, I checked out her shoes, neatly arranged on the top shelf. When we were little, we used to hide candy and tiny treasures in the toes.

I was almost at the end of the shoe search when I reached into the toes of a concert flat and felt something smooth and soft against my fingers. I pulled out a small black velvet pouch. When I loosened the drawstring and turned it upside down, a gold necklace with a heart fell into my opened palm. It was 24-karat gold. Two words were inscribed on the back: "Ever thine."

I closed my eyes, trying to recall if I'd ever noticed my sister wearing this, but I had no memory of ever seeing it. Had Hannah given it to her? That would make sense if Moura hadn't wanted anyone else to see it. But I doubted Hannah could have afforded anything this pricey. Could it have come from my sister's mystery lover? Ms. Steinberg could probably foot the bill for something like this. And then there was the inscription. "Ever thine" sounded poetic, and Brayden was a poet. Would Moura have accepted an expensive and intimate gift from someone she had no interest in? I couldn't rule it out.

I slid the necklace back into its pouch and pocketed it.

Chapter Twenty-Two

Dad and I polished off a couple of bowls of mint chocolate ice cream in the kitchen while he gave me a rundown of the night's orchestra rehearsal intrigue. Apparently, I wasn't the only one whose romance had spontaneously combusted. The principal violist had come to him in tears prior to rehearsal because the first violinist had broken up with her and taken up with the oboist. "I felt really bad for her," he said. "And frankly, I felt bad for the rest of us. The string section has never sounded quite that ... painful."

I tried not to laugh, but a snort escaped anyhow.

"It's not funny! You should have heard them."

"I know. I'm sorry, Dad! I got this funny image of these string players duking it out."

"More like screeching it out, like cats whose tails have been stomped on."

I couldn't help it. I giggled. Dad looked at me and a smile crept across his face. Then he started to laugh, too. How long had it been since we'd shared stories and laughed together? It felt good.

But after I'd kissed him goodnight and headed upstairs,

that familiar tightening in my chest started up. Damn it! I didn't want this to be the last time I sat in the kitchen eating ice cream and sharing stories with my dad.

Back in my bedroom, I dug out my cell and scrolled through my contacts until I found Richard's number. It was almost eleven. I hesitated to call him, but time was closing in on me like a vise.

He picked up right away. "Clara?" he said, sounding sleepy. "Am I dreaming, or is the hottest newsman in all of Springbrook calling me?"

"Newswoman. Cut the crap, Richard. Look, I'm sorry to call so late, but I found something in Moura's closet. It's a man's black sweatshirt with Pablo Casals on the front. Is it yours?"

"I love Casals, but that doesn't sound familiar. What size?"

"Hang on." I padded over to my closet, pulled the sweatshirt out of its hiding place, and peered at the tag. "Large."

"Not mine then. I know I have a Casals T-shirt or two, but I'm an extra-large. Have to have room for all those muscles, right?"

I smiled. Richard never lost an opportunity to tout the wonders of his buff bod. Considering the hours he spent in the gym lifting, I was amazed he had any time to practice music. And although he lacked the passion and dedication to become a great cellist, he was pretty damn good.

"How could I have forgotten those mammoth biceps of yours? Do you know anyone else this sweatshirt might belong to?"

"I haven't got a clue. Harry's the only other male cellist I know, and he's like 5' 3" and ninety pounds. He'd barely fill out an extra-small. Of course, you don't have to be a cellist to like Pablo Casals. There are more than twenty guys in Youth Orchestra, and two-thirds of them probably wear a size large sweatshirt."

I bit my lower lip, thinking about the lousy odds of finding the owner of this mystery item. "Can you do me a favor and ask around, Richard? See if anyone's missing a sweatshirt?"

"Sure. I'll put it on the orchestra listserv."

"That would be great. Can you do it soon?"

"I'm on it. I'll post it tonight."

"Super. And one more thing. Did you, by any chance, give Moura a gold heart necklace?"

Richard snorted. "Nope. No offense, but Moura never struck me as someone I'd want to give my heart to—even symbolically."

I didn't bother bringing up the obvious—the unlikelihood of Richard giving away his heart to anyone. Other than himself. "Do you recall ever seeing her wear anything like that?"

He paused. "No, but I'm not the most observant guy about jewelry.... Do you think Hannah could have given it to her?"

"Maybe, but it looks really expensive—like 24-karat gold expensive."

"Whoa! Maybe if Hannah had robbed a bank. Otherwise, I think that's pretty much out of her league."

I heaved a sigh. "That's what I thought…. Well, let me know if you get any responses to your posting, okay? Or if you think of anything else?"

"Will do…. So I take it you're still getting threats?"

"Yep. The jerk says he's aiming to get me over the Thanksgiving holidays. So the fun continues." I shifted my phone to the other ear and swiped my sweaty palm against my jeans.

"Jesus. Are you getting any protection?"

"Yeah. The police will be watching our house the whole vacation. So part of me feels like, 'Hey, what can happen with the police right here?' and the other part is scared shitless."

"Understandable. Wow." He paused, then said, "So is this a bad time to ask you out on a date?"

Clueless. So clueless. So very clueless that I couldn't even feel annoyed with him. "Gee, thanks, but my dating life is pretty much on hold while I figure out whether I'm going to have a life after Thanksgiving."

"Oh, yeah. Well, sure. So I'll ask again after the holidays, okay?"

He sounded so hopeful. I didn't have the heart to tell him that dating a gym rat, who collected girls like they were comic books when he wasn't gazing adoringly at himself in the mirror, wasn't high on my agenda.

The next day after school, I dropped by Hannah's to see if she'd given Moura the necklace—or knew who had. She answered the door and, as usual, didn't look pleased to see me. "What now?"

"I found this in Moura's room. Did you give it to her?"

Hannah examined the necklace carefully. "Like I could have afforded to give her this," she said, as she handed it back to me. "Is this from my replacement?"

"Honestly, I have no idea. I found it in her room. I don't remember ever seeing her wear it, and I gather you don't recognize it, either."

She sniffed and shook her head. I was once again awash in guilt over raking this all up for Hannah, who still looked … well, bereft.

"I'm sorry I keep bothering you. Just one more thing. Do you recall any guys you know from Youth Orchestra, or anywhere else, wearing a large black sweatshirt with Pablo Casals on the front?"

She shook her head again, her tangled blonde hair barely moving, as though it, too, had died, along with Moura. "Did you find that, too?"

I nodded.

"Did you ask Richard?"

"Not his."

"No idea then—could have been anyone. I don't know too many classical musicians who aren't Casals fans. He's like … a god or something if you love classical music."

I smiled grimly. "I know."

"Anything else?"

"No, but thanks." Under any other circumstances, I would have said, "It was good to see you," but that wouldn't have rung true. For either one of us.

Later that night, I caught Ms. Steinberg in her office right after a rehearsal. She swatted the necklace away when I tried to show it to her. "What part of 'your sister and I were not involved' don't you understand?"

"I understand I have to check out every possibility. I'm running out of time."

"Look, I'm sorry you've been getting threats. I really am. But I'm out of patience. Do you have any idea what damage you could inflict on me? Even a totally unfounded accusation could ruin my career. If you bother me again, I will call the police."

Okay, so that went well. So did my call to Brayden. "Like I'd ever use 'thine' in my poetry," he snarled. Then he spouted off all the things I could shove up my ass and hung up on me.

But I wasn't going to give up, damn-it-all. The next night, I texted Dad and told him I was working on a research project and probably wouldn't get home until seven or so. It wasn't a lie. I was doing research all right—visiting jewelry stores in the city to see if any of them carried the mystery heart necklace. Just when I was starting to get really hungry and discouraged, I discovered Loving Jewelers & Engravers. With its marble floors, Mozart playing in the background, and all the jewelry locked up under glass in cherry cabinets, this was definitely the most upscale place I'd checked out. A fortyish-looking gentleman approached me. He wore a three-piece charcoal suit, had a monogrammed hanky in his pocket, and shiny Wing Tips that looked like my dad's concert dress shoes. "May I help you?" he asked.

"I hope so." I pulled out the heart necklace. "Do you carry anything like this?"

He plucked his glasses out of his coat pocket, put them on, and peered at it. "Yes, this looks like one of our custom pieces. Were you interested in ordering another one?"

"Actually, I'm doing some research, and I was hoping you might be able to tell me who purchased this particular piece. As you can see, it's inscribed with the words: 'Ever thine.'"

"What sort of research?"

"That's confidential, but I can assure you that it's extremely important I find out who bought this necklace."

He looked at me for several seconds, and I thought I saw a glimmer of sympathy in his eyes. "I'm sorry. Our clients depend upon us to respect their privacy."

Now what? Would I have to come clean with Detective Martino about investigating to find out? Of course, maybe he already knew if Ben had been his spy. "If the police subpoenaed you, would you have to reveal this information?"

"I suppose. But even so, I couldn't be of much help. It was months ago, and many clients pay in cash. I'm sorry I couldn't be of more help, but if there's nothing else, I need to see to another client."

Feeling defeated, I headed home. I was glancing through our pile of mail sitting on the kitchen counter to see if we'd gotten any fun catalogs, and that's when I saw it—a letter addressed to me in neat block printing.

What if this is from the stalker? My chest seized up and

I struggled to breathe, as I gingerly picked up the letter and took a closer look. The printing looked familiar. And there was a return address that looked legit. Stalkers didn't include their return addresses, did they?

The tightness in my chest eased slightly, as I tore the envelope open and read:

Dear Clara,

You've made it clear you don't want to talk to me or even respond to my texts, but I need to find some way to tell you again how sorry I am.

I screwed up, and I feel terrible. I should have told you right away who my uncle is. But I was scared you wouldn't want to go out with me, and if you did, you'd be guarded around me, always wondering about my motives. I didn't want to lose what we had going, because it was like … so amazing.

I want you to know that I was NOT spying on you! My uncle had no idea we were seeing each other until I finally broke down and told him when he wouldn't stop hounding me about why I've been so down since Sunday. He says I'm the biggest "dumbass" he's ever met. Guess you two finally have something you can agree on.

I want to tell you about my uncle's past in confidence. It doesn't make how he's treated you okay, but maybe it will help you understand.

When my uncle was growing up, he was very close to Danny, his first cousin. Danny was the family superhero— star athlete, great student, and really nice guy. Danny's older brother, Ricky, on the other hand, might as well have had a big "L" for loser tattooed on his forehead. He'd barely made it through high school, and he resented the heck out of his kid brother who had a full scholarship to Ohio State to play ball. Anyhow, the summer after Danny's senior year, his mom found him dead in his bedroom of an apparent drug overdose. The whole family, including my uncle, was devastated. It was ruled an accidental death, but my uncle never believed it. He and Danny were really close, and he knew Danny wasn't into drugs. But there was no evidence of foul play.

Then years later, my uncle was at a family reunion where Ricky got drunk and told him he'd "taken care of Danny." My uncle reported what Ricky had said, but Ricky insisted he'd just been "playing with him" and talking nonsense because he'd had too much to drink. There wasn't any solid evidence, so the jerk was never charged.

My uncle would never admit it, but I think Moura being this great piano star reminded him of his superhero cousin, and he automatically focused his suspicions on you. Obviously, you're not a loser like Ricky, but from what you've told me, you grew up in the shadow of a sister who was getting all the attention at home, and pretty much everywhere else.

Anyhow, I don't even think my uncle's that suspicious of you anymore. He's just frustrated that he can't catch a break on your sister's case, and he wants to make sure nothing happens to you over Thanksgiving break.

Me, too. So here's what I want to ask you: Do you think you could give me another chance, even if it's just to be friends? Could we at least go for coffee?

I miss you. I've never felt this way about a girl before. Obviously, I didn't handle this whole thing very well. I'm really sorry. I keep wishing I could wind the clock back—or at least reset it.

Love,

Ben

I dropped the letter in my lap and buried my face in my hands. I missed him, too, damn it! God knows I wanted to trust him, wanted to believe him. But right now, I was too overwhelmed to know whether I could ever manage a "Reset."

I texted him: THANKS 4 THE LETTER. AFTER THANKSGIVNG COFFEE ALL I CAN PROMISE. IF IM ALIVE.

Chapter Twenty-Three

Fifteen days. That's all I had left until Thanksgiving. My body felt like a hostage going haywire from sheer fear and panic. One minute I'd be sweating, and then five minutes later, I'd start to shiver. I'd definitely become Queen of the Layered Look at Leonard High.

The shivering got a lot worse when I got to the newspaper office after school and Mr. B. and I found another email:

An eye for an eye ...
A life for a life ...
The end is near
For you

"The jerk's consistent, anyway," I said, as I bit down on my lower lip to keep my teeth from chattering.

"The offer stands. I'd be glad to be the one opening these. My guess is this person is getting off on imagining your reaction to these, so why should we play his game?"

I leaned my chin on my clasped hands and thought about it, then shook my head. "It's like we're in some kind of a battle, and I'm not going to crawl into a hole and pretend it's not a war."

He stood up. "Okay then. Come get me if you need me."

I nodded. "I couldn't get through this without you."

After Mr. B. went back to his classroom, I made myself respond to a freshman who couldn't understand why her parents didn't want her dating a senior hunk who'd managed to get his last girlfriend pregnant. After doing a few line edits, I came up with:

Dear Girl with Impossible Parents,

It's got to be flattering to be a freshman and have this hot older guy want to date you. And I can understand why you feel your parents are being totally unfair by not letting you go out with Senior Stud Muffin.

So what I have to say, you're not going to like. IMO, your parents have some valid concerns. First off, the difference between being fourteen and seventeen? We're talking "major" here. He's been around, had a lot more experience, and will probably expect things from you that you may not be ready for. And saying "no" can be dicey when there's a big power difference in a relationship. He's the high-status senior, right? So he'll most likely count on being in charge. That may even be part of the appeal of dating someone a lot younger.

And while he's definitely older, that doesn't make him wiser. Apparently, he hasn't yet mastered birth control, or his ex wouldn't be expecting his baby. Do you really want to be next in line for that scenario?

He may, in fact, be a great guy who is genuinely interested in you. But I can understand why your parents are reluctant to have you take unnecessary risks. Six months ago, you were in middle school! If this guy is really worth it, he'll wait for you to get older so you two can be in a relationship where the playing field is level.

—Since You Asked

I pushed back my chair and stared at the screen. I suddenly felt … well, old. I knew this girl would hate my response. When I was a freshman, I thought I was totally grown-up and ready for anything. Ha! At my first high school party, I hadn't even checked what was in the punch before I'd gulped down four glasses. Turned out, it was heavily laced with vodka. I spent the night locked in Amber Wyatt's bathroom, worshipping the porcelain goddess. Another one of my finer moments.

Funny how it's only when you look back that you realize how unready you were for stuff—like parties with booze and drugs and boys who hoped you were an easy lay, so they could improve their reps while ruining yours. Sometimes Jenny and I joked about how high school was like a field littered with landmines. You just prayed you'd make it through without too much lasting damage.

But compared to what I was going through right now? Piece of cake.

Friday afternoon, Dad picked me up after school to drive me back and forth to the Women's Project Center. I'd set up interviews with the director, Mrs. Williams, and two girls from the support group.

Mrs. Williams talked to me for a long time about the importance of not judging girls in abusive relationships who seem unwilling, or unable, to get out. "It's easy to sit on the outside and say, 'Well, why don't you just leave?' But it's not that simple. There's so much to work through: the emotional dependence, the brainwashing, and the fear. And anyone involved in an abusive relationship should be afraid, because the most dangerous time is when you're trying to get out."

I took lots of notes, and Mrs. Williams gave me a bunch of materials to take home and read before she took me down the hallway to meet Krystal, who was already waiting for me. I thanked Mrs. Williams, as she flipped a "Do Not Disturb" sign on the door. Then I followed Krystal into a small sitting room where she flopped onto a large stuffed armchair and gestured for me to sit on the love seat opposite her.

She cracked her gum nervously, and her face was nearly hidden behind a mass of jet black hair. But it wasn't so hidden that I couldn't see what I'd noticed at the support group meeting. She was very pretty with enormous dark eyes fringed with thick lashes.

"So," she said, "how are you going to make sure no one can tell who I am in your article?"

"Well, for starters, how about if I make you a bleached

blonde with small beady eyes?"

She grinned. "Sounds good…. So what do you want to know?"

"I want you to tell me as much as you can about your relationship—how it started, and anything you feel okay about sharing."

She began haltingly, telling me how "Gary" was a football star at the prestigious Catholic boys' school where wealthy families in the parish sent their sons. She'd met him her sophomore year at a dance at the all-girls' school she attended. "He kept cutting in to dance with me. It was very flattering. Irritating as all get-out to my date, but Gary was so handsome, and he poured on the charm. He told me there was no way he was leaving the dance until I gave him my phone number."

"I take it you gave it to him."

"Oh, yeah. I had one of those hot and heavy insta-crushes." She chewed thoughtfully on the remnants of a nail. They were bitten to the quick. "Within a week, we were going together. My parents loved him—still do."

"Looking back, were there any signs in those early days that anything might be wrong?"

"Like they say, hindsight is 20-20. I mean, sure. He was insanely jealous. He couldn't stand my talking to other guys, or even other guys looking at me. We were fine when we were by ourselves, but I stopped wanting to go to parties with him, because we'd always end up in fights. He'd accuse me of coming on to some other guy, which was so ridiculous, because I was only interested in him."

"Did the fights escalate?"

She nodded. "He decided he'd have to 'punish' me. Some of the other girls have boyfriends who beat them up, but Gary mostly shoves me around, pins me down, and makes me do things … sexually. Like, if he thinks I've spent too much time at a party talking to another guy, afterward, he pushes me down to my knees and holds my head down and forces me to suck his cock. He'll shove his dick so far down my throat I start to choke. And I can't help it. I always throw up afterward. Then he says I have to be 'punished' for 'making a mess.' That's when he yanks my clothes off, throws me on my stomach, and forces his penis into my rear end. It hurts something awful. I just try hard to go somewhere else—anywhere else—in my mind."

"I'm so sorry," I said, trying not to show my own horror at what she was going through. I had to remain calm, keep her talking. "Have you been thinking about breaking up with him?"

"Oh, yeah. But it's complicated—like everything else. Sometimes we can go for weeks where everything seems great. I make up excuses why I can't go party with him, and like I said, when we're by ourselves, he can be really sweet." She paused, then added, "And I don't think anyone would believe me if I tried to say what's been going on. Everyone thinks he's this great guy. It would be my word against his about what he does to me. You accuse a star athlete, especially one from a wealthy, respected family, of sexual assault, and you end up being the pariah, not him."

"Do you also worry about what he might do to you if

you broke things off?"

"It's not what he'd do to me," she said, her voice dropping to a whisper. "He's already told me that if I ever try to leave him, he'll go after my little sister, Chloe, who has a huge crush on him. She's only a freshman. She's really naïve, so innocent. I have to protect her, no matter what it takes."

Oh God. "Has coming to the support group helped?"

"Sure. You start to realize you're not alone, and you're not crazy. And the counselors have been talking to me about safety planning—how me and my sister can remain safe once I'm ready to make a move."

"Do you see yourself getting out of the relationship soon?" *Please say yes, please say yes.*

She shrank back in her seat, then chewed on another nail. "Depends on which day you ask me. Some days, I feel ready, and others, I feel paralyzed, like I'm trapped and too scared to do anything. Have you ever felt like that?"

"I'm very familiar with 'scared' and 'trapped.'"

"Seems to be going around," she said. "And these are supposed to be our carefree years."

We spoke for a few more minutes, until there was a soft knock. Opal, a willowy girl with light brown hair and somber gray eyes, poked her head in the door, and Krystal waved her in. They hugged. I gave Krystal a hug, too, and thanked her for her courage in talking to me. I assured her I'd let her see what I'd written. "One thing's for sure. You'll both be public school students, and Gary will not play football."

She grinned. "Give him a unibrow, okay?"

"Done."

After Krystal left, Opal settled into the big comfy chair and drew her long legs up, wrapping her arms tightly around them. "Where should I start?"

"How about the beginning?"

Opal's story was very different but just as heart-wrenching. She and her boyfriend, "Mike," had gotten involved her junior year when she'd volunteered for her high school's tutoring team. A chemistry whiz, she'd been assigned to tutor him. He'd shown up for their first session in a black leather jacket, low slung jeans, and an attitude that screamed, "Go ahead. Try to teach me something."

"He was this huge challenge to me. I wanted to see if I could break through the wall he'd built up around himself."

"So, did you?"

"It took a few sessions, but I kept saying, 'If you ever plan to get out of high school, you need some credits.' Finally, he started applying himself, and I realized he was really smart. And then we started talking, and that's when he told me about his family situation." Her eyes welled up.

"What about it?"

"He lives with his aunt and uncle. His dad's in prison for beating his mother to death. He was only five when it happened. He was hiding in an upstairs bedroom closet when a neighbor found him. Once he told me that, I felt so close to him. I wanted to make everything okay for him in his life, even though I knew I couldn't do that."

Opal continued, describing how their friendship turned

into romance, which totally shocked their friends, since they ran in such different crowds. "But we didn't care," she said. "Most of the time, he's the most loving person I know. It's his dark days when he goes kind of crazy, and I can never predict when that's going to happen. His eyes get this strange look, and he starts screaming at me, accusing me of things I haven't done. And lately, he's started hitting me, punching me, too. Then afterward, he cries and cries and tells me how sorry he is, and he doesn't know what came over him, how I'm everything to him and his life would be worth nothing without me. Then everything is okay, sometimes for weeks. And then it's not. The thing is, I love him."

"I'm so sorry, Opal. It sounds like he really needs professional help."

"He's afraid to talk to anybody, afraid they'll lock him up and tell him he's crazy or evil—like his dad.... The counselors here have been trying to help me sort this through. I don't want to give up on him. But one of these days, I'm afraid he's going to kill me."

By the time I left the center, I was so drained that I felt boneless, barely able to hold up my own weight as I walked to Dad's car and got in.

"You okay?" Dad asked. "You're so pale, honey."

"Honestly? I'm beat. The girls I interviewed—their stories are shattering. I don't understand how people can be so cruel to the ones they claim to be in love with. No matter how much reading I do to try to understand, it still seems so senseless, so crazy."

Dad patted my hand. "It's the curse of the human condition. We all have the capacity for love and for hate, and to act or not act on those feelings."

I ran my fingers through my hair, thinking about what Dad had said. If I looked into my own heart, dark emotions swirled and simmered there, mixed in with loving, caring ones. How many times had I fantasized about pushing Moura's murderer or my creepy stalker off a cliff? And hurting my mother as much as she'd hurt me? So far, I'd restrained myself, but I'd certainly spewed out my fury at other people—Moura, that night at rehearsal, and lately, Detective Martino, my dad, and Ben. Oh, Ben. My heart ached thinking about him. I was still so angry at him. And still so crazy about him.

I sagged back in my seat. "Sometimes being human really sucks."

Dad chuckled. "Agreed."

Saturday morning, I lay in bed for a long time. Dad was already off to a music conference in Columbus, where he was the keynote speaker. He'd come close to insisting I go with him, but I'd used the "way too much homework" excuse and reminded him that our home security system was top of the line. Which it was. He had gotten it installed shortly after Moura's murder. At the time, it had struck me as a bit like putting in a smoke alarm after the house has already burned down. Not anymore.

Finally, the urge to live and get justice for Moura was

stronger than my urge to pull the covers over my head and stay in a fetal position all day. I pulled myself out of bed, threw jeans and a sweatshirt on, and headed downstairs to the kitchen. As I swigged coffee and juice and chomped on an English muffin, I checked my texts. Richard had left me a message that no one from orchestra had claimed the sweatshirt, or knew whose it was. One more dead end. And I was running out of time.

I forced myself to walk down the hall into Moura's studio. Memories flooded back —the blood, the smell, her vacant eyes staring. I closed my eyes and sank to the floor, telling myself over and over, "Cleansing breaths. You can do this."

After several minutes, I managed to steady my breathing, and I hauled myself up. I was going to search every inch of her studio. If Moura's lover had left her anything else beyond the necklace and sweatshirt, it was most likely in here—her sanctuary.

Ever since the police had finished their crime scene investigation and the ugly yellow tape had come down, the only thing we'd done to the room was replace the rug. Otherwise, it was a mausoleum, left just as Moura left it—her music piled on the small table next to the Steinway, her bookshelves overflowing with biographies of her favorite musicians and composers, and the walls covered with photos and memorabilia from years of recitals and competitions.

I started with her music, piled up on the table beside her grand piano and in the file drawer wedged in the corner.

Then I moved to her piano bench. Tears sprang to my eyes when I found our beginners' piano books inside.

By the time I'd worked my way through Moura's extensive piano music collection, it was past noon, and all I'd found were dozens of notations in her handwriting about the pieces. No hidden love letters.

Next, I combed through her CD collection, peeking inside every single case to see if there was anything personal written on the jacket notes. Nothing. Famished by this time, I retreated to the kitchen and fixed myself a PB and J, quickly downing it with a large glass of milk.

Feeling fortified, I headed for her bookcase, one of my favorite pieces of furniture in our house. My parents had found it at an estate sale. It was at least a hundred years old, with rich dark wood and glassed-in shelves. I pulled the doors open to begin my search. Moura's collection was chock-full of books about the history of Western music and her favorite period—the Romantic era—along with a slew of biographies of famous pianists and composers. I removed them one by one, flipping through to see if there were any revealing inscriptions, notes, etc. I found several inscriptions from my parents, Dr. Lewitsky, and a couple from Hannah who carefully underlined "love" at the end of her "Love, Hannah" sign-offs.

It was when I got to the final shelf that I found it. Tucked behind the biography of Moura Lympany, the renowned British concert pianist that my sister had been named after, was a small pamphlet encased in plastic that I'd never seen before. Dated January 6, 1950, it was a Town

Hall concert program featuring Lympany performing the works of Franck and Chopin. It had to be valuable. I carefully pulled it out of its plastic wrapping and opened it. On the inside cover, someone with a large distinctive scrawl slanted to the right had written, "Someday this will be you, my darling." Below that was a quote from Ludwig van Beethoven, addressed to his "Immortal Beloved":

Be calm, only by a calm consideration of our existence can we achieve our purpose to live together—be calm—love me— today—yesterday—what tearful longings for you—you— you—my life—my all ...
ever thine
ever mine
ever for each other

I blinked, then blinked again. My breath caught in my throat as I lurched to a chair. I'd seen this handwriting before. Suddenly it all made sense.

Deadly sense.

Chapter Twenty-Four

Joel Rasher. All those hours he'd spent interviewing Moura, calling her because he had "just a few more questions." Of course. Why hadn't I connected the dots? But he was so much older—and married.

I had to talk to him. He had everything to lose if his love affair with Moura had come to light. Yet, his words had spoken of great love for her. I couldn't imagine murdering someone in cold blood whom you'd professed your love to. But hadn't I sat in the Women's Project Center listening to horror stories of romances gone violent?

I pulled my cell out, scrolled through my contacts, and made the call.

He picked up on the fourth ring. I didn't bother with any preliminaries. "This is Clara Seibert. We need to talk."

"What is this about?"

"I think you know."

"Actually, I don't." His voice sounded wary.

"You and Moura—I have evidence. You can either talk to me, or I can hand over what I have to Detective Martino. Your call."

"It's not what you think. I can explain."

"I hope so. Meet me at the food court at Lakefront Mall in forty-five minutes."

"Let me come over to your house, please, so we can talk privately. Or why don't you come out here? My wife's at the music conference in Columbus, and I don't expect her back for hours."

Like I was going to fall for that one. Did he think I was some Lifetime heroine who was stupid enough to be lured to a deserted house in the country? "No, thanks. I'd rather meet in a public place with plenty of other folks around."

"You can't think I'd try to hurt you!"

"Frankly, I don't know what to think, which is why we should talk. See you in forty-five."

I got to the mall early and snagged a corner table across from the House of Choy. It wasn't even Thanksgiving yet, but Bing Crosby was already singing "I'll Be Home for Christmas" on the mall's sound system. Groups of teenagers and tired-looking parents and grandparents loaded down with loot were scattered throughout the food court. They looked relieved to get off their feet and take a break. The aromas of sweet and sour pork, spicy burritos, French fries, and popcorn made a strange mix that seeped into my pores. While I waited, I nervously chomped on a chocolate chip cookie and swigged black coffee.

He showed up ten minutes late wearing a baseball cap, torn jeans, boots, and an old baggy sweatshirt with flecks of white paint on it. "Sorry. Took me a while to find a parking spot. Let me get a latte. I'll be right back."

I studied him as he ordered his drink. He didn't look much older than we were. But he was.

He took a seat opposite me and swirled his coffee stick around his latte, seemingly reluctant to meet my gaze.

"Why did you lie to me?" I asked.

He went into immediate defense mode. "What is it you think you know?"

"I know that you and Moura were lovers—that sitting in her closet is a Casals sweatshirt that belongs to you and undoubtedly has your DNA and traces of your cologne on it. At first, I thought it was Richard's, but it was the wrong size. And then I remembered the night you and your wife came to dinner, and we talked in Moura's studio. Your cologne that night—it had that same sandalwood scent."

"I loaned your sister that sweatshirt when we went out for coffee on one of our interview sessions early last spring. She was cold and had forgotten to wear a jacket."

"Right. And then there's the lovely heart necklace you gave her. You know, the one you had inscribed with 'Ever thine'?"

"What makes you so sure that I'm the one who gave your sister a necklace? She had lots of admirers."

"Yes. But you're the only one who gave her a Lympany concert program and quoted Beethoven's letter to his lady love on his inscription."

"Oh, come on. Half the classical music fans in the state of Ohio were in love with your sister. She played like an angel."

"Right. My sister, the angel. But guess what? It wasn't anyone who wrote on Moura's program. It was you. That day I drove out to your home, I saw your handwriting on your legal pad. You even talked about how you preferred writing your first draft by hand. That's a very distinctive scrawl you've got, Mr. Rasher. I'm sure any handwriting expert would agree."

His face crumpled. "All right! I lied. I'm sorry. But I knew if I admitted we'd been involved, you'd suspect me of killing Moura. You have to believe me. I would never have hurt your sister. I loved her, and she loved me."

"You loved her? She was sixteen! You're twice her age and married! What were you thinking?"

He let out a long breath. "I'm not sure I was thinking, or perhaps I could only think of Moura." His hand shook as he lifted his latte to take a sip, sloshing drops onto the table which he didn't bother wiping up.

"Did you actually imagine you had a future together?"

"We did! We planned it. I'd get a divorce and move to New York when she left for Juilliard. I've got a lot of contacts there for freelance work—enough for us to live on. And when she turned eighteen, we were going to get married."

"Married! She would still have been a teenager, in school, preparing for a career that would most likely take her all over the world!" I clenched and unclenched my fists, unable to believe this crazy plan.

"Moura knew I would always put her career first, always be there to help her, support her. She was destined for greatness, and she knew she needed someone who would truly understand her genius—and her obsession with music."

"Did your wife know about this grand plan?"

He took a big breath and said nothing for a moment. His shoulders sagged. He seemed smaller and almost frail. "We were waiting to tell her, but she found out about us," he said in a low voice.

"How?"

He flushed. "I … I couldn't bear to touch my wife once I'd fallen in love with your sister. I suppose that aroused her suspicions. And Moura was so uncomfortable working with her that she was thinking about switching teachers. Anyhow, my wife went through my desk one day when I was out running errands and found some poetry I'd written about Moura. She threatened to report me to the police for statutory rape. She would have ruined me and dragged Moura through the mud."

"What did you do?"

"I couldn't let her destroy me and everything Moura and I had together. I begged her to forgive me and assured her that I'd end things with Moura. I told her I'd been so bewitched by her prize student's incredible playing that I'd imagined that I'd fallen in love with her."

Actually, that last part sounded about right to me, but I wasn't going to go there. "So did you end things?"

"No. Moura apologized to her for having what she called a 'schoolgirl crush' on me and assured my wife that it was over. She offered to transfer to another teacher. But Nadia wanted her to stay. Moura was her prize student, after all. It seemed as though Nadia and Moura had made amends." He picked some flecks of the paint on his sweatshirt and shrugged. "Of course, we felt guilty about lying, but we knew we had to wait. It was too dangerous to tell anyone about us while she was still a minor."

"Do you think your wife believed that you'd ended things?"

"I think so."

"You *think* so? What if she knew the supposed breakup was a hoax? Could she have murdered Moura?"

"No! It's inconceivable that she'd destroy the most gifted student she'd ever had. I know my wife. Yes, she was upset about the affair. But she's not a violent person. And frankly, she had her doubts about you."

"I bet. So where were you the night Moura was murdered?"

"Home, working in my study. I had an article about the Columbus Opera due the next day."

"And where was your wife?"

"She was home as well. She went to bed early—said she wasn't feeling well."

"Were you by any chance playing music as you worked?"

He nodded. "I often listen to music while I'm writing. I was in a somber mood that night—playing Mahler. I've thought about that night over and over, and wondered if some part of me sensed something awful was going to happen."

"Were you listening with earbuds on?"

"Yes. I didn't want to disturb my wife."

"So it's possible she could have gone out, and you might not have heard her?"

He shook his head. "I can't imagine that."

"Here's the thing. I couldn't imagine being in my own home listening to music, blissfully unaware that my sister was being murdered two flights down. But that's exactly what happened."

His face went deadly white. "Nadia is no murderer. She's a good person. When I took her graduate seminar and my mother died, I was so depressed I wanted to give it all up. She's the one who kept me going. I don't know what would have become of me if she hadn't been there."

"That's touching," I said dryly.

"You have to believe me! Neither one of us would ever have hurt your sister. Please … don't drag us into this. It won't just be Moura's life that will have been destroyed. It will be ours."

I looked at him solemnly. "I know … I need to think." Of course, I didn't need to think that hard. I had to talk to the police, but I wasn't about to tell him that. He didn't think his wife could have hurt Moura, but I wasn't so sure. And he professed innocence, but he had an awful lot to lose if his affair with Moura had come out—his career, marriage, reputation—not to mention his freedom. Who knew what he might have done if he'd thought my sister would end the charade and reveal they were lovers? Or what he might do to me if he thought I was about to spill what I knew to the cops?

He gathered our empty cups and tossed them in the litter basket. "Let me walk you back to your car."

I held my hands up and shook my head. "No, thanks. I need to be alone right now." *So I can run to my car and then drive like a maniac to the police station.*

"Oh, come on. I'm not a monster."

I backed away from him. "I'm asking you to give me some space here. Please."

My heart pounded as I pushed past some shoppers and sped out the exit door, but there was no escape from the sound of his boots slapping against the pavement as he ran after me. Getting louder. Getting closer. Oh God, no, please no.

"For heaven's sake, Clara, slow down. I'm not going to hurt you! I just want you to listen to reason." He was panting hard, and his words came out in a broken rush.

I didn't answer—just whipped my keys out and bent down to open my car door, praying I'd make it inside and lock the doors before he caught up to me.

Then he screamed, "What are you doing?"

Before I could swivel around, the back of my head exploded in a blinding flash of light. The pain sizzled and roared in my ears—until everything went black.

Chapter Twenty-Five

My head throbbed, and I struggled to open my eyes. It was so dark, so cold. An engine hummed. My whole body vibrated as I lay scrunched up in the tiny back seat of a car traveling to who knows where. My eyes slowly came into focus. We were in my car!

My heart thumped painfully against my chest. Something was digging into my wrists. Handcuffs. I struggled to sit up, but my legs were stuck—bound together.

I lifted my head up a couple of inches, straining to see my captors. Mr. Rasher was driving. Dr. Lewitsky was pointing something shiny right at his head. A gun.

"How did you find us, Nadia? You told me you were in Columbus."

"Well, dearest, you're not the only person capable of lying through your teeth. I decided not to go. I was planning to make a house call on Little Miss Detective here, when I saw her jump into her car and drive off like a bat out of hell. I realized she must be meeting you when that little tracking device I installed on your phone let me know you were headed in the same direction."

"You were tracking me?"

"Of course I was, darling. How else could I keep tabs on you?" She sounded so smug, so sure of herself. I shivered.

"I can't believe you're capable of this! Any of this! You killed Moura, didn't you?" Mr. Rasher cried.

"We're both full of surprises, aren't we?"

He didn't reply. Minutes went by, and neither of them said anything.

Then I heard him rasp out, "What will this solve? Our lives are already ruined."

"And whose fault is that? Did you really think I'd let your teenybopper girlfriend take everything from me? My husband, my professional reputation as the mentor of one of this generation's most gifted pianists? You think I'm stupid?"

"No, of course not. But I don't understand. How could you hurt someone you'd spent years working with, caring about?" He began sobbing—great heaving howls. The car swerved.

"For God's sake, stop sniveling and watch the road," she snapped. "We're almost there."

There?

Panic seized me, squeezing my chest. My throat constricted. I couldn't breathe. Dizzy, so dizzy. No, this couldn't be happening.... Dr. Lewitsky was having her husband take me someplace to kill me.

"Dr. Lewitsky, I'm begging you," I cried from the back seat. "Please don't hurt me. Please! My parents—they're your friends! You know what they've been through."

"I'm sorry for your parents, Clara. But Moura betrayed me. Me! After I gave her everything I had musically, molded her into the gifted pianist she was—she did this to me! And you? You just wouldn't let your sister's death go, would you? Curiosity killed the cat, and now, dear girl, you're going to suffer the same fate. So sad, really, don't you think?"

"Please don't kill me." Hot tears rolled down my face, as a rush of images flashed through my head—so many people I cared about, and I'd never get to see them again. My dad—oh, how I hated thinking about him in even greater pain. My mom. Now I'd never know if she'd get better, maybe even learn to love me a little. And Jenny, Mr. B. And Ben. Oh, Ben! Not even the chance now for a reset. "Let me go, and I promise I won't tell anyone."

Dr. Lewitsky laughed. "Pull up over there. We'll find a nice secluded spot in the woods."

"Are you planning to kill me, too?" he asked.

"Don't be silly, my darling. I'm not going to kill you—I have plans for you. Last time, I had to clean up the crime scene all by my lonesome. Not to brag or anything, but it was a fantastic job. Those poor police couldn't find a thing! But this is a little more complicated, and I'm going to need lots of help. I know you won't mind—all those promises you made me about 'for better or for worse' and all that."

The car jolted to a stop. "Nadia, please. This is madness," he begged.

"Shut up, or I'll be forced to reconsider sparing your life."

My Bug's ancient car doors creaked open, and the two

of them got out. She shook the gun at him. "Loosen the chains around her legs enough so she can walk."

Dr. Lewitsky kept the gun aimed at her husband's head as he reached into the back seat and loosened my leg chains.

"I'm so sorry," he whispered.

"Please, help me!" I cried.

But he turned away and didn't answer.

"Joel, get the flashlight out of my bag."

He got it out and turned it on—a weapon, if I could somehow get hold of it. But how? My hands were still handcuffed behind me.

"Start walking! One false move, and I shoot and keep shooting until you're both dead." She nudged the gun against my back and shoved me forward. I stumbled and fell to my knees.

"Get up, you nosy bitch!" she screamed, as Mr. Rasher put his hands under my arms and helped me to my feet.

We struggled along for a quarter mile or so. Dead leaves crackled beneath our feet. Branches tore at my face, and blood from my gashes mixed with my tears. The temperature had dropped, and I could see my breath as I panted. Finally, we came to a clearing. "Let's stop here. Lovely, isn't it?" she said, as though she were admiring the view on a Sunday afternoon nature walk.

Her eyes glittered. *She's mad,* I thought, *totally and utterly insane.*

"As God is my witness, Nadia, please don't do this. We can make things good again between us. I promise!"

"Oh, promises, promises. Those don't mean too much

coming from you, now, do they, darling? But of course, we will start over after this little unpleasantness, won't we? Because you see, I'm not going to shoot Clara. You are, dearest. And then we'll be forever bound together by what we know about each other—our dirty little secrets. Like how you committed statutory rape—over and over, I might add."

"No!" he cried.

"Oh, yes, yes, indeed yes. Hand me the flashlight and I'll hand you the gun."

She took her eyes off me momentarily as she reached toward the flashlight. It was now or never. I shuffled and stumbled as fast as I could toward the trees, praying they'd give me the cover I needed.

"Stop her!" she screamed.

And then I tripped over a fallen branch and nearly choked on the ice-cold dirt.

They moved toward me. Mr. Rasher was now holding the gun, while Dr. Lewitsky shone the flashlight on me.

"Shoot her now!"

His hand shook as he lifted the gun and aimed it at me.

"Wait! Look at me!" I begged him. "Don't you see Moura? Moura!"

"For Christ's sake, Joel, don't listen to this babble. Get on with it!" Dr. Lewitsky cried.

But he stood there unmoving, tears dripping down his face. "Moura, my love!"

My whole body trembled, and I wanted to close my eyes, but I made myself keep them open, staring into his, silently pleading with him, praying.

"What are you waiting for? Shoot her!" Dr. Lewitsky said and stepped toward him.

A strange look of calm came over his face. He wheeled toward his wife and aimed the gun at her. His hand had stopped shaking.

She held up her hands and screamed.

He pulled the trigger. Over and over.

The sound was deafening. She crumpled to the ground, a startled wide-eyed expression frozen on her face.

I couldn't think, couldn't breathe. Everything moved in slow motion. Blood oozed from her chest, her arms. Would he let me live after I'd seen him murder his wife?

When I turned to him, he was actually smiling at me. It was a soft, almost apologetic smile. "I'm going now to be with Moura."

No! I opened my mouth to argue with him.

But before I could say a thing, he shoved the gun into his mouth and pulled the trigger.

Chapter Twenty-Six

The ringing in my ears from the gun shots would not stop. I squeezed my eyes shut—anything to escape from what I'd just seen. But the horrifying images played and replayed in my mind. I threw up over and over and kept heaving long after there was nothing left to expel.

The ground tilted beneath me. The trees, the bloody bodies, the broken branches swam before me. I tried to stand up, then toppled right back over. I screamed and screamed until all that was left of my voice was a whimper.

It was cold, so very cold. My whole body wouldn't stop shaking—until it did, and a delicious numbness took its place. It was surprisingly pleasant to feel absolutely nothing. *I need to stay awake, get out of here. Don't close your eyes, don't close your eyes,* I told myself, but they closed anyway as I drifted away to a soft, warm place.

Bright light burned my eyelids. "Are you alright, ma'am? Can you hear me?"

I moaned, struggling to come fully awake. I managed to open my eyes wide enough to see a youngish looking man with black eyes and a kind-looking round face hovering over me. He was wearing a uniform. Was I dreaming?

"What happened here?" he asked, the beam from his flashlight taking in the bodies of Dr. Lewitsky and Mr. Rasher.

I blinked several times. I wanted to explain. But I was so numb. I could barely make my mouth move.

"Okay, it's okay. Don't try to talk now. I'm going to run to my vehicle and get a blanket for you and radio for help. I'll be right back. Stay here, ma'am."

I spent the next two days in the hospital recovering from shock, mild hypothermia, a concussion, and minor cuts on my face and wrists.

Overnight, my abduction, the murder-suicide, and its link to my twin's murder had become the subject of a media frenzy. Dad had been inundated with interview requests from the *Today* show, *Good Morning America*, and *People*. Apparently, this lurid tale of murder and mayhem was way too good to pass up, and reporters ignored my dad's pleas for privacy. Each time the story splashed across the television screen above my bed, I switched the channel. But I had no luck turning off the images that replayed in my mind from that night.

At least the police kept the media down in the lobby, far away from my room. But that didn't mean I didn't have visitors. Detective Martino spent hours getting my statement, with Dad sitting by my side. Both Dad and I broke down at several points as I talked, and the detective let me have breaks. When we'd gone over everything for the third time, he said in a gentler tone than usual, "When you found this evidence, I wish you'd contacted me immediately."

"I figured I'd be safe if we met in a public place. And I wanted to see if he'd tell me more before I turned everything over to you. I was on my way to see you when Dr. Lewitsky kidnapped me. Didn't anybody at the mall see her grab me?"

"Apparently not. She must have been very quick about shoving you into the back seat. My guess is she had Mr. Rasher get the restraints on after they'd already pulled out of the lot."

I shivered. "I keep seeing the way she looked—that wild expression on her face. I truly think she'd lost her mind."

"Very possible," Detective Martino said.

"What really disturbs me is that Joel took advantage of Moura that way. She was still a child!" my dad cried. "To think that we trusted him, had him as a guest in our home. We allowed him to get close to her, thinking it was all for a story he was writing."

"He honestly thought he loved her and was going to take care of her," I said. "And he did save my life."

"Yes, thank God. But he was the adult here, and I can't help thinking his own actions set this tragedy in motion." A lone tear drifted down my dad's cheek. I gently brushed it away with my finger.

"Dr. Seibert, I hate to interrupt, but would you mind giving me a couple of minutes with Clara by herself?"

Dad frowned. "You're not going to harangue her, are you? I won't have her put through any more."

"Quite the opposite. I have some amends to make."

Amends? Now I really was delirious. But Dad dutifully left to get some coffee in the cafeteria, while I stared at Detective Martino.

He stared back, blinked a few times, and then cleared his throat. "I want to apologize to you, Clara. I know I've been very hard on you all these months, thinking you might have killed your sister. Not only was I wrong, but I have you to thank for solving what has been one of the most frustrating cases of my career."

My mouth hung open. I couldn't believe it. This guy had gone after me at the worst time in my life, and now I was supposed to make nice?

Well, hell, why not? Hanging on to all my anger and bitterness toward Detective Martino seemed like a big, fat waste of energy. I took a deep breath and thought about what Ben had told me, more than once. It seemed like the right thing to say. "You were just doing your job."

"I guess, but I still feel bad about barking up the wrong tree—and making your life even harder. At least now this email stalker doesn't have a reason to torment you any longer. I've made it clear to the media that we believe that Dr. Lewitsky murdered your sister and was about to murder you."

The weight that had been pressing against my chest ever since that first threatening email suddenly felt lighter. Was it really possible that the creep would leave me alone?

Still, it came down to my word on what had happened, and what Dr. Lewitsky had admitted the night she kidnapped me. "I wish we had even more definitive proof," I said.

"Officers are searching the house and her office right now. I wouldn't be at all surprised if we find more evidence."

I rubbed my forehead, deep in thought. Was there something I could do to help once I got out of here?

"Time out! I have a feeling I know what you're thinking, young lady. Now you listen to me! I really meant it when I said I was grateful to you for cracking the case. But now it's time for you to let go and let us clean up the rest. Your job is to recover and go back to living your life. Speaking of which ..." He paused.

"Yes?"

"My nephew. He's a good guy who did something stupid. But I want you to know that he didn't tell me about you, either. And he never for a moment believed that you had anything to do with your sister's death."

"I know."

"So would you be open to having a visitor? Maybe one related to me?"

I smiled, big. "You amaze me. If you get tired of this detective gig, you definitely should consider matchmaking."

Chapter Twenty-Seven

Three hours later, there was a soft knock on my door. "Yes?" I called out.

Ben poked his head in. "Okay, I know it's not after Thanksgiving yet, but I have a special delivery for Clara Seibert. May I come in?"

"Are flowers involved?"

He stepped inside and drew out an enormous bouquet of roses from behind his back with a flourish. "Voilà!"

"Oh, Ben, they're beautiful. Thank you!" *And so are you.* "Why is it that you always look amazing, and every time you see me, I look like road kill?"

He looked me over carefully after he set the flowers down on the table by my bed. "Now that you mention it ..."

I grabbed the pillow behind my head and threw it at him. He ducked, while I sank back and groaned. The room was spinning. "Guess I'm not ready for pillow fights yet."

He tucked the pillow back behind my head. "Not yet, but you will be." He pulled up a chair and gently stroked my cheek.

My skin tingled. "Thanks for the flowers," I murmured.

"Can you please put them in some water for me? I think there's an extra vase in the bathroom."

"Sure thing."

He came back a couple of minutes later with a vase full of water and stuck the flowers in. Their delicate scent filled the room.

"They're gorgeous ... Oh, Ben, I've missed you. That night in the woods, when I thought I was going to die and never see you again ..." My voice cracked, and I couldn't go on.

Ben pulled me into his arms. "You're here. You're safe," he murmured over and over.

He felt so warm and solid. I relaxed into his arms, loving the feel of him. I never wanted to let go.

But then he pulled away and gazed at me, his eyes wet with tears. "Do you forgive me for being such a dumbass?"

"If you forgive me for not listening to you."

"Oh God, Clara!" He drew me in for a long kiss that left me breathless. Then he wrapped his arms around me and stroked my back.

Maybe I really had died. This felt like heaven.

When I was more or less breathing normally, I said, "By the way, your uncle turns out to be a pretty nice guy. He was here earlier pleading your case."

"There's definitely something to be said for having law enforcement on your side."

"I'm discovering that."

After Ben left to go to work, Jenny and Dave dropped by.

When Ben and I had been on the outs, it was almost painful for me to see them together. But now it felt wonderful. I loved watching them beam at one another. And at me when I told them Ben and I were back together.

"So," Jenny admonished, "you had to nearly get yourself murdered to see reason. Well, better late than never!"

"Now, honey, don't be so hard on her," Dave said.

Honey? He was already calling her "honey"? What were they, thirty-five?

She sniffed. "I couldn't believe you were letting this amazing guy get away.... And then I almost lost you, and I was so scared." She started sobbing, and I reached for her. So did Dave. We folded her into a giant sandwich hug.

"Hey," I whispered. "You're not getting rid of me that easily.... And apparently, neither is Ben."

Getting out of the hospital the next morning felt like reliving the days after Moura's murder—only worse. Even though Dad had arranged for us to leave through a back entrance flanked by two policemen, the media found us and pounced. We were blinded by camera flashes, as reporters shouted questions at us. "How are you feeling, Clara?" "What were their last words?" "Dr. Seibert, did you ever suspect Dr. Lewitsky?" And on and on. I struggled to breathe as they pressed in. My knees buckled, and the policemen more or less shoved me into the back seat of the cruiser that would take us home.

As much as I loved the idea of becoming a journalist, in that moment, I felt ready to throw every reporter stalking us off the nearest bridge. Vultures—all of them.

They were waiting outside our house as well, though with the help of the police, we now had our lawn roped off, with a bunch of "No Trespassing" signs. Dad whisked us up to the porch and then motioned to the reporters that he was ready to make a statement.

Microphones were shoved into his face. My dad's voice quavered as he spoke: "We are very grateful to everyone who has sent us messages of caring and support in this difficult time for our family. I'd also like to personally thank state trooper Emilio Sanchez, who took the time to check out the woods adjacent to what appeared to be an abandoned car. He found Clara and probably saved her life. Until the police complete their investigation, we'll have no further comment. We ask you to respect our privacy as we work to heal and recover from the tragic events of the last months."

More cameras clicked and another bevy of questions flew at us, but my dad waved them off, and we stepped inside our home. He locked the door behind us and pulled down all the shades and curtains before joining me in the living room. I'd already collapsed on the couch.

After years of wondering what it would be like to become a celebrity, now I knew for sure. Even five minutes of fame totally sucked.

I slept fitfully for most of the rest of the day, in between talking to Ben and Jenny on my phone. Dad went to visit Mom that night, but I stayed home, binging on reruns of all my favorite detective shows.

At breakfast the next morning, I was feeling better and

was in the midst of pestering Dad about going back to school when the doorbell rang. "So help me," Dad says, "I'll take a restraining order out if it's one of those news people! They're driving me crazy!"

But Dad opened the door and said, "So glad it's you!" I hurtled out of the kitchen in time to see Dad taking Detective Martino's overcoat to hang it up.

"Clara, how are you feeling?"

"A lot better. Want to come in and have some breakfast with us?"

"Coffee would be great." Then he smiled at me. Smiled! I searched my brain to recall if Detective Martino had ever smiled at me before. Nope. A definite first.

"Glad you're feeling better, and I have something to tell you. It may be upsetting, but I also hope it will be somewhat of a relief and give you even more closure than you already have."

Dad took off his glasses and rubbed his eyes. "What is it?"

"We found the murder weapon—the missing bookend from Moura's studio—in the attic of Dr. Lewitsky's farmhouse. It was in a box she had all taped up, marked, 'Old Piano Scores.'"

Quite a message there. She'd had a score to settle with her old piano student all right. "Was there any ... you know, blood, or anything on it?"

He nodded. "Preliminary tests indicate it's a match to your sister's. And Dr. Lewitsky's prints are all over it. Between your testimony and the forensic evidence, we have enough to close the case. I wanted you both to know before we make an official statement. I'm holding a press conference at two. If you're up to it, I'd like you both to be there."

My dad and I looked at each other and then he shook his head. "We are very grateful to you, but this is difficult. I think I'd be more comfortable watching you on television in the privacy of our home." He turned to me. "How about you, honey?"

I nodded and clasped Dad's hand tightly. "Can we write something out that you can say on our behalf?"

"Of course."

Dad went to get his trusty legal pad, and Detective Martino poured himself a cup of coffee. "So Ben and I were wondering," he said, a twinkle in his eyes as he looked into mine, "what do you and your dad have planned for Thanksgiving?"

I had to admit that Detective Martino cleaned up well. When Dad and I tuned in to his press conference that afternoon, the first thing I noticed was that he'd put on a freshly pressed suit. It didn't even have any buttons missing. And I was glad to see Trooper Sanchez standing proudly beside him. Detective Martino made a big point of thanking him for finding me.

Sanchez flushed and said he'd noticed one of the car doors was ajar. He wanted to make sure no one was in trouble in the nearby woods. "I'm just glad we got her help right away."

Detective Martino went on to lay out the case in as unsensational a manner as possible, even though there was no way to dress this up as anything other than the soap opera it was. "It appears that Dr. Lewitsky was upset that her husband, Joel Rasher, had become involved with her piano student, Moura Seibert. This was apparently her motive for murdering Moura. Then, her concerns about what Clara, Moura's sister, might be uncovering in an investigation she'd begun after receiving some threatening emails, led Dr. Lewitsky to kidnap Clara and try to force her husband to shoot her. Instead, Mr. Rasher turned the gun on his wife, and then himself."

He paused and cleared his throat. "Clara nearly lost her life, and I ask that private citizens leave the detective work to us. Whoever is sending Clara threatening messages, please stop. You can rest assured that we have identified the perpetrator of this heinous crime, and Clara was not involved. So you have no need to bother Clara Seibert ever again."

When the press conference was over, Dad turned the television off and looked at me. "At least we've hopefully seen the last of that deluded stalker of yours, honey."

I said a silent prayer that Dad was right.

"You know what I'm looking forward to?" he asked.

"What?"

"Talking about normal things—like what we should plan for Thanksgiving."

I leaned forward and gave Dad a kiss on the cheek. "I've been meaning to talk to you about that."

Chapter Twenty-Eight

That night, I went with Dad to see Mom at the hospital. When we walked into her room, she was sitting in a chair by the window and staring at the inky sky. On her lap, she held one of our old photo albums, its brown leather scratched and worn. Dad must have brought it over.

She actually looked at me when I approached her with my usual greeting and kiss on the cheek. "My God, Clara, look at your face!"

"The doctors say all the scratches are superficial, Mom. I'm lucky. There should be no lasting scars."

"Well, that's something! What were you thinking trying to go after those people by yourself?"

Gee, thanks, Mom, for the "Thank God, you're all right." "I thought if I met Mr. Rasher in a public place, I'd be okay."

"Well, you certainly miscalculated on that one."

"Lucille, that's enough! Had it not been for Clara, we might never have learned who killed Moura. Let's focus on being thankful that Clara—so brave, so smart, and yes, impetuous and foolish—is still here with us." He pulled me toward him, then leaned toward Mom. *No, please, you are not going to try for a group hug, Dad. That will never fly.* But he just touched her shoulder lightly and then released me. He took a seat on the edge of the bed, and I pulled up a chair across from Mom.

"That's true," Mom said. "I'm glad you're all right, Clara." Her flat tone made me feel like I was the booby prize she'd gotten stuck with after the real one had been snatched away. Which it had.

Tears glistened in her eyes. "You know what I can't stop thinking about?"

"What?" Dad said.

"Why Moura never told me what was going on with Joel Rasher. I thought we were so close. I could have helped her, guided her. She was so innocent." She reached for a tissue and mopped at the tears that had begun streaming down her face.

Innocent? When it came to her personal life, Mr. Rasher was more like the tip of the iceberg. But I wasn't about to add any more dirty laundry to my family's growing load.

I sighed. "Anyone want a Coke? Or coffee?" Mom shook her head, but Dad asked for coffee. I slipped out the door, glad to get away from Mom's hand-wringing about what she hadn't known about her darling daughter Moura. Who was it who'd said, "The more things change, the more they remain the same?" If anyone ever questioned the truth of that statement, I'd simply say, "See Exhibit A: My mother."

Dad insisted I spend one more day resting at home, so I spent Thursday ignoring the handful of remaining reporters who rang our doorbell by the hour. I organized my notes and then roughed out the opening for my dating violence story. Mr. B. always emphasized hooking readers immediately, so I started with a quote I hoped would draw them in: "The first time he pinned me against the wall, he held my arms so tight that he left bruises. I begged him to stop. 'You're hurting me,' I told him. 'You asked for it,' he said."

It felt good to get back to work, even if the subject was incredibly depressing. When I was writing, I got drawn into a whole other place. And it was a relief to escape my own world for a while. When I wasn't working, I had too much time to think—and relive things I wanted to leave behind. The awful scene in the woods had also brought back memories of the night I'd found Moura in vivid Technicolor. Seeing her lying there—so still, so lifeless, like a discarded rag doll—it was beyond awful. And the smell. I'd been too cold in the woods to smell much of anything, even my own vomit. But the smell of Moura's blood that night in her studio was etched forever in my mind, my whole being.

Our family doctor had given me some meds to help me sleep, but the meds didn't prevent my nightmares of being chased in the woods. I knew that the bad dreams and awful memories would recede over time, and I would eventually start to feel better, more like myself. But it was still hard. I vacillated between being euphoric that I was alive and feeling shell-shocked from all the horror and death I'd witnessed. Dad had made an appointment for me with the therapist I'd seen after Moura died. I knew I needed it.

The first day back at school was both wonderful and strange. Our French teacher, Madame Auld, welcomed me back warmly and couldn't resist commenting on Ben hovering protectively beside me: *"Ah Clara, nous sommes très heureux que vous soyez de retour saine et sauve avec nous. Et apparement, quelqu'un de notre classe est partciulièrement heureux de vous revoir."* (Ah Clara, we are so glad you are back safe and sound with us. And apparently, someone in our class is especially happy to have you back.)

Ben blushed, and I figured we looked like a matching set of over-ripe tomatoes. But despite his evident embarrassment, he flashed a big smile and said, *"Vous êtes très perspicace, Mme. Auld."* ("You are very perceptive, Madame Auld.") And yes, his accent was awful. And somehow, all his imperfections were so endearing. Whoa, did I ever have it bad.

He also turned up after every class to walk me to the next one, even though I told him I really didn't need babysitting. Not that it didn't feel absolutely great to hold his hand and know he had my back, especially when students I barely knew sidled up to me and said stuff like, "I can't believe what you've gone through. Tell me everything!"

I tried to be nice, explaining that "It's still really fresh for me—not something I feel like going into right now." When that didn't work and they kept pressing for details, Ben would glower at them and nudge me along. "You make a great getaway sidekick," I told him.

"As long as I can get away with you, it's all good," he said.

How had I ever almost let this guy go? Well, I knew how. He'd been a jerk, but hey, I'd had my jerky moments as well.

"Ben?" I looked up at him, not wanting the bell to ring before I got this out.

"Yeah?"

"Let's never keep stuff from each other again. And I promise to talk things out with you when you make me angry. Deal?"

He grinned. "Sounds good, but a major deal like this must be sealed with a kiss."

My eyes darted around the hallway. "Not here!"

Before I could continue my protests that PDAs were not allowed in school and we couldn't be late to class, he swooped in and pressed his lips against mine. My pulse was on fire. It felt too good to stop.

But then the warning bell sounded. Ben began backpedaling down the hall, a sloppy grin on his face. "Gotcha! Now it's a deal!"

Chapter Twenty-Nine

Sunday night, Ben and I went out to dinner by ourselves at Giovanni's, a cozy bistro where we ate delicious linguini with white clam sauce and fettuccine Alfredo. We took turns feeding each other from our respective plates. "I feel like those dogs eating spaghetti in *Lady and the Tramp*."

"My mom loved that movie!"

"Did she? I wish you'd tell me more about her."

And he did. He talked about how she gave really great hugs and loved to laugh. "Even toward the end. She'd lost all of her hair, which had been beautiful—thick, wavy."

"Like yours," I said, unable to resist the impulse to reach up and push a lock of his dark hair out of his eyes.

He grinned. "Yeah, but my mom's was really something. ... Anyhow, she even joked about that. 'This is my latest cost-cutting discovery,' she'd say. 'Look at all the money I'm saving by never needing to get my hair done.'"

"She sounds very gutsy."

"Yeah ... And she was a real history buff. She's the one who got me hooked. For years, I didn't even know there were cartoons on television. I thought TV meant the

History Channel."

I laughed. "You'll be at least as entertaining as the History Channel. Your students will be so lucky to have you."

"I hope so." He reached over and brushed my cheek with his warm fingers.

"Touch me like that again, and you'll have to explain to the waiter why your date needs to be peeled off the ceiling."

He beamed at me and held his hands up. "I'll just have to join you up there."

"You are too much!"

"Can't help it. You have that effect on me."

"Good to hear," I told him.

After dinner, we sat on the couch in my living room. He put his arm around me, and I burrowed into him. Safe. I felt so safe with Ben.

"Tell me how you're doing with all this," he said. "It's got to be overwhelming."

Something about the gentle tone of his voice sent me into a meltdown. "Oh God, do you really want to hear all this?"

"Please. Talk to me."

I closed my eyes and started to talk. It all tumbled out— the dreams, the flashbacks—all the things I'd held inside.

My tears began to fall and didn't stop for a long time. Ben held me close. He didn't try to tell me to calm down or say that everything was going to be okay. He just let me cry for as long as I needed to.

I loved him for that.

The final three days of school before the break were crazy as usual. Students had basically already checked out, and most of the teachers had that, "Can we all just get out of here?" look. I'd emailed my draft of the dating violence story to Tony, Mr. B., and Mrs. Rivera. Tony didn't say much, but Mr. B. and Mrs. Rivera were effusive. "You nailed it, kiddo," Mr. B. told me Tuesday afternoon when he dropped by the office.

"Thanks. I felt good about this one."

"Well, you should have. It's solid and heartfelt." He took off his glasses and pulled a crumpled tissue from his pocket to clean them. "I want you to think about doing more features—not just the advice column. I know they're a lot of work, but you've got a good feel for this."

My heart raced. "Really? Well, yeah … Of course! I mean, I really got into this. And I have some other ideas I want to pitch at the next staff meeting."

"Good. Meantime, you'd better run this by everyone at the center."

"Will do. Mrs. Williams said to email a copy to her, and she'll run it by the group as well."

"So after that, you should go home, take a break from all this."

"Not a chance! There might be some folks needing advice. You never know." I opened my inbox and, sure enough, a couple of letters had come in. "See? An advice columnist's work is never done!"

Wednesday afternoon, students poured out of the building like a stampede in an old cowboy movie. Ben and I lingered by his locker as the place emptied out.

"I wish I didn't have to work tonight," he said. "I'd much rather be with you."

Impulsively, I nestled into him and planted a row of kisses up his neck to his ear. "Ditto," I murmured. "But we have tomorrow. Dad and I will be over as soon as we visit Mom. What should we bring?"

"Just yourselves. There will be enough food for a small army. Every Martino and Marchetta within a sixty-mile radius is coming and bringing food."

"Okay, so this time, it's my turn to bring the flowers."

"Uncle Luis will like that!"

Somehow, I'd never thought of "Uncle Luis," AKA Detective Martino, as a flowery kind of guy. But I guess we were both learning that first impressions weren't everything. Besides, Ben's uncle and I now had two things in common: We were relieved we knew who'd murdered Moura, and we were both crazy about Ben.

"Call me on your break, okay?"

"Always."

I went upstairs to the office for one last writing session. I'd already drafted a response to one of the letters I'd gotten from a student who was crushing on her best friend's boyfriend. But I still needed to respond to the second letter that had come in from a student whose girlfriend ignored him whenever her girlfriends were around—which, apparently, was all the time.

The place felt like a tomb—just me and the janitor I'd passed on my way upstairs. Even Mr. B. had left early. But

I didn't mind. I liked the quiet when I was working.

I opened my email before I settled in to write. No new letters, and thank goodness, no more threats. It really was over! I wondered if I'd ever know his or her identity. Maybe it didn't matter, as long as the jerk ball didn't move on to some other poor victim. I wouldn't wish that on anybody.

I took a deep breath, did a couple of neck rolls, opened a fresh document, and started writing:

Dear Ignored and Getting Pissed,

I'd be getting pissed, too, if my girlfriend treated me like I was the wallpaper in the room every time her friends came by. Not cool.

IMO, you've got to talk to her. Tell her how you feel. It's possible she's not even aware she's ignoring you, and her "you don't exist when my friends are here" act isn't intentional.

I guess I'd also want to know why. Is she embarrassed by you? Worried about losing her closeness with her friends? What's the deal here?

*Hopefully, you'll know more after talking with her. And if she's not willing to stop treating you like you don't exist when her BFFs are around, that's some pretty major info for you. What kind of a friend is she to you? Bottom line: A girlfriend is supposed to be a **really** good friend.*

You deserve that! Good luck, and let me know how things turn out.

—Since You Asked

I chewed on my pencil. I knew from experience it wasn't easy to confront people. But if his description of the way she was acting was accurate, she wasn't about to win any awards for "Caring Girlfriend of the Year."

I was still making a few line edits when the door creaked open. I jumped a mile. "You startled me! What are you doing here, Tony?"

"Bringing my favorite advice columnist a latte to kick off the break."

"Thanks. This is really nice of you."

He put his feet on the desk and took a swig of his latte. "I have an idea for a project I want to run by you. Then, I'm doing a whole lot of nothing. I've had a hell of a semester."

"Sorry it's been hard. Hang on a minute, and let me send this to Mrs. Rivera."

I read over my edits one more time, then pushed "Send" and turned around. "I'm all ears."

"I want us to do a series on the whole college acceptance-rejection thing—you know, follow five seniors as they go through the whole waiting process. And then, how they cope with the results. I mean, there's so much pressure …" He droned on, and I tried to concentrate. This was a good idea, something right up my alley. But his words seemed to be coming from farther and farther away. They were all mushing together….

"It's a great idea, but I'm feeling a little weird. I hope I'm not getting sick." I stood up and swayed a little. The room was spinning. I closed my eyes and sank back down.

"Are you okay? You look kind of ill all of a sudden. I

hope you're not getting the flu."

"I hope not." I pressed my fingers into my forehead. "Not right before Thanksgiving."

"It's been going around, you know."

I nodded, bleakly.

"Let me get you home." Tony handed me my backpack, and I pushed myself to standing. My legs felt like Jell-O.

"Help me?"

"Of course," he said. I clung to him as he half-dragged, half-carried me to his car. "Giving you a ride is no trouble at all."

His voice sounded miles away. I closed my eyes and leaned back in the seat. The words, "No trouble at all," echoed in my mind until I drifted off.

Chapter Thirty |

The smell of burning wood mixed with the faint aroma of mildew and cologne filled my nostrils. I groaned and struggled to swim to full consciousness. I'd dreamed of being thrust into a bottomless dark pool. My eyelids felt so heavy. And my arms ... What was digging into them? Why couldn't I move?

I forced my eyes open and stared down in horror. My breath came in jerky rasps. I was tied to a chair with thick rope, my hands bound behind my back. Tony had his back to me, bending over to thrust a log into a wood-burning stove a few yards from where I sat. He'd put on one of those thick woolen lumberjack shirts, as though he were auditioning for some folksy Thanksgiving family special.

This was special all right. He was whistling the tune to "Over the River and Through the Woods."

Oh God, no, please no, please! I had to get out of here! I glanced around. The door couldn't be more than ten feet away. I leaned forward and lifted the chair legs up, so they wouldn't scrape against the floor. I tried to scoot myself with my feet.

I'd managed to move within a couple of feet of the door when Tony yanked a handful of my hair and slammed his fist into the side of my head. My ears were ringing, as he dragged my chair backward. He moved around to face me, then bent down, so that his face was inches from mine. There was no escaping his nauseating cologne or heavy breathing. "So I see Sleeping Beauty has woken up."

My heart pounded. "Where are we? What's this about?"

"You're my special Thanksgiving guest! Welcome to my family's cabin, where you and I can have some special alone time. No one comes up during the winter … well, except for us."

"What's going on? What did you do to me? You drugged me, didn't you?"

"Well, obviously. And surely you can figure out what this is about. It's payback time, Writer Girl." He straightened up and moved back to the stove to add another log.

"I don't understand!" I cried. "You're the one who sent me all those messages? Why? Did you really think I killed my sister? But now you know I didn't! What's going on?"

"'What's going on?' he mimicked in a high falsetto voice. "For a bright girl, you're not too swift on the uptake, are you? This has nothing to do with your sister! You ruined everything with your stupid-ass advice in that ridiculous column." He began to pace back and forth in front of me.

Despite the heat filling the room from the stove, I shivered. "What advice? What are you talking about?"

He moved behind me and tipped my chair back and thrust his face inches from mine. I trembled and tried to avoid looking at him, but he screamed at me. "Look at me, you bitch! You convinced my girlfriend to break things off with me, not once—but twice. Where do you get off playing God in people's lives?"

He shoved the front of my chair down. My spine felt like he'd just jammed a fist through it. He circled around me, his arms moving like pistons in the air as he punctuated every statement. "You turned her against me, you arrogant piece of shit!"

"Your girlfriend. She's the one who … ? But I don't understand. How did you find out about those emails? Nobody knows my password to the column inbox, and her letters were never published."

"You don't think I was keeping tabs on my girl? It was pretty easy to figure out her password and read *her* email." He threw a log into the stove and moved back to perch on the arm of his chair.

"Are you talking about Sheri?"

"She's something, huh?" For a moment, his eyes gleamed, but then the sparkle evaporated.

"You still want to be with her, don't you?"

His jaw clenched. "It's all I think about. But she's blocked me on her phone and on Instagram. She's cut me out of her life."

"I'm sorry."

"You're sorry? This is all your fucking fault! You ruined my life. Now I'm going to ruin yours."

Oh God. What is he going to do? Kill me? What do I do? I had to convince him I was on his side. I took a deep breath.

"Look, I'm sorry about Sheri. I get it—I see how much she means to you. What if I called her, told her we'd talked, and you were really sincere in wanting to change, be the kind of boyfriend she wants? You said yourself she took my advice very seriously. Why wouldn't she again?"

Tony leaned forward and stared at me intently. "You trying to trick me, Clara? Get me to let you call Sheri, so you can tell her where you are, get rescued?"

I took a sharp intake of breath, and then let it out slowly. "I'd like to get out of here—no question about that. But I'd also like to help you. I can ask her to come up here—suggest the three of us talk about how we can make things better for the two of you. I could offer to be ... you know, like a mediator."

He ran his tongue over his lower lip and seemed lost in thought for several seconds. Then he stood up and walked over to his backpack and took out a long serrated knife. He brought it over to me and held it inches from my nose. "No funny business, or you'll be the one I carve for Thanksgiving. Are we clear?"

I blinked, then nodded.

"Well then, let's give Plan B a try," he said, straightening up. "Where's your phone? She won't answer mine."

"Should be in my backpack."

"Right. Left yours in the car. Be right back—now, don't go anywhere!" He laughed at his poor excuse for a joke and then opened the door. A burst of cold air rushed into the room. I closed my eyes and willed myself to stop trembling. This had to work. I didn't want to put Sheri's life at risk, but I was desperate. And if he thought she was willing to consider taking him back, they'd cycle back to the honeymoon stage, and she'd be safe. At least for a little while.

Tony stomped back in, carrying my backpack.

"Phone's in the side compartment," I said, praying he wouldn't empty my backpack and come across the pepper spray I carried with me. There was always a chance I could get to it—if, that is, I could convince Sheri to come out, and Tony agreed to untie me for our little mediation session.

He pulled my cell out and checked my messages. "Ben wants you to call him when you get a chance," he reported with a sneer.

Ben! Oh, Ben—was it really only a few hours ago that we'd talked about celebrating our first Thanksgiving together? I'd dreaded the thought of all those Marchetta and Martino cousins looking me over as "the new girlfriend." Now that sounded positively relaxing.

"I should call him, so he won't worry. We were planning to go out tonight after he got off from work," I lied.

"Not happening."

"Well, can you at least untie me, so I can call Sheri?"

"Not necessary. I'll dial, and then hold the phone up next to your ear for you to talk."

Great. This would be comfortable. And what if she didn't answer? What, then?

He punched in the number, pulled his chair up close to mine, and held the phone to my ear. Miracle of miracles, she picked up on the fourth ring.

"Hello?"

"Hey, is this Sheri?"

"Yeah … Do I know you?" she asked, sounding wary.

"You've probably seen me around school. My name's Clara. I write the 'Since You Asked' column."

"You're kidding," she said, her voice sounding several degrees warmer. "I can't believe I'm talking to you. I love your column! And you really helped me! How did you know who I was? How to call me?"

I bit my lip. "Actually, that's a long story. Do you have a minute to talk?"

"Sure."

"Well, when you wrote to me, I had no idea your ex was Tony. I guess you know he's the editor of the paper. Anyhow, the two of us took a run out to his family's cabin to hang out and talk about some new ideas we have for features." Okay, this was sounding lame. I rushed on. "You know, like Tony had this great idea for following five seniors over the next several months as they apply to colleges and go through the process."

"Just make sure he doesn't try to tell everybody where they should go. He got really upset when I told him I wanted to go out of state, instead of to Ohio State where *he* was planning to go. Typical Tony," she added, bitterly.

This was going to be a tough sell. "Actually, speaking of that, Tony and I got to talking about our own lives, and he told me about what happened between the two of you. He feels so bad about how he messed things up. He really broke down.… He knows he has to change for real. He's willing to go to the men's group at the center, get into therapy, do whatever he needs to, to be the boyfriend you deserve.... "

Tony's jaw dropped at this, but I mouthed, "Trust me," and he shrugged.

"Are you sure he's not pulling your leg? Tony's a pretty smooth talker," she said.

Was I ever familiar with *that*. "I really don't think so," I lied. "He truly loves you, and I realize now I was off base in my advice. It was a definite wake-up call for him when you told him you wouldn't go back with him. Now I think he's ready to commit to changing."

She didn't say anything for a few seconds. "I don't know," she said, finally. "He always swears it will be different, but it never is."

"I totally get where you're coming from, but I feel like we made a breakthrough. I think he finally gets it. Is there any chance you can drive out here and maybe the three of us can talk together?" I held my breath.

"You're at the cabin?"

"Right. Do you know how to get here?"

"Yeah. Tony and I used to go up there to be alone. I'm not sure. Put him on, okay?"

"Sure. Tony, can you come over here? Sheri wants to talk to you."

He grinned wildly, grabbed the phone away from me, and took a few noisy steps around the room before putting the phone to his own ear. "Sheri? I know it's late, but can you come? Clara's really been amazing to talk to. I love you so much...." He listened for a few seconds. "I understand ... You're right, baby. Okay then, I'll put her back on." He handed the phone back to me.

"Are you okay? Is this on the level?" she asked.

"*No.* It's no problem at all," I said. *Would she notice I hadn't answered her question?* "I can't wait to talk to you in person. By the way, my phone's about to die. Would you mind calling Gino's Deli and telling Ben Marchetta that something's come up, and I'm sorry I can't make our date tonight?" Ben wasn't stupid. He'd know something was wrong if she called him about a date we didn't have.

Tony ripped the phone away from my ear and glared at me. "Sheri?" he said. "Don't worry about calling Ben. Clara can call him on my phone. We both lost track of time and had no idea we were going to get into such a heavy discussion. But I'm glad we did."

He listened, then said, "Great. See you soon." He clicked the end button, threw the phone down, and slapped me hard across the face. "I told you, no funny business! You were trying to get your boy Ben to rescue you, weren't you? Bitch!" He slapped me again.

Chapter Thirty-One

Tony guzzled the last of his beer and smacked his lips like he'd just won the lottery. "Sorry your deli boy won't be riding to the rescue," he said, picking up the knife and running his tongue along it. "But you've still got a chance to convince me to let you live. Let's see how you do helping me get back together with Sheri, and convincing me I can trust you to keep your mouth shut."

"Trust is a two-way street," I shot back. "Sheri needs to know she can trust you. Which means I need to look like I'm *not* your hostage. I have to use the bathroom, and you've got to untie me. Or Sheri's never going to believe I came here willingly to shoot the breeze about the paper and our love lives."

He scrunched up his face and looked at me closely. "You look like shit all right." He stood up, knife in hand, and moved toward me. "Try anything, and this knife will cut up a lot more than these ropes."

"Okay, okay," I said, my breath coming in short gasps.

He yanked the rope away from my body and sliced it, then moved around to the back of my chair and cut the loop of rope around my wrists. I wiggled my hands in relief and then rubbed them over and over, trying to coax the circulation to kick back in. "Thank you." I stood up and the floor tilted beneath me. I clutched the chair and took a deep breath.

"You okay there?" Tony asked lazily.

"Yeah, no problem." Feeling a smidgen steadier, I slowly moved toward the love seat near the door, where Tony had dropped my backpack.

Tony roughly yanked me to a stop. "Where do you think you're going?"

"I'm just getting my comb and brush. They're in my backpack."

He waved the knife in front of my nose. "I'll get them. You stay here."

Oh, shit.

He grabbed my pack and emptied its contents on the couch. "My, my," he said, holding up the can of pepper spray. "What do we have here? I don't think you'll be needing this, do you?"

He opened the front door and hurled the can into the woods.

"I always carry spray. I wasn't going to use it on you," I said, praying I sounded convincing.

"Sure you weren't. And I'm your best friend."

"Whatever. I have to pee. Now please! Hand me my makeup bag. It's that blue thing."

He unzipped it and studied the contents. "Don't think you can do any damage with what's in here," he said, as he zipped my pouch back up and threw it over to me.

"Ladies first. Then my turn. Gotta look good for my girl." He waved me toward the bathroom, knife in hand. "Don't close the door all the way, or you'll be very sorry."

Great. I moved into the tiny bathroom and left the door ajar only an inch or so. I sank down on the seat, turned on the water, and sighed in relief as I peed. And peed. How many hours had it been?

I washed my hands and face, gulping handfuls of water to drink. Then I stared at myself in the mirror. I looked like a hunted dog. My hair was in tangles, my face was blotchy, and there was a swollen red mark on my left cheek where Tony had slapped me.

"Hurry up in there," he yelled.

"Give me a minute. Gotta comb my hair." I pulled out my brush and struggled to untangle at least a dozen knots. I felt like I was massacring my own scalp. When I finally had my hair more or less smoothed out, I spread a ton of blush on my cheeks, hoping it would camouflage Tony's handiwork.

"Took you long enough," he said, as I emerged from the bathroom.

"Sorry."

"I'm keeping this door wide open, so don't get any ideas. I'll even let you peek while I take a leak."

"Gee, thanks," I said, glancing around and noticing that the ropes that had bound me were nowhere to be seen. Neither was Tony's beer can, or the contents of my backpack that he'd emptied on the couch. Apparently, he'd been busy spiffing up the place for Sheri. It looked downright homey.

"Sit in that armchair there, where I can see you," he ordered. I sat and closed my eyes as I heard him unzip his pants and pee, opening them only after I heard the toilet flush and the sound of him zipping back up. After he'd washed up, he spritzed his mouth with breath spray and slicked his hair back. Then he doused himself with more cologne. *Gag me.*

"So you get off on telling everybody else how to run their lives. What should I say to Sheri when she gets here?"

Was this a trick question? I paused, then offered, "Maybe you should ask her what she wants, what she needs from you."

He grinned at me. "Genius! She'll eat that up. I don't think I've ever asked her that."

Why didn't that surprise me? And if I were such a genius, why was I the prisoner of this nut job? "Great. Well, I think that's the way to go—really focus on listening to her."

"Sure, sure," he said. "Got it." He walked out of the bathroom, waving the knife around as though it were a baton, and he were an overly enthusiastic conductor.

"You might want to put that thing away when she gets here. I'm not sure she's going to buy into the new, sensitive you if you're packing."

"You don't pack a knife, stupid. You pack a gun."

"Still …"

Headlights shone through the front windows. Tony strode over to his backpack and dropped his knife inside.

"Showtime," he said over his shoulder to me. Then he flung the door open and pulled Sheri into his arms.

Chapter Thirty-Two

Tony helped her take off her parka. Her cheeks were pink from the cold, and she wore an aqua tunic that brought out the blue in her eyes, along with skin tight black jeans and boots. She was all soft curves, and her long blonde hair hung down her back like spun gold. Tony had one thing right—she was beautiful.

She turned to me, took my hand, and grasped it in both of hers. She looked over at Tony and said teasingly, "I had my doubts about coming up here, but the chance to talk to the writer of 'Since You Asked' in person was too cool to pass up!"

Tony threw his arm around me and squeezed my shoulder. Hard. "Yeah, Clara's amazing all right."

Sheri looked around expectantly. "Anyone else here?"

"Why would there be anyone else?" Tony asked, a sharpness creeping into his voice.

"No reason! I thought maybe Ben might have driven up to join Clara, since you said you'd call him."

"Nah, I promised him I'd take good care of his girl and bring her home later," he said with a smug smile.

I looked at Sheri closely. She had settled herself on the couch, kicked her boots off, and drawn her legs up beneath her, as though she were getting comfy for a cozy chat. She was either a hell of an actress, or she truly believed nothing was wrong. "Got any hot chocolate?" she asked.

"Probably some in the cupboard." Tony started to get up from where he'd parked himself next to Sheri and then hesitated. My bet was it occurred to him that leaving the two of us out here to talk might not be the brightest move. "Actually, Clara, would you mind getting it? Everything's in that cupboard to the right of the sink. Sheri and I have a lot to talk about, and we'd better get started." Apparently, he'd decided that letting me snoop around the cabin's kitchen was less risky than leaving me alone with his lady love.

"Don't be silly, Tony. Clara's not our servant. It will just take a minute. Let's all go."

Tony, in his most charming syrupy voice, said, "You're right, babe. Sorry, Clara."

Ten minutes later, we'd all settled back in the main living area with steaming cups of hot chocolate. I sat across from the lovebirds, trying to keep my hand from noticeably shaking as I lifted my mug to my lips.

"So where do we start?" Sheri asked, looking directly at me.

Before I could summon a response, Tony jumped in. "Let's start with what you need, what you want, babe. I know I've been a lousy boyfriend, but I want to start over by doing a lot less talking, and a lot more listening, to you." He sounded so sincere that even I almost believed him.

Sheri's jaw hung open. She turned to me. "Did you tell him to say that?"

"I might have made a suggestion or two."

She turned back to him. "I want you to keep talking to Clara. That's the first time you've asked me what *I* want, instead of telling me what you think I should want."

Tony hung his head, then looked up at her with puppy dog eyes. "I know. I'm sorry, but it'll be different now. So tell me, talk to me."

And she did. "For starters, I don't want to be your possession. I don't want you telling me what to do, who I can see. And I don't want you checking up on me every five minutes. I'm not your personal property that has to be guarded twenty-four seven." She pointed at his chest and added, "And most especially, if you ever, ever put a finger on me again—unless it's to hold me or kiss me because that's what we both want—I'll not only refuse to ever see you again, but I will press charges. Understood?"

Tony nodded so vigorously I thought his head might fall off. "Absolutely," he said. "I can change. I know I can."

Sheri continued to talk. And talk. She wanted him to be her friend, her equal, to support her passion for art and not try to prevent her from choosing the art school that was best for her future. And she said she wanted him to face his demons. "I see how your dad treats your mom. That's not okay. That's not how I want to live."

Tony stiffened, and for a moment, I thought the mask was going to come off. "You know I don't like it when you bring up my dad."

"That's just it," she said, solemnly, as she unfolded her legs and pulled away from him slightly. "If you're not willing to get into therapy and deal with what your dad is doing to your mom, and you won't talk to me about what's going on inside for you, then this is never going to work."

"Okay, okay," he muttered. "I know you're right. I'll do the therapy. I'll work on it. I promise." He grabbed her in his arms and drew her toward him for a long, lingering kiss.

I sat there, wondering if I should bolt for the door. But I couldn't just leave Sheri alone with a guy who could turn on a dime and had a humongous serrated knife in his backpack.

When their kiss was finally over, Sheri turned to me. "Sorry! I guess we got a little carried away. I really do want to thank you for helping us through this."

"Glad to help," I said. What I really wanted to do was scream, "I'm the one who needs help! Please!" But I kept silent.

She looked at her watch and said, "Oh, my gosh, it's late. I promised Mom I wouldn't stay long." She began to pull on her boots.

"I wish you didn't have to go so soon," Tony said, nuzzling her neck.

"Actually, I need to get going, too. Would you mind dropping me off, Sheri?"

She looked up at me and smiled, but before she could say anything, Tony said, "No need. I'll take you. I promised Ben, and a promise is a promise."

"I appreciate the offer, but if Sheri's willing, I wanted

to turn the tables on her and ask her for some advice about an issue Ben and I are having. I need a girl's perspective."

"I'd be honored!" she said. "I can't believe you're asking me for advice! Of course, you can ride with me."

"No, Clara! Have you forgotten we have some unfinished business?" His eyes darkened, and I sensed he was on the brink of breaking his "I'm a sensitive, sane guy" persona.

"Of course not. I'll get all those ideas written up over the weekend and have them on your desk by Monday."

I started to move toward my coat and backpack when Tony grabbed me from behind. He pulled me tightly toward him, his fingers digging into my shoulder. "I really have to insist, Clara. I'm sure Sheri would be glad to get together with you some other time."

I couldn't help it. I flinched. The color drained from Sheri's face. "Not five minutes ago, you promised you'd change. And I almost fell for it. Let her go! She's leaving with me, Tony. Now! We are so done!"

He released his grip on me and started toward Sheri, yelling, "Neither one of you is going anywhere!"

I jumped on his back and jabbed my fingers into his eyes.

He howled like a feral animal and threw me off him.

I fell backward, landing hard on my butt.

Sheri jumped in and clocked him on his thick skull with her mug. He went down, hot chocolate splattering everywhere.

"Run!" I yelled to her, as I struggled to get to my feet.

She hesitated, then turned and sprinted out the door. In the distance, sirens screamed.

"You bitch!" he yelled.

I stumbled toward the door and my hand gripped the handle as he tackled me. We both went down. I screamed.

The siren shrieked, closer now. Headlights streamed through the windows. Tony looked up and loosened his grip just long enough for me to shimmy around to my back. I drew up both my legs and kicked him as hard as I could in the balls. He howled and rolled away from me.

"This is the police!" a voice boomed out over what sounded like a loud speaker. "Come out with your hands up!" I knew that voice—Detective Martino.

I crawled toward the door. "C ... c ... coming," I cried out. I reached for the knob, jerked the door open, and held up one hand in the air. Then I collapsed.

Detective Martino nearly tripped over me as he rushed past to get to Tony. He grabbed his arms roughly and cuffed him. "You have the right to remain silent. Anything you say can and will be used against you...." He droned on with the rest of his spiel, as Tony lay splayed out on his stomach, still groaning. Then Martino pulled out his cell, called for backup, and yelled for Ben, who burst in the door.

"Clara! Oh, my God." He swept me up in his arms and lowered me down into the love seat. I clung to him. I didn't ever want to let go.

"What the hell happened? What were you doing out here?"

"Sheri!" I cried. "Is she okay?"

"I'm here," a thin voice said from the doorway. "I shouldn't have left you. I'm sorry! I was so scared."

"I told you to run! I'm the one who should be apologizing for luring you out here. I'm sorry. I was just so desperate to get help!"

She moved over and sat next to us. Her face was drained of color. She touched my arm gently.

"I still don't understand," Ben said.

"Tony's the one who sent me all those messages. He said my advice had broken Sheri and him up. I told him I'd help him get back with her if he'd let me live."

I took a deep breath and grabbed Sheri's hand in mine. "I still feel so guilty for putting you at risk like that."

"Hey, you did what you had to."

I nodded bleakly, then looked up at Ben. "How did you guys know where to find us?"

Sheri broke in—"I wanted to think this was on the up and up, but I wasn't sure, so I called Ben. I could tell he was worried when he insisted on my giving him directions to the cabin." She turned to Ben. "How come it took so long for you to get here, anyway?"

He flushed. "Long story ... had to talk to my boss, track my uncle down, and then we missed the turn the first time around. Talk about a hidden driveway! Some hero I am, huh?"

He looked so mortified that I reached up and kissed his cheek. "We managed," I said.

"Right up until I saw he wouldn't let you go, Clara, there was part of me that still wanted to believe he'd changed,"

Sheri said. "How stupid is that?" Tears filled her eyes.

I pulled her into an awkward hug with the two of us. "You can't beat yourself up over that! You cared about him. I don't think any of us realized how messed-up he was. I sure didn't."

She sniffed. "I guess ... got to find my phone and call my mom."

I snuggled into Ben. "I need to call Dad, too."

"Okay ... give me one more minute to hold you." His arms tightened around me. "You know, it's kind of hard to be your hero if you're going to keep saving yourself."

I sighed, contentedly. "Oh, come on, you know you like strong women."

He leaned down, lifted my chin, and stared down at me. "I always thought my mom was the strongest, gutsiest woman I'd ever known. But you are something else. It just might be a tie."

Tears sprang into my eyes. "From what you've told me about your mom, that's the biggest compliment anyone's ever given me."

"You deserve it. You know how you said Moura was the big star of your family, and you were the afterthought?"

I nodded.

"Well, in my eyes, you're the real star, the real thing."

I opened my mouth to thank him for saying that, but no words came. Tears poured down my face. I started to swipe at them and then gave up in favor of hugging Ben harder.

In the distance, we heard more sirens. Detective

Martino said, "That'll be the officers who'll take Tony in." I looked over to see Tony slumped in the armchair. His eyes looked unfocused, dazed. "We'll take Clara and Sheri in our car to the station for statements."

Ben nodded. "You okay to go out on the porch with me to wait?" he asked me.

"Still a little wobbly," I admitted.

"Good excuse to lean on me." He helped me get my parka on and handed me my backpack. "You hold this, and I'll hold you."

He carried me out to the porch steps and we sat together. He held my hands and kissed them. I nestled into him and closed my eyes, listening to the reassuring sound of his heartbeat.

The words I wanted to say finally came.

"All my life, I've felt like I didn't matter much. But you've helped me feel like I do, like I'm special, too, in my own way. I am so thankful for *you*."

"You don't need me to feel special."

"Oh, Ben." I clung to him, amazed that in the worst year of my life, this beautiful, wonderful guy had appeared.

"I really think our folks would understand if you weren't up for inspection tomorrow at the big family dinner. You up for a private celebration?"

"It's the first Thanksgiving without your mom—and my sister. You should be with your family, and I need to be with my dad."

"I guess," he said, sounding reluctant to be separated even for a few hours.

"You know what else?"

"What?"

"It may not do any good, but I think I'm going to tell my mom about us, start sharing some of my feelings with her. Who knows? Maybe things can get better."

"Hey, even if you get nowhere, you know that has nothing to do with you, right?"

"Yes, Dr. Phil!" I managed to give him a shaky poke in the ribs.

He grinned at me.

"Now about that private celebration," I said. "How about later tomorrow night?"

His dark eyes shone as he looked down at me. "We'd better follow our new tradition and seal that with a kiss."

"Mmm," I murmured, as he lowered his face to mine.

Acknowledgments

I feel so grateful to the folks who helped make my dream of writing *It Should Have Been You* a reality:

First and foremost, I'm incredibly grateful to my first editor at Page Street, Alyssa Raymond, whose honest and perceptive feedback made this a much better book. Thanks go as well to the entire Page Street team who has been so great to work with, including publisher Will Kiester, acquisitions and editorial manager Marissa Giambelluca, YA editors Lauren Knowles and Ashley Hern, publicity and marketing director Jill Browning, publicity and marketing assistant Madison Taylor, and copyeditor Sheelonee Banerjee. Many thanks also to Deb Shapiro for her publicity efforts on behalf of Page Street's inaugural YA line.

As for my extraordinary agent, Katie Shea Boutillier, what can I say? Your encouragement, unwavering professionalism, and wisdom have sustained me through months and months of revising and reworking this manuscript. I feel truly blessed to have you as my agent.

I'm so lucky as well to have had amazing mentors at Seton Hill. Multi-published novelists and master teachers

Barb Miller, Anne Harris, and Lee McClain taught me so much about writing, the writing life, and about the importance of revising. I will forever be your fan! Thanks also to my SHU critique partners China DeSpain, Erica Millard, Karie Jo Milburn, and Sarah Buechele, whose feedback on early versions of this book was so helpful. And I am so grateful to V.M. Burns, Beth Fantaskey and Christina Hoag for their reviews of my manuscript. Additionally, my former SCBWI critique group cheered me on and made helpful comments about beginning drafts, so thank you Teesue Fields, Amanda Forsting, Elaine Hansen, and Bobbie Larkin.

Kudos as well goes to my dear brother-in-law, Richard Johnson, for all of his technical assistance over the years, and to Steve Bennett, Ken Wiesner, Kristine Hanson, and Laura Spinella at AuthorBytes.

Above all, I am thankful to my husband, Alan, always my first reader and my forever encourager-in-chief.

Lynn Slaughter is the author of *While I Danced.* She earned her MFA from Seton Hill University in Writing Popular Fiction and teaches part-time at Indiana University Southeast. She is the proud mom of two sons and grandmother of four.